KARINA HALLE & SCOTT MACKENZIE

ROCKED UP

First edition published by Metal Blonde Books
May 2017

ISBN-10: 1546747508
ISBN-13: 9781546747505

Cover design: Hang Le Designs
Interior formatting: Champagne Formats
Edited by: Kara Malinczak
Proofed by Laura Helseth, Mariana Ruiz, Dawn Sousa Birch, Amy Clowdsley

DEDICATION

For those who haven't forgotten how to dream.
And for Bruce.

PROLOGUE

LAEL

Seven Years Ago

"He's *so* hot." I glance over at Shelby who's staring down at the cover of Seventeen magazine with a crazy smile on her face. "Like, so hot."

"I know," I tell her. That's all we've been talking about this entire limo ride to the venue. It's all I've been talking about ever since I first heard Brad Snyder's voice playing from the speakers in our house, let alone from the moment I first saw his face.

Brad Snyder is the lead singer and guitarist for one of my favorite bands, *And Then.* I would totally love the band even if Brad wasn't in it, and especially if they weren't represented by my dad's record label, Ramsey Records. They've just got this killer sound, heavier on the rock than what normally does well on the charts, and it speaks to my soul. It makes me want to be a rock star more than anything.

Of course, my father would be the one to do that but he doesn't take me seriously at all. He says I'm too young (I'm fourteen) and that I don't know what I want yet. I always point out that he discovered Brad when he was the same age, but he just dismisses me as he always does.

At least I'm finally going to see them live. It's taken a year of extreme begging for this to happen. I mean, considering who my father is, you'd think that I'd have seen them a bunch of times already, but no. And every time the band has been in the office—they've even been in our house!—I've been at school.

My boyfriend, Ken, didn't want to go with me to this show. I think he's totally jealous of Brad, he just won't admit it. I can't blame Ken for that. I mean, Ken is cute, but he's fifteen. I used to think it was so cool that he was a year older than me, but come on, he's no Brad Snyder.

But Brad is way too old for me, even if I ever did have a chance. He's twenty. Super fit, super hot. He's not the type to strut around the stage shirtless or pose for steamy pictures like the rock stars with sweat dripping off their abs and stuff. He's not like that. He's just himself. And even though his fangirls would profess to know him, I really *do* know him.

My father doesn't tell me anything, of course, even who he's dating (though it seems he's always dating some hot young actress or singer), but I know on some weird level who Brad really is. It's like I feel connected to him through his music—like his songs speak just to me and me alone. There's a lonely boy behind the hot façade, and I can understand someone with loneliness.

At least my friend Shelby doesn't think I'm nuts when I talk about Brad that way. If I'm his number one fan, she's probably number two. Or three. Not as obsessed as me, and definitely without the connection I feel, but she knows all their songs by heart and has posters of Brad on her wall.

My obsession is subtler, maybe because it seems super weird with my father being in charge of them. I don't have their posters on my walls, but I do have a sketchbook I keep for magazine cut-outs and sheet music—plus when I feel like doodling (usually sketches of the two of us) or writing my own lyrics, I jot it down in there. I keep the notebook under my bed—not that anyone would care to find it. My father barely knows I'm alive most days.

Which is why I'm surprised he bothered getting us backstage passes for the show. It's not even my birthday. The only problem is that we're meeting my father at the venue, so it's not like Shelby and I will be able to run around unchecked.

The concert is at the Palladium Theater in Hollywood, a long limo drive from my house in Calabasas which has given Shelby and I plenty of time to giggle and get super nervous.

"Do we get to go on the side stage?" Shelby asks, even though she's already asked me this a million times.

"I think so," I tell her. Last time I told her yes, the time before that I told her maybe.

"Do you think we'll be able to talk to the guys?"

By guys, she means Brad. She doesn't care about the other guys in the band, Switch, Calvi, and Nick. I don't really care about them either. They're all older than Brad, and Calvi is like some Italian mobster wannabe. But they're all integral to the sound, even though sometimes I think they could be easily replaced. The only one who can't is Brad. He's everything.

"I hope so," I tell her, twirling my hair around my finger. I've got stick straight long blonde hair that I'm dying to do something rebellious with. Like dye it my favorite color, teal. Or chop it all off into a Miley Cyrus look. But my father would hate it. My mother had long blonde hair and he used to say that we looked alike. He doesn't say it anymore. He doesn't talk about her at all. She died from cancer when I was only four years old, so my memories of her are pretty much nonexistent.

The only memory I have is of her taking me to my first dance class. My chubby tummy in a bright pink bodysuit and pale pink tights. Dancing is the only thing I've really stuck with over the years, and I like to think it's because I know it's what she would have wanted.

But even though my father never talks about her, I know he misses her. At least, I like to think he does. He must be terribly lonely sometimes, having to work all the time and boss people around. I imagine my mother must have made him more human, at least for a little bit.

"Oh my god," Shelby cries out softly, a big toothy smile on her face. "What if your dad introduces us? What are you going to say? What are you going to do?"

"What are *you* going to do?" I retort, giving her a look. I know she thinks I'll turn into a screaming blubbering mess like those fans did in the sixties when they saw The Beatles, but believe me, I have complete control over my emotions. She's the one who's going to lose her mind.

"I'm going to play it cool," she says, trying to sound cool and failing miserably.

Yeah freaking right.

By the time the limo pulls up and goes through the gates at the back of the theater, I'm practically having a panic attack.

We're in the place where normal people don't get to go! All my friends from school are out there beyond the fences lining up or maybe already in the venue. Maybe even hanging around one of the entrances, trying their hardest to catch a glimpse of one of the band members. And yet here we are, feeling like rock stars ourselves.

We say goodbye to the driver and I double-check my last text from my father. He said Arnie, the band's famous English tour manager, would be outside the door, but so far I just see a scraggly-haired bouncer with a thick neck and a couple of roadie-looking types smoking cigarettes.

I feel like such a little girl, surrounded by these people who seem so much cooler than me. They might even be nobodies, but it doesn't matter. I'm super nervous too, that maybe I'll say the wrong thing, or that Arnie will never show. I don't know why he's meeting us and not my father. I exchange an anxious glance with Shelby, and I can tell she's thinking the same thing. Worst case scenario, I'll call my father and just hope he sees it, wherever he is.

But then the door swings open, fluorescent lights shining out into the darkness, and I see Arnie's silhouette. I've only met the guy once, in passing at our house, but I recognize him more from all the pictures I've seen of him with the band. The main website I follow, And Then We Were Fans, has tons of photos of him.

"Lael Ramsey?" Arnie asks in his thick accent.

Shelby points at me because I'm apparently speechless.

"Great, come on in," he says, holding the door wider and gesturing for us to go inside.

This is the moment of truth. At this moment I stop being Lael and start becoming the me I've always wanted to be.

I step inside with Shelby and stare up at Arnie as he starts searching his pockets.

"I've got your passes here," he says, "somewhere, bloody somewhere."

I giggle. So does Shelby. Arnie is totally intimidating, not just because he's older and wiser—I mean with his long beard and hair and glasses, he totally resembles a wizard—but because he's infamous. Aside from managing *And Then*, he's also been overseeing U2, Foo Fighters, and NIN on their tours. He's a legend.

And in the presence of a legend, I become a giggling pile of nerves.

Way to be cool, Lael.

Thankfully he fishes out the laminated passes and thrusts them into our hands. "These give you access almost everywhere, okay loves?" he says, looking us both in the eye. "Everywhere except their dressing rooms. Unless you're invited in. But don't count on it. They know you're part of Team Ramsey. All right, I better go check on Switch to make sure he's not doing a mound of..." he pauses, looking between the two of us, "chocolate."

He starts walking off.

"Wait!" I cry out, finding my voice. "Where do we go? Can we watch from the side stage? Where's my dad?"

"Can we meet them?" Shelby asks, her voice extra high-pitched with hope.

"Your father had business to attend to, so you're both on your own. Yes, you can watch from the side stage, though I have to warn you, the sound isn't the best there.

And if you do happen to run into them," he says, "don't be afraid to say hello."

And then he disappears up the stairs.

I look at Shelby and we both squeal in unison.

Backstage is the kind of nirvana I've only dreamed about. And I've dreamed about it a lot. In my fantasy, I'm roaming around backstage, a little older than I am now, and Brad sees me by myself. He walks up to me and asks me who I am and what I'm doing and why I look so sad. I tell him that I'm sad because I understand what loneliness is and that we should be lonely together.

In this fantasy I also smoke for some reason, wear red lipstick, and have a short black bob. Basically, I'm Uma Thurman in *Pulp Fiction* crossed with *Amelie*. A million miles from who I really am. But the point is, Brad sees that I know the real him and then he falls madly in love with me and we get married and I have his babies. The end.

And I know it's totally just a fantasy and it could never happen, but maybe I'm special. Maybe he sees something in me that he doesn't see in anyone else. That hope keeps the fantasy alive for me, the *what if*. Nothing in this world is impossible if you wish hard enough.

But the further that Shelby and I explore backstage, the more I realize that the fantasy will probably stay that way. It's a beehive of activity and we are far from being the only girls there—we just happen to be the youngest.

Everyone seems so much prettier, skinnier, cooler. I look over at Shelby with her hair pulled back in a ponytail and round cheeks and I realize how young we really are. Why would Brad ever be interested in a child like me?

Shelby, though, doesn't seem to be thinking the same thing. She's still practically jumping up and down, and after a while, I am too. There's no use playing it cool anymore. How can all the people here pretend this isn't the greatest thing that's ever happened to them?

We stick together like glue, afraid to be without each other. It's exciting, it's scary. I'm staring at everyone here with big eyes, even the ones who are pretending to be cool.

Then I see Jerry Cantrell standing off to the side. I mean, the freaking legend, the guitarist from Alice in Chains.

"Oh my god!" I grab Shelby's arm. "It's him."

"And he's going off to the side stage!" she squeals. "Let's follow him!"

We trail behind Jerry, trying to be casual. Even though we're allowed back here, I still feel like we're going to get caught at any moment.

We nervously stand beside Jerry until I work up the nerve to ask if he can take a picture with us. He's tall and looks like he did in all those 90s videos.

He's also the silent type—he just smiles and nods and poses with us while we take a selfie.

After that we're buzzing, on the moon, and I'm so tempted to send the pic to everyone I know, but I don't want him to see that I'm nuts.

Plus, the lights lower and more people crowd on the stage around us.

The show is starting.

I'm a bit sad that we didn't have a chance to find the boys before the show but maybe afterward is better. I would think Brad and the band wouldn't be socializing beforehand and just concentrating on the music.

And then it happens. Shelby elbows me and I look beside us to see Switch getting behind the drums, followed by Calvi going over to his guitar, and Nick picking up the bass.

The shadows of the stage create imposing figures.

Then comes Brad, and the moment I see him I feel my heart stop.

He's so beautiful, his eyes focused on his mic stand, slipping his famous Gibson SG guitar over his shoulders as he walks over to the middle of the stage to plug it in.

Shelby makes a sound that's half a whimper, half a squeal.

I can barely breathe.

And then the lights shine on the stage and the band kicks off with "Young Demons."

For the next hour and a bit, I'm transported to another place, another world, another galaxy I never knew existed. I know Arnie said that the sound on the side stage isn't the best but honestly there's no place I would rather be. Being here makes you feel like you're one with the band, like you're one with the world, with every single musical note.

I want this.

I want what Brad has.

I want to come up on stage and play an instrument and have the crowd fawning over me, screaming over me. I want the power that Brad has to bring someone like myself to another world.

And most of all, I want him.

For once, I don't feel overwhelmed by the impossibility of my fantasy, of my wish. I feel good, right, like I'm supposed to be here and feeling these things. That this is the start of something wonderful. The start of the real me.

This will happen, I tell myself. *You know you can make this happen.*

I keep repeating it to myself, spending half the show in some pocket of self-awareness, this drive and resolve building inside my heart. Then I realize I need to pull myself into the moment, into what I'm witnessing.

I watch the band, bobbing my head in time with everyone else on the side stage (Jerry included), and sing my heart out.

When it's all over my throat is raw and I feel high. Better than the glass of wine I had once, better than the joints I've smoked a few times. Better than my best dream. I'm floating and I never want to come down.

"That was amaaaaaazing!" Shelby yells at me, looking just as euphoric as I feel. Though her voice does sound a bit muffled and far away, which makes me realize how loud the show must have been. "That was the best thing in the world! I'm so happy right now!"

I nod, and while I feel all she's feeling, it's almost too personal for me to put into words. "Let's try and find them," I tell her, noting they walked off the stage already.

"Okay!"

But we're not the only people with this idea. Their dressing room door is closed, guarded by some security, but people like Jerry Cantrell and the drummer from Tool are able to waltz on in with no problem.

Jerks.

But we're nothing if not persistent. The show has given me new confidence, bolstered me into believing we'll meet them and that everything is going to be all right.

Then it happens. An hour has passed with us loitering outside, listening to their cheers and debauchery from inside the dressing room, and then the door opens and Jerry steps out.

He gives us a polite nod—we're old friends at this point—before walking away and then Switch comes out to talk to someone, beer in hand.

Before I know what's going on, the entire band is out in the hallway with us.

Including Brad.

My whole body jolts in his presence, like I've been plugged into a lightning bolt.

But he starts to walk off, away from us.

Shelby says softly, "Oh no."

I won't let this happen.

I cry out, "Brad!"

And he stops.

Turns around to look at us.

Looks into my eyes.

My knees start to shake. He's so beautiful, that thick dark hair, those arched sexy brows, that sweet mouth that I bet kisses so well.

And he's looking at me expectantly.

Or, he was.

He just gives us a polite smile and a wave and turns to walk off again.

We're just two little girls to him.

Then Shelby yells, "This is Ronald Ramsey's daughter!"

I could kick Shelby right now. She yelled it so loud that everyone turned to look at us.

But I can't kick her. I can't even glare at her or say anything.

I can't move. I am frozen—a statue.

My heart is going a mile a minute on the inside, but on the outside, I might as well be made of ice.

I'm not sure I can breathe either.

That's even more apparent as Brad starts walking toward us.

"You're Lael?" he asks, his voice rich and low as he stops a few feet from us.

I can't even nod.

"She is," Shelby says, nudging me.

I'm still slack-jawed. I can only stare at him.

His dark eyes take me in and I feel a million volts of intense current run between us.

"I'm Shelby," she goes on. "You guys were sooooo awesome tonight. That was the best show ever."

"I'm glad you liked it," he says to her before shifting his eyes back to me. "Are you okay, Lael?"

My name. He said my name again! It sounds so beautiful coming from his lips!

And no.

I'm not okay.

Everything is starting to go grey around the edges.

His eyes darken with concern and he gives me a wry smile. "Breathe," he says. "Just breathe."

I try and take in a breath but nothing seems to happen.

Oh my god. I can't breathe!

Oh my god. I think I'm passing out!

"Lael," Shelby says in frustration. "You're being ridiculous! Stop embarrassing me."

"She's looking a little pale," Brad says, taking a step closer as he examines me. "Maybe you should sit down."

I open my mouth to say something just as the world begins to spin and I tilt to the left.

I don't feel anything but I hear Switch's voice in the distance.

"Looks like we've got another fainter, people!"

The world goes grey, then black.

Then grey.

Then white.

"Lael?"

I open my eyes to see Arnie beside me, handing me a glass of water. Shelby is on the other side, hand at my back.

I'm sitting on a couch in a dressing room.

We're the only ones in here.

"What happened?" I ask, taking the water from Arnie and gulping it down.

"You fainted, love," he says.

"It was so embarrassing," Shelby says.

I place my head in my hands, feeling so angry and sad and mad and shamed. I've never fainted before, ever!

"It happens to a lot of people," Arnie says. "Believe me. There's a fainter at almost every show. Brad just has that effect on some people. Who bloody knows why."

Because he's too good to be true, I think to myself.

I look up at Arnie. "Where is Brad?"

"He left," he says. "He doesn't stick around for that long after shows. He doesn't party much or drink much either. Keeps to himself."

"Will you tell him I'm sorry?"

Arnie pats me on the back. "He doesn't care. He thinks it's flattering, and he's used to it. Don't worry about it, love. But I do have to tell you that the limo is waiting outside to take you back. Hope you both enjoyed the show."

"We did," Shelby says, and even though I know she's so mad at me, she helps me to my feet.

We say bye to Arnie and then make our way down the hall. Switch and Calvi and Nick are still there, drinking and laughing. They don't pay us any attention which is a relief. I walk past them, and we head out of the theater and into the night.

"Way to go, numbnuts," Shelby says to me as we get into the waiting limo. "You meet Brad and then you faint. You were supposed to play it cool."

"I don't know what happened."

She rolls her eyes. "He knocked you unconscious with his hotness, that's what happened."

Then she starts laughing hysterically.

I start laughing too.

We laugh all the way back to my house where she stays the night and we have a sleepover. We go over everything that happened, every single moment of the night, so that we'll never ever forget it.

And I start planning on ways to see Brad Snyder again.

Next time, it's going to be different.

ONE

LAEL

My knuckles on the steering wheel are bone white from gripping it so hard.

I don't think I've ever been this nervous before.

Okay, so I can think of a few times, but even so, my nerves are stretched to the max.

And it doesn't help that traffic on the 405 has slowed to a crawl and everyone is honking at each other even though no one is going anywhere. You'd think people in LA would be used to this shit day-in and day-out but I guess honking and getting angry are just part of the deal. If you don't spend hours in traffic releasing your anger on other drivers, do you really live?

Normally I wouldn't be driving toward the airport on a Monday nearing rush hour, but when my father called me an hour ago, I couldn't refuse.

And I didn't want to.

Even though seven years have passed since I was that

awkward girl who fainted at the *And Then* show, and even though I've learned to let go of my adolescent fandoms and obsessions (let's not forget how I stalked Thirty Seconds to Mars all around the country when I was sixteen), this is still something pretty amazing.

I'm on the way to pick up Brad Snyder from the airport.

Yes. The Brad Snyder.

That Brad Snyder.

The man who turned me on to music to begin with, who put that shred of hope in my soul, and made me realize I could do anything I put my mind to. Without Brad's own music to inspire me, I never would have picked up the bass guitar, never would have paid for my own lessons behind my father's back, never would have filled notebooks upon notebooks with my own songs and lyrics.

Never would have been given this opportunity…

I push it out of my mind and concentrate on not slamming into the car in front of me. The fact is, I'm not just picking him up—I also have to be the bearer of some sad news for him.

Which makes this all really weird since I don't know Brad. At all.

Yes, we met at the show at the Palladium when I was fourteen, and yes I fainted. And after that I met him a few more times. My father had a large party for them at my house when one of their albums went platinum, and I also went backstage a few times after that. But that was all when I was still in private school, still just a teenager. I'm twenty-one now, and even though I know I'm still young, I don't feel it. And for Brad's sake, I hope I don't look it.

The moment I graduated, I was out of Los Angeles

in a second. I'd had enough of the city—something about growing up here as the daughter of one of the country's most successful record producers makes you grow real jaded of the whole scene. I backpacked across Europe, working odd jobs here and there, and then spent my last year in Southeast Asia and Australia doing the same. I managed to score a job picking grapes (under the table, of course) in the town of Mildura, in Australia's Victoria province, and wouldn't you know it, I actually kept working there for a few months until I felt I had enough of getting dirt under my nails.

All that time I was traveling, I had my bass guitar and my special effects pedal with me. Whenever I had a second I would either be practicing or joining local bands and playing live shows. Sometimes it was just solo—like the awkward show I did in an expat community in Bali. Other times I would be in a band of sorts. Because I stayed in Mildura for so long, I officially joined the Kumquats (I didn't name them) and played around Victoria and New South Wales. It was mainly pub shows in rural areas, but the band was psychedelic and really let me experiment with sound.

That's when I realized I had something to bring to the table. I was finally moving past being that bass player that just follows the same prescribed rhythm. I wasn't D'Arcy from The Smashing Pumpkins, just nodding her head and strumming those same notes over and over again. I was Mlny Parsonz from Royal Thunder or that chick from White Zombie, rocking the bass but not fading into the background. I had something to contribute, a sound and a method all my own.

Yes, it was those shows, as small as they were,

sometimes only playing to one drunk farmer in the corner, that taught me more than school ever could.

But you can only run away from life for so long. I knew I couldn't illegally pick grapes and play in dusty bars forever. I had to come back home and find a life for myself, even though what I really want to do isn't that practical.

Or, it wouldn't seem that practical in any other family. In this family, however...

So, I came back to LA. Instead of living back at home in my father's sprawling mansion in Calabasas, I chose to be as far away from the Kardashians as possible. I found a roommate, sharing a simple garage converted into a guest house that we rent in Sherman Oaks, and got a job as a waitress at a restaurant down the street.

I wanted as little of my father's help as possible.

That was three months ago. In that time I've kept up with my bass, been busy writing songs, playing with various artists, and I managed to adopt a dog, a tiny Chihuahua called Baby Groot, all while working and trying to figure out just how to make happen what I need to happen.

Then I heard the news of what happened with *And Then,* how a few weeks ago they fired their bassist Nick. It wasn't a surprise—anyone who followed the band knew that Nick had been asking for it for some time. Fame goes to people's heads, and sometimes it goes to the wrong people's heads. I don't care how big you are, no fan likes it when someone from the band berates them while on stage.

So then I asked my father for one of the biggest favors of my life, something I know I'll always be in debt to him over.

And to my total surprise, he said he would see what he could do. That's the thing about my father. For better or worse, he can make almost anything happen.

Which is the reason why I'm so nervous on this drive, along with the fact that I have to tell my hero Brad Snyder some bad news when I'm pretty much a stranger to him, *and* I'm going to be late to pick him up because of the damn traffic.

I sigh and brush a piece of hair behind my ears, its bright color catching my eyes in the rear-view mirror. I know I certainly don't look like the young kid with straight blonde hair and the gap-toothed smile. My hair is dyed teal, my favorite color, and today I played with beachy salt spray to make it wavy. I may have also done a YouTube tutorial for my makeup before I left the house, and now I'm wondering if I went overboard with the contouring. Nothing says trying too hard like stripes of brown on your face.

I lick my fingers and try to wipe it off until it's subtler in the harsh light of day. I know it's totally silly and I shouldn't be worried about how I look, but I can't help it. There's a part of me deep inside that feels like I'm fourteen all over again.

God, if only I had an idea back then how unreal things are about to get. Hell, if only I knew I'd one day be picking up Brad Snyder and putting him in my car.

If only I knew I'd be one step closer to uncovering the mystery of this man.

The man, the myth, the legend…and all that fucking jazz.

Fuck. I hope I don't faint.

TWO

BRAD

Sometimes I still feel like that hopeless child, that worthless little fuck I was before Ramsey made me a star. I was nothing, a skinny kid wearing sneakers that were two sizes too big because the Salvation Army didn't have my size, always wearing that stupid yellow t-shirt that hung over my ripped jean shorts. I can hardly blame my mother for not loving me—when I picture that twelve-year-old loser, it still makes me cringe.

Don't get me wrong, my mother wasn't perfect. When I think of her I see her in the corner of our garbage-filled apartment with a nee dle in her arm. Sometimes she had boyfriends that gave her money, and they were always surprised to see me, leaving after an hour or so. I called her by her name, Suzanne, because she said I sounded stupid when I said *Mommy*.

I *was* stupid.

Sometimes the police would come and Suzanne would

be taken away screaming. She always yelled at me and said it was my fault. It probably was.

A nice lady that spoke to me like I was a puppy would be there and I would leave with her. She knew I wouldn't leave without my guitar; I left the apartment holding her hand, dragging it to my temporary home.

My father, a musician, gave me that guitar. I didn't remember him much but as a kid I thought the world of him. I figured when he got out of jail I'd show him the songs I made with that very same guitar, a Gibson. I had to steal it from a pawn shop more than once after Suzanne sold it to that creep that ran it.

That was the reason the police came that last time, so it really was my fault. Suzanne said she needed money for her medicine. She also said I should burn in hell, and that's the last I heard from her.

The nice lady who treated me like a puppy stopped working at the house where I was living. She never said goodbye, and I always wondered if she hated my guts. Probably. Over the next three years I would move around. I never had friends, except Kevin Robson. He was an old guy that gave me music lessons for free. Mr. Robson, as I would call him, was the closest person to me.

He would always say the same thing when I walked into his recording studio with all the buttons and machines.

"Did they let you out of your cage?"

He sounded mean, but he wasn't, and I would roll my eyes. He would usually shake my shoulder and say something about me being skinny and not eating enough. Then he would give me a few bucks to get us some burgers at Dilallo across the street. I would leave my Gibson guitar with him when I left – Mr. Robson was the only person I trusted with it. I didn't have to ask him what he wanted, I knew. It was always the same routine; Mr. Robson would give me ten dollars and make a point of telling me to bring back the change. I always laughed at his jokes even if he wasn't funny, partly because he was old and I wanted to be respectful. I liked him, I never knew why he was so kind to me. Perhaps he took pity on the pathetic loser that I was.

Mr. Robson worked as the sound man for the old theater where all the popular bands played. We were never allowed to eat our Dilallo burgers near all his fancy machines, so we would sit in the red little seats and look at the stage while we ate. It was a magical place; it looked so different during the day before the people poured in and fake smoke and colored lights filled the stage.

"It should look like a dream," Mr. Robson would say, referring to the lights and smoke they were testing for that evening's act.

We would play guitar together after lunch in his sound booth. The first thing he taught me was an E pentatonic scale, and after that, it was history. I would show him songs that I wrote at home, while my mother was out, and for whatever reason he always liked them and would tell the other workers to come and listen.

"You have to make people feel something, kid, that's all that matters," he would tell me.

If I finished a song completely, he would set me up on stage and I would play it for the crew while they worked. I liked how my voice sounded grown up coming out of the big speakers and how my acoustic guitar filled the room. Sometimes the lighting guys would turn down the house lights and light me up if they had time.

It felt good at a time when very few things did.

"Use the whole stage, kid. Don't be shy to scream that last note," he'd say, giving me courage. It always helped that I sounded great after he fixed up my voice with his recording equipment.

"Who's playing tonight?" I would ask as if I wasn't fishing for an invite. I would never show up without him saying it was okay, and he invited me almost every time. Then I would show up early and help set things up.

Looking back, Mr. Robson and that theater were my entire world. Later, I often felt guilty that I was having such a good time while Suzanne sat in jail.

Over the course of those three years, I saw countless bands. Mr. Robson would tell me what the bands did right and what they did wrong at the end of the night while we were cleaning up. There were all kinds of acts—I will never forget the burlesque one-woman show that completely mesmerized the crowd. Her name was Ms. Sugar.

"Now that's a real performer, kid. She had 'em in the palm of her hand right to the end," Mr. Robson said.

She would come by every few months and all the stage workers really liked her, for obvious reasons. I liked her because she was the only one who called me Brad instead of "kid."

I later found out that Mr. Robson was a loner who never married. I guess it was pretty obvious there was no Mrs. Robson considering he lived on fast food and spent every waking hour in his sound booth. Either way, I'm pretty sure, after a while, he was as close to me as I was to him.

When I turned thirteen, I got my first official birthday present.

"Now this is from everyone, kid, not just me. We all chipped in and got you something."

Mr. Robson presented me with an electric guitar, a Gibson SG like my acoustic. It looked like it was meant for rock and roll. It was orange-brown near the pick-ups and faded to black around the edges. I remember my throat feeling really small and tight and my eyes watering a little. I didn't understand why I felt the need to cry, but somehow I kept the tears in. I just stood there like a statue, staring at the perfect guitar, trying to hold it all together.

I think Mr. Robson noticed so he spoke for me.

"This kid is going to be a star," he said to everyone, and they all applauded in response, the noise overwhelming the small room. "Happy birthday, kid."

That birthday was probably the best day I'd ever had up until that point. Mr. Robson said I was being silly about feeling guilty for having such nice things while my mother was locked up.

After receiving the electric guitar, my lessons with Mr. Robson were mostly plugged into an amp rather than on the acoustic, and the songs I wrote were based around that awesome electric sound.

Mr. Robson would say, "Don't always play with the volume at ten, they won't feel anything when you do that. For something to sound loud it has to be next to something quiet."

Depending on who was playing the theater that night, we sometimes would have to set up a backline. A backline is a set-up of all the equipment that we had at the theater, and the band would just show up and play on our amps, keyboards, and drums. Usually smaller bands would do that, or maybe when there were multiple acts and tearing down and setting up a new equipment for each band wasn't practical. Anyway, those days were the best because the crew would get a chance to jam on the equipment during the day. Sometimes, we would play one of my songs and I got to be front and center. It was amazing to play with a full band, drums pounding, bass rumbling, my guitar sounding exactly how I wanted it to when it was plugged into the Marshal amps.

The more we played, the more often they would ask me to take center stage. They weren't as old as Mr. Robson, but they were still pretty up there. Even though they had grey hair, they acted like teenagers when they played, and they were really good musicians. One time we had fun with the smoke machine, using up all the dry ice. Mr. Robson gave us some trouble for that.

So, after such an epic thirteenth birthday, I would be lying if I said when I walked in a year later I was wondering if they would do something similar for my fourteenth.

"Did they let you out of your cage?" Mr. Robson asked without fail. I laughed and started coiling up some cables. I pressed on like any other day, not feeling bad that Mr. Robson didn't know it was my birthday, but feeling bad that I had some kind of expectation. As if the electric guitar wasn't enough. I quickly sorted myself out and tried to forget it was my birthday. I noticed they were setting up a backline so I hoped we would get a little jamming in.

"I was thinking of trying that burger place across the street," Mr. Robson said jokingly as he handed me a ten-dollar bill.

"Bring back the change," I said before he could and laughed at the scowl that melted into a smile.

"Who is playing tonight?" I asked as I walked away.

"Never heard of 'em, kid. Take a look at the marquee on your way out," he said.

As I walked out of the grand theater and into the foyer, I saw one of the crew members on a ladder beginning to put the black letters up outside. Still curious about who that night's act was, I walked into Dilallo Burger and was greeted by the older couple that always worked there.

"I'll take the usual," I said to the smiling lady who took my money. I sat in a rickety chair and listened as they spoke in a language I couldn't understand. I never could tell if they were arguing or not.

"Kid!" The man who did the cooking shouted and handed me a paper bag with the burgers. The bag had a shine from the grease soaking through.

"Thank you," I said, and walked toward the exit.

"Hey, kid!" the chef shouted again.

With one hand on the door and my other hand cradling the greasy goodness, I turned my head toward the smiling man behind the counter.

"Don't forget about us when you're famous!" he shouted.

I had no idea what the hell he was referring to. His wife smiled and pointed to the marquee across the street where the night's acts had been posted. The crew member was walking away with his ladder in hand.

In big bold black letters, the marquee read:

Iggy Pop

Ms. Sugar

Brad Snyder

I threw the door open and stood on the sidewalk staring at the sign in disbelief. My heart was racing and I felt my throat tighten up. Alone, on the sidewalk, I shouted for joy like a wild man and ran across the street getting honked at by the cars I was cutting off.

I stumbled into the theater out of breath and smiling.

"Happy Birthday, kid!" Mr. Robson cried out joyfully.

I was completely overwhelmed. I had never played in front of anyone, and this was going to be a full house. I was sweating and probably looked a little green.

"Sugar said she would go on first and get them ready for you. You're going to do great."

I must have looked like I felt because Mr. Robson took me by the shoulder and guided me to a seat.

"Relax. You're ready, so just have fun with it. The guys will meet you backstage and you can decide what you want to play. Just do twenty minutes tops. You'll do great."

I didn't respond—I just stared at the stage in disbelief and ate my burger like a smiling idiot.

I met Iggy Pop briefly, and he was nothing like I thought he would be. He sounded like a grown up and was actually very nice. Mr. Robson said I could learn from him but complained that he kept the volume at ten too much.

I watched Ms. Sugar from the side of the stage. She would give me a wink here and there. I had a crush on her even though she was twice my age, and I think she knew it.

I wondered why so many fans would want to watch a show from the side of the stage. The sound was awful. I tried to poke my head out to see if I could see Mr. Robson, but the lights were blinding, making it impossible.

"Ladies and gentlemen," Sugar said in her sultry voice. "It is with great pleasure that I announce the next act. I have a feeling that you all will one day be able to brag to your friends that on June 7th, opening for Iggy Pop, you saw this young man's debut performance here in this the-ater. This boy is going to be star, and we all get to witness where it all started, right now, on this stage before you. Ladies and gentlemen...Brad Snyder."

The crowd applauded politely as Sugar strutted off the stage carrying her clothes, a large feather boa wrapped around her neck and pasties on her nipples. She leaned over and in an airy voice spoke into my ear, "Don't forget to have fun, Bradley."

A stagehand handed my Gibson SG to me and I walked to the mic with a fraction of the confidence Sugar walked off with. I kept on trying to see Mr. Robson, but the lights were too powerful. The applause had fizzled out and the room was quiet. I plugged in my guitar and it made a crackle that filled the room. I remembered Mr. Robson's lesson about looking confident. The microphone gave some feedback when I put my lips close. The band looked like soldiers holding for their command. Mr. Robson said it's best to just get playing when you walk out, so I counted off and we slammed into action.

I can barely remember that first show. I do remember that I could hardly figure out what side of the guitar to hold when I first stepped out onstage, but somehow after I played the first note I glided along.

It was the perfect escape. I felt love. Mr. Robson may have been my only friend, but at that first show I felt like everyone in the theater was my friend. I wasn't a stupid kid with big sneakers that screwed everything up, I was some-thing very different.

That's when it started for me.

That's the day I was born.

When the house lights came on at the end of my last

song and I said thank you and good night, I spotted Mr. Robson at his sound booth. He was smiling and waving his hands in the air. Seeing him so proud of me is one of my nicest memories.

Over the next year and a half I played at the theater often, and sometimes I would play other venues in town with Ms. Sugar. She always looked out for me and I could tell she wanted me to do well. It was she who got in touch with Ramsey Records.

At seventeen I was actually making some money. It wasn't much, but at least I could pay for the Dilallo burgers sometimes. Sugar would always give me a few bucks at the end of the shows and Mr. Robson said there were more people there to see me and that's why I played last. For some reason, he didn't seem so sweet on Sugar anymore, but he didn't talk about it.

People seemed to know me around town because one of the shows I played made it on TV. I hoped my father was allowed to watch television in jail and would recognize me. I wasn't spending any time at foster homes anymore because I would get in trouble for coming in so late after shows, but I had friends in the city that let me sleep on their couch. More often than not I would sleep at the theater in the backstage area. Mr. Robson pretended not to know I did that.

It was a rainy winter evening the day Sugar introduced me to Ronald.

That night, I said goodnight to the crowd and smiled at Mr. Robson in his sound booth who was clapping and waving his hands as enthusiastically as ever. I walked off-stage and Sugar greeted me with a funny smile.

"There is someone I think you should meet, Brad."

I followed her backstage and out the back door into the alley behind the theater. The cold winter rain made everything dark and there was a black limo with tinted windows parked in front of us. Sugar opened the door to the limo and slid in, motioning for me to follow her.

"Ronald, darling, how are you?"

Sugar spoke differently than usual as she addressed the large man sitting across from us. Ronald didn't look at Sugar; his eyes stayed on me.

He looked at me like he and I were aware of some kind of amusing secret. I smiled and nodded as if I were agreeing to something, but the truth is I had no idea what was going on.

"Brad, look, I'm hearing good things, and I liked what I saw tonight. I'm willing to work with you. How old are you?"

"Seventeen," I answered.

Ronald smiled. "Do you know who I am?"

"No," I answered truthfully.

"My name is Ronald Ramsey. I own Ramsey Records and I can make you a star. With your talent I can see big things. Huge things. But, look, it won't be easy. It will be work. Hard work. Are you willing to work for me?"

I looked at Sugar who was nodding yes and motioning me to answer Ronald.

"Yes?" I answered.

"There is nothing wrong with playing these small clubs," he said. "You can have fun with that for now, but what I'm talking about is making you an international star. I can't do it for you, Brad. At the end of the day, you have to put your heart into it. There will be times when it's hard and you'll be tired. There will be times when you might want to give up, and I need to know that you won't give up on me if I'm going to invest in you. I need to know I can trust you. You're not a quitter, are you, Brad?"

"No."

"What about drugs, do you do drugs?"

"No."

"Drink?"

"No."

"Look, I'm not trying to scare you, kid. You have talent. I'm not worried about that because it's clear you have something special. I just need to know you won't let me down."

Ronald leaned forward so I could see him better. He had a shock of blonde hair and a chubby red face. He was smiling, but it was hard to tell if he was happy or angry. He was a large man and I thought about how it must have been hard for him to get in and out of this limousine. Ronald kept his gaze on me nodding his head up and down like he was having a conversation in his own mind about me.

"I won't quit playing, Mr. Ramsey," I told him, still taken aback about it all.

"Ronald. Call me Ronald."

"Ronald, this is all I want to do. I have a ton of material no one even knows about and..."

He cut me off. "Come to the office tomorrow and we'll talk more."

I took the business card he was holding out for me and stepped out into the cold winter rain. I gave Sugar a nod as she lit a cigarette and gave me a wink, and I closed the heavy black limousine door.

I walked away from the car barely noticing the awful weather, my leather jacket open and my long dark hair soaked and sticking to my face. I needed to go for a little walk before I went back into the theater. I needed for everything that just happened to sink in.

I walked into the night smiling. I knew this was the beginning of the rest of my life.

Fast forward to today, and I'm sweating nervously on a turbulent flight from Austin to Los Angeles. I'm twenty-seven years old and nothing like the kid with those cheap sneakers and the second hand t-shirts.

Ronald kept his promise. He had made me a star.

Over the past ten years since that fateful day in Ronald's black limousine, I have been on countless flights, and even though the pills they give me keep the anxiety under control, I just can't get used to flying. I had never been on a plane until I signed with Ramsey Records, so who would've known I have such a fear? It's probably the only complaint Ramsey Records can make about me.

For example, I'm pretty sure most musicians wouldn't be putting up with the shit I'm going through right now. I try to be a nice guy and play along with the games they play with the media, and so when they asked me to fly down to Austin to do a duet with Lindsay Wilder, I obliged.

Lindsay is a young starlet on Ramsey Records who is supposed to be my on-again off-again girlfriend. It's all a ruse. Everything is a fucking ruse these days. One time, on another flight, I sat next to one of Ramsey's henchmen who had too much to drink. She told me my entire working life is mapped out. If it looked like I cheated on Lindsay, or got in a fight with a security guard, or even got arrested, it was all for show. Everything is planned to keep just the right amount of exposure and intrigue.

The duet with Lindsay was lame. She wasn't even there.

She recorded her parts last week. I'm sure they will do some photo trickery to make it look like we were in the studio together having a ball.

Other than flying, I don't have any major complaints. I don't agree with most of what the record company does, but it's still good work if you can get it. It doesn't feel that long ago when I didn't have my own bed, and now I have a house in the hills with a pool and everything else you can imagine. Funnily enough, after a decade Mr. Robson is still my only real friend. He still complains that I don't eat enough, and he still makes the same jokes on cue when I see him. I just wish I saw him more often. With all the recording, touring, photoshoots, and interviews, I barely have the time.

You would think with all the fake show business stuff, I would have lost my passion for music, but that's totally not the case. Somehow I manage to keep the two separate. My last single, "Violent Little Things," went to number one. Ramsey Records can manipulate the entertainment media as much as he wants, but at the end of the day all that matters is the music. I still write all my own material, except, of course, when I'm doing a lame duet for a starlet's record.

"Ladies and gentlemen, we will be beginning our descent into Los Angeles shortly. Please remain seated with your seatbelts fastened."

I feel the engines power down and my stomach knots. Usually I have my bandmates with me, but I was on my own for the hellish experience in Austin and this one too. I fucking hate landing. I also hate take-offs and everything else in the middle.

When the wheels touch down, all my tense muscles relax and I let out a deep breath.

We all know that there is an alarming number of musicians that die in their twenty-seventh year, most of them in plane crashes.

I guess that wasn't the flight that will kill me.

I only have a carry-on, so I quickly make it to the arrivals gate and look for my driver who is normally waiting for me.

To my surprise, I'm greeted by someone else.

Lael Ramsey.

Ronald's only daughter, a fresh-faced beauty with brown eyes and long hair dyed teal. I haven't seen her in a few years.

When we first met she was just a teen, so it's strange seeing this young woman who must be at least twenty by now.

And far more attractive than I bargained for.

She spots me and stretches her arm up high, waving at me with a smile.

"Well, well, well, what do we have here?" I ask as I approach her, smiling back.

"Hi, Brad. How was the flight?" she says.

"Are you my ride?"

"I am. C'mon," she replies, grinning, and I follow her out of the airport, trying not to stare at her ass. No sir, this is definitely not the bratty young girl I remember.

That said, it is unusual that she's here picking me up. Something's wrong.

"Look, Brad," she says slowly as we approach a small blue electric car in the parking lot. "I have bad news. I just don't know how to say this…"

"What's up?" I ask, my stomach turning with nerves. This isn't going to be good.

"It's your friend, Mr. Robson," she says quietly. "He died last night."

It takes a moment for the news to sink in. I'm not sure what I feel, or if I'm even feeling anything. I just stare at nothing, trying to understand. Actually, what I'm feeling is almost the same as the day he gave me my first present, the guitar I still play. My throat is tight, my body is growing hotter by the second, my eyes are starting to water.

Only this time, unlike back then, I can't stop it. It hits me all at once, like a tidal wave. I break down and cry like I've never cried before, surrounded by this massive, lonely parking lot.

I barely realize it when Lael, Ronald's daughter, a girl I hardly know, is pulling me into her arms.

I hold on to her like she's the only person left in my life.

THREE

BRAD

It's not unusual for Ramsey Records to request I come in for a meeting at its head office just outside of Hollywood. The building is a twenty-story circular high-rise that was built in the early eighties. At the very top of the building, large metal letters spell out Ramsey Records. I've been on the roof and I have seen the rusted old framing holding up that massive sign, and sometimes I imagine what it would be like if those heavy letters got loose and tumbled to the ground. I wonder what would happen if I kicked them.

As usual I just sit there at the meeting without saying a word while a team of people shout back and forth about this or that.

"We need more poolside shots."

"Sex tape."

"He should make an appearance at a global warming protest. That is so hot right now."

"For fuck's sake, we need more talk shows. Has

Corden replied?"

"Let's piss off Australian Customs, that news goes global."

"How about some shots of him leaving that sex club? Madeline's, is it?"

So I sit and eat the sushi while they play with my life like I'm just a product. No wonder it's increasingly rare that I'm invited to these nasty brainstorm meetings. It's also rare that Ronald would attend, but there's Ronald at the opposite end of the table with his elbows on the desk and his hands making a triangle shape just under his chin. He looks stoic, seemingly unimpressed with what's happening, but it's also his default face.

"Okay, that's enough for today," he announces. "I want Brad's face on the cover of every magazine when his album comes out this spring. That's still a few months away so don't exhaust your resources. Stay focused on the tour, only play your games in the cities he is playing. Brad, stick around, I need to talk to you."

Shit.

The crew shuffles out of the room exchanging looks that only exist in the competitive corporate world. They look like wild animals in nice clothing, completely willing to kill the person they were holding the door open for if it suited them. I preferred when they ignored me—whenever they did speak to me through their smiling teeth, I knew it was trouble.

"How was the duet with Lindsay?" Ronald asks from across the long boardroom table covered with a mountain range of sushi. It's strange being so far away, and I anxiously do a quick drum roll with my chop sticks before setting them down.

"Good. I felt like we made a real connection," I shout at him.

Ronald smiles and stands up, flattening his tie over his rounded belly, slowly walking toward me as he speaks to the ceiling.

"Look," he says. "I am sorry about Nick. I know you got along. It's not about who threw the chicken, and I don't care about that lady's car. It's his attitude. No one wants to work with the guy, I knew he had to go."

"He threw the chicken."

"It was never about the chicken."

Nick, our now ex-bassist, was involved in a bit of an incident.

I sit there looking up at Ronald standing next to me and we share an awkward pause that seems to last for days. The room is so quiet I can hear him breathing.

"I hear you still won't work with the song writers. That's okay," he finally goes on. "As long as you're writing hits you won't have any problems from me. It's just that we haven't heard anything from you lately and we need that album ready for spring. We need a summer hit, a summer love song,"

"Okay. I'll call it Summer Love Song," I answer sarcastically.

"I like it," Ronald answers, choosing to ignore my sarcasm. He sits down next to me and says earnestly, "We don't need another one of your avant garde projects. I don't care if those hipster magazines love it, it doesn't pay the bills. That shit doesn't pay for your fancy condo in the hills. What the fuck did you call that album again?"

"Stomp Box," I answer.

Stomp Box was an album completely comprised of

analog guitar effect pedals swirling and driving ambient sounds for an hour and a half. Not a single chorus or hook, just one long track of me manipulating twenty effect pedals and playing my guitar. By the end of the track I had every pedal on. I'm not usually into smoking pot but after that session you could barely see the instruments through the smoke.

"Yeah, that fucking shit, enough with that," he says. "Now, look. It wasn't easy, but you don't have a single flight for this tour so you are in for quite the road trip. This means you will be living on your bus for over two months. I expect big things on this tour. Really big things. The venues are getting bigger, and we are selling out faster. You need to step up to the plate. When you get back it's straight to the studio to get that album ready for spring, so I need you to be ready for that, too. I told you the day I met you, over ten years ago, there will be times when it's hard and you will want to give up. I'm just reminding you, it's not going to be easy over the next few months. I promise you that. I need to know you won't give up. I need to know you will see this through."

"This is what I do. You have nothing to be worried about," I assure him.

He clears his throat, avoiding my eyes. "We have a new temporary bass player for you. She'll be with you for this tour while we look for someone to fill the position full-time."

"She?" I question. What the hell is he talking about?

Ronald looks uncharacteristically defeated.

"She wants to be a musician," he says quietly, almost wincing. "I think she's caught up with some kind of romantic idea of what life on the road is like and there's nothing like two months on a bus during winter to get it out of your system."

"Uh, who are we talking about, Ronald?"

Ronald stands up and stalks over to the door. He opens it and sticks his head out into the hall, bellowing, "Come on in." Then he turns to look at me. "Brad Snyder, meet your new bass player."

Lael Ramsey steps into the boardroom.

No one says a word. Ronald smiles, looking back and forth between Lael and me.

What the fuck is going on?

I know I should say something, and it has to be the right thing or else I'm dead. This is his fucking daughter here.

"I didn't even realize you played bass," I manage to say to her.

Her fake awkward smile breaks for a moment and she opens her mouth to say something.

"She's a fantastic player," Ronald says, cutting her off. "And I think she will be a great part of the team. She'll have her own bus to travel on and her own security. Other than sound check and the actual shows, she won't be bothering you and Twitch."

"Switch," I correct him on the name of my bandmate.

"Sure. Look, this is really a non-issue. Lael is very capable, and there is no reason you, Mitch, Calvi, and her can't have a professional working relationship. You guys will travel together as usual and Lael will meet you at the venue at the appropriate times."

Ronald looks at Lael and puts his hand on her shoulder.

Lael gives him an awkward smile and nervously whispers, "Yay…"

"Good," he says with a nod, happy with her fake enthusiasm. "I think we're done here. Lael, darling, I know you have somewhere to be so I won't keep you. Your assistant will let you know when the first rehearsal is. You'll see Brad, the other guy, and Stitch there and I am sure it will be great."

I exchange a look with Lael, trying to let her know everything's fine. She returns my gaze with fear in her eyes. I can't blame her. Perhaps I look the same.

Ronald ushers her out the door, closing it behind her, and once again Ronald and I are alone in the boardroom.

He sits next to me with a grave expression. "I've invested more in you than any other artist in the history of my company. I'm not going to say I own you—that wouldn't be right—and I'm not even going to say you owe me anything. You've held up your part of the deal quite well. But, young man, I want you to know, I will take it all away if you let anything happen to Lael. You and anyone else from the crew are not to socialize with her, okay? This is a working relationship. In fact, I've told Lael that you are basically her boss. And I have eyes and ears everywhere, so don't fuck this up. She doesn't belong on the road, I don't want that life for her. It just has to be this way for now. Remember, it has nothing to do with the chicken."

And with that he smiles, stands up, and heads out of the room, leaving me alone at the big table.

I can only sit there, dumbfounded, trying to make sense of this. I don't like this situation being forced on me. The boss's daughter following in her own bus for a two-month tour? Nepotism at its finest. Or perhaps at its worst.

"Hey," says Lael, her voice soft and concerned. I look up to see her poking her head in the door.

"Hey," I tell her, not sure what else to say. Shit, this is awkward.

"Look," she says, "I just asked my father if I could audition. I didn't want things to be like this."

She seems embarrassed, and I have no doubt she's telling me the truth. This is one hundred percent her father's doing. It has nothing to do with her.

"Are you my ride home?" I ask with a sigh.

"Uh-huh," she says warily.

"Well, all right then, take me home," I say, giving her a small smile, and together we walk out of that miserable office building.

I like being in her tiny car. It's very much an extension of her, at least the her that I know so far. There's teal everywhere and it smells like coconut sunscreen.

We glide away without a sound. She's concentrating on driving through traffic so I take the opportunity to stare at her profile without being noticed. Her long blue-green hair is pushed back by her sunglasses, completely revealing her face and neck. She has a profile that is hard not to stare at—a perfect nose, full lips, young, sunkissed skin. By any standard she is beautiful, but she does not look like the next bass player of *And Then*.

"Like I said, this wasn't my idea," Lael says after a while, keeping her eyes on the road. "And I know you're upset about it, so I'll go to my dad's office tomorrow and tell him I won't do it."

I don't have the heart or energy to respond. I'm suddenly so tired of dealing with things like this. So I put my head back against the seat rest and watch the city pass by.

I have to admit, I'm strangely comfortable with Lael. When I first met her she was just a kid who used to stare at me with heart eyes. She's still a bit younger than me but miles away from that kid that used to hang around me so shyly.

Her words are still hanging in the air, prompting me to say something.

"Good idea. Talk to your dad tomorrow. Call it off," I tell her, still looking out my window.

Now it's my words that hang in the air. I was probably a little harsh, but it needed to be said. I'm not going to take this girl on tour when there's someone out there better suited for the gig. We strive to be one of the most bad-ass bands in the world and Lael is too…pretty.

"I will," she says. "Like I said, this was not my idea. You don't have to worry about taking care of the boss's daughter for your entire tour. Not that I need taking care of, but it's a stupid idea and you don't have to worry about me being around."

Lael's tone is that of a teenager's toward an authority figure. I give her a side eye and don't entertain her with a response.

We're not far from my old stomping grounds. The theater that I used to call home is just minutes away. I haven't been there for a while, and with Mr. Robson having passed away, it feels like it's time to walk down memory lane and say goodbye to my dear friend.

"Do you mind taking a little detour?" I ask.

"Where?" she asks with total attitude.

"The theater where it all started."

"We can do that," she says in a calm, sober voice, her expression softening as she puts on the turn signal.

We don't speak on the way to the theater. It's been ages since I've been on this street in the afternoon, and it looks different with the sun high in the sky. It's quiet too. This part of the city comes alive at night and sleeps during the day. Lael's able to park on the street almost directly in front of the theater's main doors.

"Hungry?" I ask.

"Starving."

We cross the street and get a couple Dilallo burgers. To my surprise, the couple working there are as lively as always. They remember me immediately, offering their condolences for my loss. Lael seems less than enthusiastic about the greasy white bag that they hand her, but I can tell she's charmed by the hard-working couple.

Burgers in hand, we cross the street to the theater. The moment I enter the foyer, the smells instantly bring me back to my late childhood.

Then, stepping into the theater area I see it: Mr. Robson's sound booth, looking painfully empty, flowers laid out all over his equipment.

I run my hands over the flowers that were obviously left by the crew but I know Mr. Robson would have hated having them near his equipment.

I let out a deep breath and close my eyes. I can hear his voice in the depths of my mind: *Did they let you out of your cage?*

"Are you going to be okay?" Lael asks.

I meet her eyes, warm and filled with concern. I make a promise to myself not to break down on her again.

"I will be. C'mon over here. These are the best seats in the house." I direct her to the seats where I always sat at with Mr. Robson.

We sit down and look at the beautiful empty stage, save for an old friend, Ross Duncan, who's on a ladder fixing some lights, the sound of his tools clanking filling the room.

We eat in silence for a while, though my mind can't seem to focus on one thing.

"That is the best thing I've ever tasted," Lael says with a little laugh after she scrunches up the empty burger wrapper and drops it into the bag.

"Right?" I say, amused by the grease around her mouth. I pause. "So, what's it like being the daughter of a tyrant?"

My question doesn't seem to shock her.

"I don't know, what's it like working for one?" she replies, arching a brow.

I clear my throat. "It just surprises me that you want to be a working musician. Aren't you supposed to rebel against your father? Become, like, a doctor or something?"

"My father *hates* that I want to be a musician," she admits. "He sees them as the bottom of the food chain. No offense."

I gave her a crooked smile and a thumbs up, supporting the claim.

She continues with a sigh. "It's like I'm an extension of him rather than my own person. Sometimes I feel like a ghost—a guest in someone else's life."

I'm thinking of how Mr. Robson gave me a chance. I can't imagine where my life would be if he hadn't mentored me. And even though Lael and I grew up on different sides of the tracks, I can see we have some things in common. Most obviously, we're both trapped under the spell of Ronald Ramsey. She's bound by blood and I'm bound by legal contract.

Honestly, I'm not sure which is easier to break free from.

And yet, I know she's sincere about being a musician. I

can feel her youthful drive, know what she's feeling by the way she's gazing at the empty stage.

"The only time I can be the person I need to be is when I'm onstage," she says. "That's when I'm in control. I can self-destruct or I can shine."

I finish chewing before saying, "Self-destruction is very nineties. I would shine if I were you."

"I was born in the late nineties, so I missed that stuff," she says with a shrug.

I imagine how Mr. Robson might react to Lael if he were here with us. He would have done everything he could to encourage her.

Suddenly I feel the weight of responsibility, as if Mr. Robson is standing over my shoulder.

I know what I have to do.

"Alright, young lady," I say to her, and she scrunches up her cute nose at my choice of words. "Why don't you come for an audition? I won't tell Switch or Calvi who you are. You'll be just another bass player auditioning. And I'll go with whatever they say. That way this has nothing to do with your father. It's based on your talent. It's what's fair for all of us."

A smile slowly crosses Lael's face, her eyes still looking at the stage. In an easy, confident voice she says, "I can do that."

FOUR

LAEL

"I can't do this."

Christy turns around from the stove, stirring the giant pot of cabbage soup she made last night. "You can do this," she says calmly. "Why are you getting all freaked out now? You were as cool as a cucumber an hour ago."

"Because," I tell her, standing in the kitchen doorway, unsure of where I should go, what to do with myself. "An hour ago I wasn't an hour closer to my impending doom."

Christy snorts and goes back to paying attention to the soup. "You're so dramatic, Lael. What happened to the positive, confident ball-buster that I know?"

I sigh and look down at my legs where Baby Groot has wriggled his way in between them, staring up at me with big eyes. He wants food. He always wants food.

I scoop him up and give him a kiss on the nose. "But what if I do get the job," I say, more to Baby Groot than to

Christy. "Then what am I going to do with you?"

"Aunt Christy will look after him just fine," Christy comments. "We have a ball when you're at work." Christy works from home as a graphic designer, so when I'm out waiting tables, she's keeping an eye on him. Sometimes I feel we practically share the dog, which makes me feel only a little bit better at the potential of leaving.

But I'm getting ahead of myself. An hour ago I was blisteringly confident, totally convinced I'm going to have the band eating out of the palm of my hand. Now I'm just twisted nerves, thinking I'm going to mess it all up.

No, I tell myself, putting Baby Groot back down on the floor, *you won't mess it up. You know what you're doing. They just might not want all the baggage you bring—the Ramsey name.*

And that's so true. I felt so mortified at the way my father just sprung all of that on Brad, as if he didn't have a choice. What makes it worse is I don't think Brad *does* have a choice. What my father says goes. I've heard him say in many different ways that he discovered Brad and he owns Brad, and knowing my father's team of henchmen and lawyers, I'm sure it's completely true. I just hate that my father would impose me on the band like that.

When I said I wanted to have a chance at playing bass for the band, that wasn't my intention. I just wanted a chance—I didn't want to be forced upon them without any say, and I certainly didn't want it announced like that. I mean, Brad just found out one of his oldest friends and mentors died, so of course my father had to add this whole disruption to the mix.

Luckily, Brad is a pretty easygoing guy. Quiet as anything but still fairly decent. I mean, that's probably an understatement. I'm trying not to dwell on the fact that I actually had him in my arms momentarily as he grieved over Mr. Robson, something that completely caught me off guard. In that moment, he stopped being Brad Snyder, my idol, the man on the pedestal, the rock god of my dreams, and became something decidedly more human. A little bit less of a mystery.

Anyway, the audition idea is what I was hoping for in the first place when I asked my father. Just a chance to prove myself fair and square.

Only now, I'm freaking the fuck out. In a way, it would have been easier to have been forced upon them because they'd be stuck with me and I'd finally be able to live out my dream of being a working musician, playing live shows beyond my wildest fantasies. In time they would see how much I rock, what an awesome addition to the band I would make.

But that way comes with resentment. I had enough of that growing up, the way people treated me because I was Ronald Ramsey's daughter. True, the private school I went to had a ton of kids who had famous and powerful parents, but even so, my father has a reputation for making and breaking people.

I know everyone always assumed I would coast through life because of my father, but that's part of the reason why I left the US and went backpacking for so long. I wanted to put distance between the girl I knew and the woman I would become. Cheesy, I know. But I couldn't figure out who I was without being on my own, away from my father's cold and domineering shadow.

Now I know who I am and what I want. It just sucks that what I want to do with my life—play music!—is so intertwined with what he does. It's like I'll never escape. And I'm sure I could have moved to New York and tried to do it all without him, just as I did when I was backpacking, but the truth is, sometimes you have to stop being stubborn and use the helping hands offered to you. You should never let your pride stop you when your dream is on the line.

"You're going to be fine," Christy says, pouring herself a bowl of the soup and sitting down at the table. She's been on a cabbage soup diet all this week. Every month it's something crazy even though the girl doesn't need to lose any weight. "You know you rock. You know you're talented."

"But they might not see that," I protest. "Because all they'll talk about is how I'm Ronald's daughter. Do they really want me on their tour? They'll think I'm a snitch or something. Or like some kid they have to drag around. They're going to hate me. Plus, what if they don't like my sound? I know what I can bring to the table but they might not want it. And who the hell knows who else I'm auditioning against?"

"Damn, girl," Christy says, shaking her head. "You sure fucked up big time when you came up with that audition thing."

"Actually, that was Brad. And I had no choice. I could see in his eyes that this was the last thing he wanted. You have no idea how long I've dreamed about an opportunity like this—"

"You mean dreamed about *him*," she says wryly. I may have only known Christy for three months but we've become pretty close as roommates, especially when we have a bottle of wine between us. I may have mentioned Brad in a sexual way on more than one occasion. But she won't stop talking about Chris Pine, so whatever.

"Anyway," I push on, giving her a steady look, "this is my dream come true and I didn't want to get it that way. I wanted to earn it, to win it."

"And you will," she says. "And if you don't, then there's something else. That's what you always tell me. Better things are always just around the corner."

I know that's what I tell her, but right now I can't think properly. I just nod and head back into my room, shutting the door on Baby Groot. Normally he goes wherever I go, like my shadow, but I'm about to practice on the bass some more and make sure the pedal is working for the millionth time, and he hates it when I play. He'll be scratching to get out of the room in a hot second. I try not to take offense.

I sit down on the corner of my bed and go through the motions. I know all their songs by heart. I even know the songs from the avant garde solo album that Brad did. I can play everything in their catalogue with my eyes closed.

I try and think about what I can bring to them. What can I, just a lowly bassist, bring to a band that's on top of the world, a band that has everything?

Stability is one thing. They want someone the opposite of Nick, someone they will get along with. During the audition they won't have a clue who I am, at least that's what Brad said. I know Arnie will know, but he's a nice man and he doesn't really count. He likes me. But after they learn the truth, if I'm accepted at all, I have to bring a sense of ease to the band that they didn't have before.

Luckily, even though I do have natural showboating tendencies, I can keep that under wraps. I can keep my head down and let everyone else shine. That's what I can bring to the band.

Sound-wise, though, that's trickier. The band already has a signature sound that they never really stray from—it's probably why Brad branched out and did a solo project, just so he could deviate for once. Now, taking in my penchant for fuzz and effects and noting that Brad's solo effort had a lot of that, I bet I may just have the sound the band didn't realize they wanted or needed.

Of course I'm getting ahead of myself here. I'm just Lael Ramsey. As a bass-player, I'm pretty much a nobody.

But I believe in myself. And when you believe in what you do, that's how you become a somebody.

I take in a deep breath, finding strength and courage in the air, letting it fill me from head to toe.

Then I pack up my pedal and guitar and get ready to do this.

FIVE

BRAD

"Okay, it's time to talk about bass players."

I'm talking to my bandmates in our studio. We all have our usual spots: Calvi and I sitting next to our amps, and Switch behind his sparse drums. Of course, there is an empty chair where Nick used to be. It took me so long to fire Nick because I was avoiding the painful process of finding his replacement. We're auditioning four bassists today. I have no doubt they'll all have their individual sound and will play the songs with ease, but there is way more to consider than the sound that comes out of their amp. This is going to be someone we have to live with in a bus for months on end.

Things to consider could be:

Are they easy to be around?

Do they have stage presence?

Do they show up on time?

Do they represent And Then well?

Are they professional?

Are they into drugs?

Most importantly, we need a guy who we have good chemistry with.

Or, perhaps, a girl.

I spoke to my manager, Arnie, and had him arrange for Lael to be added to the audition roster today. I can see him through the soundproof window sitting in the control room behind the mixing console, talking to someone out of sight. His long grey hair has barely thinned over the years, and his beard is always perfectly groomed to the point I often chuckle at the thought of this biker-looking dude choosing what high-end leave-in conditioner he's going to try next.

I'm waiting for Switch or Calvi to respond to my question about the bassists, but as usual, I'm getting nothing. The room is silent save for the hum of an amplifier and Calvi quietly tuning his gold-top guitar. Switch was closer with Nick than Calvi was but he seems to be used to the idea that Nick is gone. I think he totally understood why I had to let Nick go—he started to believe in the myth of rock and roll and all the standard clichés, such as:

Sex with groupies

Depravity

Violence

Trashing hotel rooms

Arrogance during interviews

Drunk on stage

Throwing televisions out of hotel windows

Heroin

The chicken incident

Mr. Robson briefed me on the heroin thing at the start of my career and I believe his words to be true. He'd said, "Kid, if you do it, you will never be the same for the rest of your life."

Nick definitely was not the same after he got into heroin, and eventually I had to say goodbye to my old friend.

"How do you guys want to approach this?" I ask, directly now.

They both shrug and after some more silence, Switch speaks up. "Let's just jam with each of them, shoot the shit, and see what happens." With his head tilted back and his eyes in a squint I can tell he's going to be tough on them.

Calvi takes a break from tuning his guitar and adds to the conversation, "We don't have to choose any of them if we don't want. If we settle, we'll be back in the same situation next year."

I make eye contact with ol' Arnie though the window. I can tell our first victim is somewhere in the control room out of my eye line because Arnie's body language has changed. Like my bandmates, he has been with me since the beginning and I know him well.

Arnie stands and walks out of sight. I take a deep breath and wait for the door to open.

"...That's how we did it in the old days," Arnie says, finishing his conversation with a rather tall, dark haired, pale skinned character.

"Boys," Arnie says, "this here is John Beddis. He's stopped by to jam."

Arnie has the guitar tech set John up as he sits down in Nick's old chair, next to Nick's old Ampeg SVT amplifier. Even sitting down, John seems to tower over the three of us. His long face makes him look perpetually unimpressed.

Switch, Calvi, and John make idol chit-chat, and I, too, go through the motions of greeting this gangly monster. I can tell the chemistry isn't right before we even play a note. We do a song called "Rust in My Bones," and although he plays his bass with precision, he has the energy of a mortician and I'm happy when it's time to say goodbye.

"Thanks for coming by John. We'll be in touch," Arnie says with a smile, keeping things light.

Next up is none other than *the* Jazz McKinnon.

I'm actually starstruck when he floats into the room with his personal guitar tech, assistant, *and* publicist. He's fifty something years old with overly-styled blonde hair and a scarf wrapped around his neck, draping over his leather vest. Jazz may be over fifty, but he's in better physical condition than we are. Jazz McKinnon is the only guy on the planet that can pull off leather pants, a leather vest, a scarf, and dyed blond hair. He smiles, exposing his toothpaste commercial teeth.

"And Then…" he says, gesturing to us. "Love it. Look at you guys. I'm a huge fan. Let me get this straight though. I'm not here to replace Nick. I just want to jam with you guys."

Jazz keeps his eyes on me and holds out his right hand while his guitar tech scrambles to put his guitar in his hand. I still can't believe he's here—he's a legend in the rock world, having helmed some of the biggest names of the eighties and nineties.

Looking at my bandmates, I can tell they're just as blown away. I exchange a moment with Switch and we both manage to keep from giggling like children. Calvi is locked in a stare with Jazz, smiling like an idiot.

Jazz's assistant looks up from her phone and makes an

announcement. "We've scheduled a brief photo shoot, gentlemen, if you don't mind."

Somehow I'm not surprised. Regardless of what happens with Jazz, this is a moment that needs to be commemorated.

Jazz ignores the large lights, reflectors, and other equipment pouring into the rather small jam room.

"Over here, please," a photographer orders and ushers all of us around the drums where the lights are shining. Calvi and I put our guitars down and obey. Switch stays seated on his throne behind the drums, completely hidden by Jazz standing directly in front of him. Calvi and I exchange a fan boy laugh behind him. Jazz is strutting around like a rooster, front and center. The camera's flash seems like a strobe light and they must take a thousand pictures even though the shoot only lasts about two minutes. When it's all over and the equipment is dragged out, Jazz's assistant pulls me to the side.

"Hi, Brad," she says. "I know we only have an hour so I'm keeping the press to a minimum."

"Press?" I question.

"Yes. Modern Bass Player magazine is going to do a piece on the audition."

"Okay," I say slowly, not sure what the hell is going on. Then I turn my head, and I don't believe my eyes.

I don't see how it's possible but Jazz is in a completely different outfit right down to his shoes. Perfectly torn jeans, sneakers, a graphic t-shirt, blazer, and a network of necklaces. I think his damn hair is even a little different. Houdini would be impressed.

"Thanks again for having me," Jazz calmly says as he floats by me toward one of his entourage who sits him down with a journalist from the magazine in the corner of the studio.

Calvi, Switch, and I are no strangers to this aspect of the job, but this is next level. The three of us stand in the opposite corner from Jazz and his intimate interview and wait. Arnie walks in smiling and says to Jazz's assistant, "Time flies. We only have five minutes left."

She nods and walks over to the interviewer, whispering something into his ear.

"You know, I always wanted to meet him," Calvi says.

"Me too," I say, though who would have known it would be like this.

"I like his haircut," Switch adds.

Jazz walks across the room, looking from his phone up to us and says with a confident smile, "I have a book tour in a month so I can't do the last leg of the tour. I wanted to be clear on that. I'm really digging your song 'Rust in My Bones.' I feel like I have rust in my bones sometimes. Anyway, that went well. Take care, boys."

"Wait," Calvi says and then stops him for a quick selfie before bidding him farewell.

Jazz and his entourage (that has seemed to grow significantly since his arrival) stream out the door, and we are left with just the three of us again.

"Wow, right, what a dude," Calvi says, clearly taken by his childhood hero.

Arnie walks in to give us an update. "Sorry, boys. That ran a little late and we'll have to jump right into the next audition. I told him it would be a little shorter than planned so you can have a little break before our last one of the day. Bruce Ross, And Then, And Then, Bruce Ross."

We all greet Bruce with casual greetings after the

pointless introduction. We all know him already. He has his own progressive funk band, and we have run into him many times on the festival circuit. His sets are usually one long bass solo broken by nasally vocals that are almost always about fishing. Bruce walks up to me to shake my hand and I get an up-close look at his iconic bowler hat and the greasy mustache that is waxed into points.

"Thanks for the chance, man," Bruce says as he squeezes my hand tight and holds deliberate eye contact through circular blue tint glasses that make him look extra intense.

"Yeah, man. For sure. Cool guitar," I tell him, referring to the bass guitar hanging from his shoulders. The wood curled and twisted wildly, I think Bruce is the only person I know that wouldn't look out of place playing the strangely shaped guitar. Then again, the man looks like a reject from a Charlie Chaplin film.

"Do you know 'Rust in My Bones'?" I ask him.

"You mean the song that's playing nonstop on every rock station in America? I think I might have heard it." I catch a tinge of bitterness in his voice which doesn't bode well.

Still, we jump into the song, and in true Bruce Ross form, he turns the tune into one long bass solo. I don't even sing because Bruce doesn't leave any sonic room for me. Don't get me wrong, it's amazing—Bruce is probably the best bass player on the planet in a technical sense.

Calvi and I take a seat when the song is done and Switch is the first to speak.

"Duuude, that was so fucking good."

"Thanks, partner. I know you guys are busy and I have my snake in the car, so I'm going to run," Bruce answers in a nasally voice and presses his blue glasses up from the end of his nose.

"Thanks for that, Bruce," Arnie says as he walks Bruce out.

"What a weird guy," Calvi says as soon as the door closes and we're alone again.

"Yeah, but shit the guy can play," Switch adds.

I give them both a dry look. "I would rather eat broken glass than be on a bus with that character for two months, wouldn't you?"

We share a laugh and spend the next hour or so eating sushi that was delivered, Arnie playing back the recording of John and Bruce's auditions. Obviously, we can't listen to Jazz because he didn't play a single note.

I had debated whether to tell my bandmates about Lael but thought it was best to keep them unbiased.

"Oh, would you look at the time," Switch says, pointing to a clock on the wall. He's obviously referring to my rule that we can't start drinking until after one o'clock in the afternoon.

"Beer me," I tell him. It's been a stressful day and beer is usually the answer.

Switch goes out to the kitchen and comes back with a case of ice cold beer. He rips it open and throws one to me and one to Calvi.

"Who's the babe sitting in the hall?" Switch asks as he falls into a worn out leather couch.

I know very well who's sitting in the hall and I consider telling them that she's both our last audition of the day and the daughter of Ronald Ramsey, but decide to leave out the latter.

"Oh, right," I say casually. "We had an open audition online and this girl was the winner. She seems pretty good."

"A girl? Hmm," Calvi responds stiffly, staring into nothing, thinking of god knows what.

"A girl?" Switch repeats, his eyebrows scrunched together and the corner of his lip curled into a smile.

"Yeah, a girl…so…" I answer.

Knock-knock.

Here comes the moment of truth.

Arnie opens the door and in walks Lael with bass in hand with all the ease and confidence of a professional, her thick teal hair looking striking. She's dressed to impress. Lael glances at the three of us lounging with beer and chopsticks in hand and gives us an unimpressed look. Then she scans the room and struts over to Nick's old Ampeg SVT amplifier.

Leather pants look much better on her than on Jazz McKinnon. Her sleeveless shirt has a White Zombie graphic, and the collar is artistically torn and split, exposing her tawny skin.

"I'll have the engineer set you up," Arnie politely says to Lael.

"Thanks, but I'm good," Lael responds, keeping her attention on the bass amp that's taller than she is.

She takes off her small purse that's the exact same shade of teal as her hair and pulls out a guitar effect pedal. Mr. Robson used to call those pedals dirt boxes. She gets down on one knee and plugs her guitar into the pedal that happens to be the exact same color as her purse and hair.

She then plugs another cable into the opposite end of the pedal and stands up to finally plug into the large amplifier. With a snap and crackle, the amp comes alive. Lael reaches up and twiddles the knobs on the amp.

Then she slams her foot down on her pretty little effect

pedal and the sound that comes out is anything but pretty—a mean growl shakes the room. Her knees bend slightly every time she hits the top string of her bass. Her right arm rises up and slams down aggressively every time she hits the note. Finally, she turns toward us sitting at the edge of our seats, where we are watching her every move, and puts one hand on her hip.

Arnie knows very well who she is, but we agreed we would keep her lineage a secret for the audition at least. The band has never had to meet or deal with her before, and even if they did, it would have been back in the day. Arnie stands between us and Lael like a social referee and makes his introductions doing his best to ignore the strange energy in the room.

"Lael, meet Calvi, Switch, and Brad, collectively known as the band And Then. Gentlemen, meet Lael. She's here to audition to be the interim bassist for the upcoming American tour. I will let you get acquainted."

Arnie opens the door and walks out backwards, giving me a smile just before it closes.

"Hey," Calvi says to Lael after an awkward silence.

"Hey," Lael responds, just as casually.

"You have a pretty killer sound there," I speak up.

"Thanks," she says, trying not to smile.

"What kind of pedal is that?" Switch asks.

"It's one of a kind."

I stand up and walk toward Lael, extending my hand. She takes it, and while we shake hands and hold eye contact, she very briefly breaks away from the tough girl routine.

"Nice to meet you, Lael," I say with a smile.

"You too," she says almost shyly.

I'm tempted to wink at her but I don't.

"Lets have some fun, fellas, shall we?" I say and walk toward the equipment.

Switch walks behind his drums and Calvi to his guitar. Switch does a few rolls and hits on his drums as he always does, as if to make sure they still make a sound when you hit them. Calvi tunes his guitar. I feel like if I don't just count off the song they'll be adjusting their instruments all day.

"All right. Rust in My Bones, in one, two, three, four."

We've played the song a thousand times but it's never sounded as good as it does right now, with Lael on the bass. She is fucking *wild*. Her overdriven sound makes the song meaner, heavier, while she adds notes, slaps and slides in the perfect spots. She holds a wide powerful stance, like she owns the room, owns the song, as her bass guitar hangs almost to her knees. Her entire upper body thrusts into each and every note. At every change in the song, Calvi, Switch, and I exchange a look of amazement and joy and begin to play with more enthusiasm, trying to match her. Lael's over-the-top approach is infectious, and by mid-song the whole band is playing at full throttle.

Toward the end of the song it's like we're all competing to be the component with the highest energy. Switch is standing up when he rolls along the toms, and slams his drums harder than usual. Calvi has his foot on an amp, playing harder than he normally does. Rather than tapping my foot, my entire leg bounces up and down.

The song usually has a tight ending but this time we hold the last note for what seems like days, everyone building and building. Lael reaches down and makes her teal pedal go into oblivion.

Finally, with our guitars raised high in the air, Switch does his final roll on the drums and we all slam down and end the long crescendo. For some reason, as it sometimes happens when we're jamming, we all laugh.

"*Duuude,*" Calvi says to Lael.

I'm still laughing, overjoyed and completely blown away as I reach for my beer. I take a long swig and exchange a look with Switch. It seems he feels the same way too.

"That was pretty bad-ass," I manage to say to her when I'm done swallowing.

But Lael is already unplugging her pedal and putting it back into her purse, ready to go.

Arnie opens the door and addresses the room, "Thank you, Lael. That was fantastic. We'll be in touch."

"Thanks for having me. See ya, boys." She smiles at each of us and heads through the door that Arnie is holding open for her with the same confidence she walked in with.

When it clicks shut, the air in the room changes.

"I never really thought about having a girl in the band, but why not, I think it's cool," Calvi says while he rests his guitar on a stand.

"I like her," I tell them. I liked her before, but after seeing her actually play? Shit, we would be fools not to take her.

Well, aside from the messy complications of who she really is.

"Yup," Switch agrees.

Arnie, however, doesn't share the same enthusiasm. I can tell he's being a little cautious with her, and for all the right reasons.

"You know," he says carefully, brushing his long grey hair behind his ears. "She's pretty young. Maybe she needs a little more experience. I mean, it's a long tour and demanding as hell. I thought Beddis sounded pretty good."

But in this moment, there doesn't seem to be any choice. I choose to ignore Arnie's warning as we all take our seats, open fresh beers, and look at each other with confirming smiles.

"All in favor of Lael say aye," Calvi says, raising his beer, insinuating if we agree it will be a binding contract.

"Aye," Switch says, holding up his beer. They both turn to me.

"Aye," I say and hold up my beer. Then we bang our cans together.

"Majority rules, motion passed," Calvi says with a laugh.

Arnie stands in front of us with his arms crossed, stroking his long grey beard.

"Oh boy," he says under his breath.

SIX

LAEL

My life has come full circle.

Well, if full circle includes me with my hand over my mouth, feeling like I'm going to vomit. Because I might just do that.

I'm backstage with *And Then,* hanging around outside their dressing room at the Palladium Theater, just as I did back when I was fourteen at their very first show.

Only now I'm part of the band.

I'm officially their bassist.

I have been for a few weeks now.

And this is our first show.

It doesn't matter how many times I've rehearsed with the band (not enough, in my opinion, it's like trying to herd cats), or how many times I've done it on my own, I'm not ready.

How could I ever be ready for this?

"Breathe," Brad says, and I look up to see him staring

at me with a bemused smirk on his face.

I try, but all I can do is gulp for air. Does he even realize that he said that exact same thing to me all those years ago in this same exact place?

It's hard to tell with Brad sometimes. He keeps mainly to himself, even at rehearsals, and while he's not stingy with the praise and has been pretty encouraging, it usually stops at that.

"I'm trying to breathe," I tell him. "God, weren't you this nervous for your first show?"

He shrugs. "Maybe. I hardly remember it."

"How can you not remember it? I think this will be branded in my brain for the rest of my life."

He scratches at the stubble on his chin. Sexy stubble, I might add. Brad's dressed pretty low-key for tonight's show: a black t-shirt that shows off his muscles and black jeans just tight enough to show off his ass. His hair is pushed back off his face, and his eyes are dark and smoldering as always. Sometimes I wonder how I'm able to play my bass, let alone talk to him, without drooling.

But I have an image to obtain and that's one of being a consummate musician and a total professional. Of course, I feel like I'm failing at both right now. Because, you know, wanting to vomit and everything.

"I'll tell you that I remember playing the first show ever by myself. I opened for Iggy Pop…somehow." He grins at me, flashing pearly whites that make me weak in the knees. "The stars aligned that day. My birthday. Anyway, that show I'll never forget. But all the rest of them kind of blend in with each other." He gives me a sly look, leaning in closer. What little breath I have hitches in my throat. "I'll tell you something. Before every show, I go into a zone of sorts. It's probably why I don't remember them all so well. But it gets the job done."

"Are you in the zone now?" I ask quietly, conscious of how close we are to each other.

"I will be in a few minutes. So don't take offense if I seem a bit standoffish."

"I would never. You do what you need to do. I'll…just try not to throw up."

He puts his hand on my shoulder and gives it a squeeze. I feel waves of mild current flow through him to me, heating my skin. I know it's all in my head but I'm feeling so alive right now, so who knows. Everything is heightened for good or bad.

"You're going to do great, Lael," he says to me. "Trust me. You wouldn't be here if I didn't believe in you. You want to know the trick?"

"What?" Yes. Yes, give me all the fucking tricks.

"Show them no respect."

I frown. "Ummm…"

He explains. "The reason you're nervous is because you care too much about what they think. The audience. The crowd. This isn't about them. They're here to see you, but you're not here to see them. Give them no respect. Play for you. Don't worry what they think. You have a story to tell and a show to give, and you'll do it because they're here for you. Don't forget that."

"It sounds a little crude."

He shrugs casually. "Rock and roll is crude, baby."

I smile at him, feeling some of my nerves wash away. "That it is."

"Now, if you'll excuse me," he says with a wink, "I'm going to get into beast mode. I'll see you on the other side.

And remember, you're going to do fine. Just be yourself."

"And show no fear."

"No respect, but that works too."

Then he turns and walks off toward the back wings of the stage.

Oh shit. Oh shit, does that mean it's almost time? What do I do?

I catch Arnie walking past me, his face furrowed in concentration, staring down at his phone.

"Arnie," I call out, running beside him. "Where do I go? When do we start?"

He glances at me briefly. "Oh, it's you. Just find the rest of the band."

"Brad already went on stage."

"He's in the zone."

"I know. So what do I do? How much time till we go on?"

He glances at the phone. "Two minutes, love." Then he walks off.

"Two minutes!?" I shriek.

Just then the dressing room door opens and Switch and Calvi and one of the guitar techs step out.

"Hey, you didn't run off," Calvi says with a smirk.

"No, I didn't," I tell him, narrowing my eyes. "I'm ready. At least I think I am."

"You're as ready as you'll ever be," Switch says, patting me on the back and turning me around toward the stage. "Come on. The stage is this way."

Fuck. I'm not calm, not even in the slightest. The minute Brad went into beast mode and walked off, all my confidence went with him. I have to repeat to myself over and over again, as crude as it sounds, show them no respect, show them no respect.

By the time I'm waiting in the wings of the stage beside Switch and Calvi, Brad off in his own world, looking like a madman, I'm practically shouting the mantra to myself.

Show them no respect!

And yet there they are. I can see the audience. They're loud and the show is sold-out and absolutely crammed full, from the fans being squished against the barricade to the line of photographers between them and the stage, looking bored out of their mind as they wait, to the people up in the rafters practically leaning over the railings. This is utter madness.

This is my dream.

A mix of adrenaline and anxiety and pure fucking joy courses through my veins until I'm sure I might just explode right here, and all that'll be left will be Lael pixie dust. Something I'm sure Calvi would snort up his nose right away.

"You ready?" Switch asks as one of the techs goes out and starts adjusting Brad's microphone, saying, "Check one, check two, check, check" and the crowd goes absolutely wild.

I shake my head, biting my lip, though I can't tell if it's because I'm trying not to puke or trying not to smile.

This is unreal.

This is so unreal.

"Ready or not," Switch says, "it's showtime."

He glances across the stage where Arnie is standing, arms folded across his chest, and he nods, giving a signal.

"We're not going to huddle or something?" I ask Switch in a panic, pulling on his sleeve. His t-shirt already feels soaked in sweat and he hasn't even started drumming yet.

"Huddle?" he says, then his eyes turn salacious. "I'll gladly give you a private huddle, darling."

I put my hand on his shoulder and push him out of the way. "Pass. You go drum your drums."

"You go rock that bass."

And then Calvi stalks off into the darkness of the stage, almost in a huff, and I know I have no choice but to follow and find my mark and my instrument, just as we went over during sound check.

It's surreal.

That's the only way to explain it.

I walk through the blue dark of the stage over to my bass while the crowd gets louder and louder. I try not to look at their faces—I try to pay attention to just the bass strap going around my shoulders.

But I can't help glancing at the crowd. Harsh blue light shines down on them, and I know they can't really see me, but they're waiting. Waiting for when Brad walks on stage, when the main lights go on, when we launch into "Fuzzface," our first song.

I'm waiting too.

Heart pounding against my chest.

Stomach swirling.

Breath hitched in my throat.

This is it.

Then the crowd roars, a crescendo that climbs higher and higher, and I feel like my soul is being lifted up on a wave.

Brad is on stage.

Though I can't see his face, he glances over his shoulder at me and nods.

The lights go on.

We go on.

And just like that the crowd only exists to feed me. I go into my own version of beast mode. I am a monster that thrives on cheers and cries and the sweat of everyone in this theater.

I pummel the bass, whipping my hair around, putting every ounce of energy into every note, and for now I feel limitless, like my energy has an endless reserve that can never be exhausted.

And through it all, I feel intensely connected to Brad, more than I thought I could. I feel connected to everyone. On the stage, in the crowd, we're all one, all feeding off each other, all lifting each other until we come together in the song.

It's the best feeling I've ever had in my life.

And I know I want to keep doing this until the day I die.

"This is a little ridiculous," I yell up at George, the driver of the bus.

As in the driver of *my* bus.

As in, I have a fucking bus all to myself because my father doesn't want me riding with the rest of the band for who knows what reason. He probably thinks they'll be a bad influence on me, as if I can be so easily coerced.

Either way, it's ridiculous.

"I know," George, a heavy-set guy with a perpetually sweaty forehead, says. "Believe me. Every single tour is an even greater pain in the ass. Why the hell can't Brad fly? I mean, a private jet? Your father would surely get him a fucking private jet. So he's afraid of flying? Just drug him up."

"You know what they say about rock stars and airplanes," I tell him, coming up to sit beside him in the passenger seat. I sigh as I look ahead of us, at the back of the tour bus that the rest of the band is on. My band.

"This is just another way to segregate me from them," I say, crossing my arms. I've been floating through most of the day on a high from last night, but now that it's stretching into the evening and we're speeding up the I-5 to Seattle, I'm losing a bit of the buzz.

Mainly because I'm annoyed.

I don't know at this point if it's my father or the band who really want me traveling back here. After last night's performance, I was certain that I would feel one step closer to the band. I certainly did when I was on stage.

But when we walked off stage after the encore and everyone went their separate ways. There were no pats on the back, no jobs well done. Nothing. It's like the show didn't even happen. We just got on our separate buses and that was that.

Fuck it. I don't need the band's approval to tell me I did a good job. I got enough from the media. I've spent most of the day going through all the concert write-ups of the show, trying to see how we appeared to everyone else.

The good news is, everyone loved it. Specifically, they loved me. Sure some said that it seemed I hadn't found my place on stage yet and was both a bit rusty and a bit green, but most said I brought a new energy to the band and that I was a breath of fresh air after Nick.

The bad news is, I'm not sure how much the band likes all the focus being on me, nor do I know how the fans feel.

I mean, I should know, I'm still one of their biggest fans, even though I'm in now in the band. But I also know what it's like to love the original lineup and hate change. Nick was a dick, but he was what they knew and expected. I'm not sure the fans know quite what to do with me yet, and obviously there's going to be a lot of talk over the fact that I'm Ronald's daughter and probably bought my way in. Plus, some rock fans can be pretty misogynistic when it comes to a girl wailing on the bass and holding her own. I think I'll have to prove myself over and over again.

Eventually we stop at a hotel in Oregon for the night. We're doing things the long way, driving up from LA to Seattle, then working our way down the coast. Normally, Arnie and George take turns driving through these long hauls but in this case, since there's now a stupid extra bus on account of me, we have to stop for the night.

At least it gives me an opportunity. The minute I exit the bus and see the band getting off, I beeline it over to Brad.

"Hey," I tell him, grabbing his arm lightly. "Can I talk to you for a moment?"

His eyes light up when he sees me, which is a good sign.

"Sure, what's up? How's the bus?"

I pull him aside so that we're out of earshot of Switch and Calvi who are giving us looks.

"About that," I say. "I think it's fucking ridiculous."

He bursts out laughing. "Tell me how you really feel."

"I'm serious. It's costly and pointless."

"It's your father's bill. And his wishes."

"So? Do you always do what he says?"

He cocks a brow at me, studying me for a moment. I

think I may have hit a nerve there.

"No," he says. "You're here because you wanted to be here fair and square. You won that audition."

"What I mean is, I'm a grown woman." At that, his eyes skirt down over my body and I feel myself blushing from head to toe. I swallow hard and push on. "And I can make my own decisions. It's not up to my father to decide that I should travel in another bus, which not only keeps me purposely excluded from the band I should be connecting with, but adds to the stress of the journey. We could get places quicker on one bus with Arnie and George taking turns as they used to."

Brad sighs and runs his hand over his face. "I know," he says, looking off toward the hotel.

"Plus, don't you want me to get to know you guys better? Become a real band? I can't do that if I only see you on stage every night. Our music, our shows, they'll be a thousand times better if I get to be around you all more often. We need to act like a unit. The audience isn't stupid, they can tell when bands know each other, like each other. There's a synchronicity in the air."

He looks at me curiously. "Is that so? You were great last night."

"I wouldn't know," I tell him pointedly. "After the show, you guys all just went your own ways."

"We don't sit around and congratulate each other."

"Well, I could use the encouragement. It was my first show with you guys. Shit, it was my first show playing to more than twenty people."

"Well, you did good," he says with a nod. "And you'll do better every night. And yes, I agree we should get rid of the bus. Hell, I want to get to know you better too."

I bite my lip, trying not to smile. It's funny how certain words and looks from him have me fangirling all over the place. I need to pull it together. I need to ignore that smile that makes my toes curl, those dark eyes that make my skin feel hot.

"But for tonight," he goes on, "let's get you checked into your room. I'll tell Arnie and George what's up. Just so you know, we may have to have the other bus trailing behind as a decoy for a few more days."

"Decoy?"

"Hey, I'm not scared about disobeying your father's orders, but I'm not going to fuck with anything this early in the tour. Believe me, your father has eyes everywhere. He'll be asking about the bus for a while yet. You just won't be on it."

I laugh. "It's still ridiculous then."

"Welcome to the world of rock and roll," Brad says. He places his hand at the back of my arm and steers me toward the hotel. "Come on, let's get you settled in. Tomorrow we play Seattle, then Portland, then San Francisco. Those crowds are going to be insane, so you need your rest. The best is just ahead of us."

SEVEN

BRAD

I was never good at sleeping on a moving bus, especially when Arnie is driving. Arnie spent a great deal of his early twenties rally car driving and he seems to think the I-5 is a race track. I much prefer our normal driver who is the opposite of Arnie in every way. George is the calmest person I have ever met, and the bus seems to float along the highway when he's driving. But ol' Arnie is flying along, yelling at cars as he passes them, his accent deepening with his road rage.

Get off the road, ya Wanker!

Learn how to drive, plonker!

The drive from Portland to San Francisco is ten hours, and Arnie splits the driving with George for the long trips so we don't have to stop anywhere. We couldn't keep up this schedule otherwise.

But I can't blame my insomnia entirely on Arnie's driving—I have a hard time winding down after any show.

My adrenaline doesn't switch off when I step off the stage. Instead, it lingers like an idling race car engine, maybe like the cars Arnie used to race. It rumbles along in my chest as I lie in my bunk and watch the dark Oregon forest fly by.

Switch snores. If he wasn't such a great guy to be in a band with, it would be a deal breaker. I take his snoring like he's showing off, boasting at how easily he can sleep on this bus. I go through an internal emotional journey until I can't take it anymore and consider hitting him right in his rumbling nose. Then the tone of his snoring changes and I feel like he's making an effort even though he doesn't know it.

Calvi is showing off too, that bastard. This one actually smiles like a weirdo while he sleeps. We could have had the worst day of our lives and the bus could be on fire and this smug bastard would still smile away in his slumber. Sometimes he even giggles in his sleep, though he always says he doesn't remember what he dreams about. I think he's just laughing at me and my insomnia.

I've been trying not to stare at Lael ever since she joined our bus. She's created a happy home within the confines of the tiny space of her bunk. Right now she's wrapped up perfectly in a blanket that she brought with her, her phone lying next to her like a loyal companion. Her purse is tucked in the corner by her feet and a notebook and some magazines are under her pillow.

I have to admit, she's hard not to stare at. She has my full attention more and more these days. I trace the lines of her lips, the curve of her nose, her eyebrows, her chin—I barely blink as I take her in.

The race car in my chest turns off its engine.

I hold her in my gaze and I feel…calm.

She slowly opens her eyes and looks over at me as if she knows I have been watching her.

I don't look away.

We share a moment, our heads resting on our pillows as we look at one another.

She smiles.

I sleep.

I feel like I merely blinked but somehow it's morning, and judging by the colorful buildings I can see from my window of the parked bus, I know we have arrived at our destination.

I sit up and rub my eyes. Lael's bed is made up and one of her duffle bags is in the corner. The other two vacant bunks are left in a twisted mess.

I've always liked San Francisco. The sky, when you can see it, is a slightly different shade of blue, and the ocean air always feels clean. Today it's sunny, and considering it's mid-December, the sun feels warm. I don't mind the bus sometimes, but a hotel room with a hot shower is in order at this point.

"Morning, young man," Arnie says as he climbs up the narrow steps into the bus. He offers me a very large coffee and a familiar piece of paper—our itinerary for the day.

"You're a good man, Arnie," I respond as I take the coffee and sheet of paper, glancing at it.

9am - Interview at 865 Battery Street, Live 105 radio show

11am - Hotel check-in, 181 3rd St., W Hotel

12pm - Lunch with App designer at 27 Hotaling Pl., Villa Taverna

1:30pm - Band meeting and rehearsal at venue, Warfield

Theater, 982 Market St.

    2:30pm - Interview with full band, Rolling Stone magazine

    3pm - Meet and greet with VIP ticket holders

    3:30pm - Sound check

    6pm - Dinner at Boulevard Restaurant, 1 Mission St.

    7pm - Wardrobe

    7:30 - Group video message for And Then Fan club website stream

    8pm - Meet and greet with VIP Elite plus members

    9pm - Showtime!

    After party: Kirk Hammett's house

I look over my morning orders, rolling my eyes and shaking my head at each item.

"Lunch with an *app designer*?" I question.

"Don't you remember? The Brad Snyder App. They'll get a notification every time you take a piss," Arnie answers.

"Is there really an after party at Kirk Hammett's house? I mean, *the* Kirk Hammet. Guitarist for Metallica?" I ask.

"Yeah, mate. I guess he's a fan. He invited you and the boys over. You know he's a collector of horror memorabilia and his house is like a museum full of the shit."

"Really?"

"Really. Now, let's try to stick to the schedule today. No flaking off, especially for the interviews. The other turkeys have already started their days. Time for you to get on with it. There's a driver waiting outside to shuttle you around. I'll leave you to it and meet you at the Warfield after lunch."

Arnie leaves the bus like he's late for something. I know it can't be easy for him, keeping all of this going. It would all fall apart in a minute if it weren't for him herding us like cats.

I rummage through my storage space to find some clean clothes, quickly wash up, and step out of the bus with coffee in hand, squinting at the morning sun.

"Mr. Snyder."

A rather short man with a middle-aged face and the body of a boy is standing next to a black Suburban. My driver.

"Hello," I greet him with a smile and step into the vehicle. I can barely see him from my back seat so I'm concerned he can't see over the dashboard. His small hand reaches up to adjust the rearview mirror, and I meet his eyes.

"Okay, Mr. Snyder. First stop is 865 Battery Street. Away we go."

We pull away and I stare out the window, sipping my still hot coffee. This will be a fairly standard day, save the party at Kirk Hammett's house, which sounds absolutely unreal. I've learned to take things one step at a time. I tend to be a good boy and do all that's asked, but on occasion I put the itinerary in the waste basket and disappear for the day, only to show up when it's time to play. I wish today was one of those days.

Especially when it comes to the first stop. I *hate* morning radio shows. There's nothing worse than fake enthusiasm and sound effects. I guess the only good thing is there are never any curve balls—all the questions are standard, a couple call-in questions from listeners that have been screened, some fake laughter, and you're done.

Our vehicle is at a stop due to heavy traffic, and we're only a couple of blocks further down the street from where we started. My driver has his attention on his GPS, where he's looking for a better route.

"Don't worry, Mr. Snyder. We'll be on time."

I wasn't worried. I try to worry as little as possible. I'm content just people watching out of the tinted window from the confines of this Suburban.

Then I see Lael walking back toward the bus, her hair tied up under a hat, large vintage sunglasses covering half her face. I roll down the window and shout to get her attention.

"Lael!"

She smiles when she sees me and walks over to the stopped Suburban.

"Good morning, Brad," she says, polite as always. Even though I've slowly been getting to know her better, I still get the impression that she's not letting her guard down around me. Not that I would blame her, being Ronald's daughter and all.

"So what does your day look like?" I ask her, curious.

"Just going to take it easy, maybe use the gym at the hotel if I can stop being so lazy."

"Take it easy?" I raise my itinerary. "You didn't get one of these?"

"No. Arnie just told me to meet at one-thirty at the venue."

"Well, it doesn't seem fair that the new kid gets the day off while I'm running all over town alone. Care to join me? We can get through this together."

I smile and she gives me a cautious smile back, mulling it over.

I open the door. "Come on."

Lael slides in and I give her the itinerary to peruse.

She looks it over and her eyebrows raise.

"Kirk Hammett?" she asks.

I laugh, and before long we're moving again.

We arrive at the radio station just in time. Everyone that works there is fake smiling and completely obnoxious in their excessive energy.

It was an easy interview in the end, but it wasn't without some annoyances. When Lael and I first walked into the studio and put our headphones on, the DJ, Stuntman Jim, made a comment about my girlfriend being too young for me. I corrected him and introduced Lael as the new bass player but his opening remark lingered in my mind for the entire live broadcast.

When I'm asked at the end to do some sound bites for the radio station, I tell them that Lael will do it instead. There was a time I got a thrill out of doing these live interviews, but that enthusiasm has long since gone. But watching Lael's excitement is refreshing and fun, like a parent seeing Christmas again through their child's eyes.

She does more takes than anyone should, her nerves getting the best of her while the jackasses at the radio station increasingly lose patience. Even their fake smiling stops while our laughing increases until Lael and I have tears in our eyes. Finally, she nails it so we can move on.

This is Lael Ramsey, the new bassist for And Then and you are listening to Live 105.

We laugh at the ridiculousness of the moment, and just like that the tone is set for the day. We find amusement in just about everything on our way back to the hotel: the wide-smiling receptionist, our little Italian driver... It's like we're kids on a field trip, amused solely by our own laughter.

In the hotel lobby we sign a few autographs and run into Switch, dressed in a leather jacket with a fur collar and aviator sunglasses. Switch enjoys the attention and tries to goad the paparazzi into taking pictures of him every chance he gets.

"Hey, man, what are you up to?" I ask Hollywood Switch.

"I have an interview downtown," he answers, turning his head so the fan taking a picture with their phone gets his good side.

"Right on. Who with?" I ask and motion to Lael who is walking by to wait for me.

"Costco," he says.

I raise my brows. "Like the store where you can buy six packs of underwear?"

"Yeah, dude, they have their own magazine."

"All right, man. I'll see you later."

Have fun with that.

I walk with Lael to the elevator and head up to the top floor. All I can think about is a warm shower and a little downtime.

And yet…

Lael's room is directly across from mine, and as our backs are to each other, putting in our key cards, I say, "I hope you don't think you're done." I pause until she turns around to look at me with an open expression. "What's next on that silly list?"

Lael holds the door open with her foot while she takes the itinerary out of her pocket.

"Let's see," she says, looking it over. "Ah, right, you have a lunch at noon to discuss the Brad Snyder app with an app designer."

I bow my head, shaming the concept.

"I think that's exactly what the world is missing," she says with a playful tone. "A Brad Snyder app."

"We'll skip that one," I tell her quickly. "I'll tell Arnie it's a no. Let's just go to the wharf and get some chowder or something."

"Are you sure? Playing hooky seems awfully rock star of you."

"If the shoe fits. So are you in?"

"Hell yeah."

We both smile, somewhat still giddy from earlier. I find myself not wanting to say goodbye to Lael. Her face has a glow from all the laughing and fresh air, and she looks beautiful. I wonder what would happen if I invited her into my room. For a moment we stand there holding open our doors, letting the possibility hang in the air, subtle but undeniable.

"Rest up, mister. I'll knock on your door in an hour," she says with a smile. Then she winks and disappears into her room. I stare at her closed door for a moment before I retreat into mine.

Luckily, it's not long before I've had a shower and freshened up and the two of us are back out there. It's high noon on a sunny San Francisco day, and we're walking along the wharf looking for a place to have a bite.

It's an odd moment for me. If it wasn't for the occasional looks I get when people recognize me, I'd feel like I'm just a normal guy sharing a sunny afternoon with a pretty girl. I have to say, it's interesting getting to know someone new, even though Lael isn't exactly new. She just feels new.

People will always surprise you if you let them. No one's exactly as they seem, and Lael is no exception.

As we stroll along the busy walkway dodging strollers and tourists, Lael talks and talks, which is a nice change of pace. It takes the pressure off of me. Just when I think she's run out of things to say, she keeps going. She's refreshingly open, the opposite of me, and covers her entire life, every relationship she's had, where she has been, where she wants to go. And her deep respect for Prince.

"I mean, look at Prince. He lived and breathed what he did. He nearly put out an album a year for his whole career," she says, totally passionate. "His music is not what he did—it's who he was. Anyway, about my roommate, Christy…"

It takes some focus to follow her and her wayward trains of thought, but it's nice to see her so comfortable with me. I almost feel honored, though I have a feeling this is just the way she is.

She finally takes a deep breath when both of our attention goes to a very cinematic moment on a bench just in front of us. A very young girl is accepting an ice cream cone from her mother, her smile, and her star-shaped sunglasses catching the attention of everyone walking by.

"Aww." Lael clutches her chest, looking in love with the scene. She looks at me with a big, silly smile. "Can I have an ice cream, too?"

"After!" I respond and point to the chowder joint to our right. "Real food first."

"But ice cream *is* real food," she protests. "It's the *only* food."

After we settle at a long table overlooking the small marina and the ferries heading out to Alcatraz and other islands in the bay, Lael takes a breath and for a moment becomes self-aware.

"Am I talking too much?" she asks.

"No," I answer truthfully. I'm actually enjoying her blabber. She has an unusual approach that's entertaining.

We sit side by side facing the water. Lael shows no sign of running out of things to talk about, so I make myself comfortable. I can't be sure if she notices that our legs are touching beneath the table, and the way she is leaning into me is causing our arms to touch as well. I don't pull my arm or leg away; rather I slightly lean into her, drink my tea, and enjoy this very genuine moment I'm sharing with my new bass player. There's something about the perfect blue sky and the ocean air blowing her familiar scent toward me that makes me want to take a mental picture.

I'm definitely not one to pull out my phone and snap a photo, but once in a while I make an effort to not let a moment pass me by. I live in the now, taking everything in, and try to file it away wherever memories are kept. I'm doing that right now.

"What are you smiling at, Snyder?" Lael asks with amusement.

I don't answer her right away. I raise my hands innocently while I try to come up with a response, but my mouth opens and the words fall out, skipping the filtration process.

"You."

"Am I making you smile, Mr. Snyder?" she asks coyly.

I clear my throat and nudge the conversation in a different direction.

"I was just thinking about the pranks the fellas have in store for you," I elaborate, hoping she buys it.

"What?!" she asks, her voice high pitched with worry. "What pranks?"

"I don't know."

"Brad!"

"Honestly, I don't know, I just thought I would give you a heads up so you at least have a chance," I say with a laugh.

Lael grabs me by the collar and playfully pulls me toward her. I play along and pretend she's hurting me.

"What are they going to do, Snyder?"

It's during this playful moment that I notice the sniper with the camera taking our photo. I have no doubt he's been following us for some time.

Lael turns her head to look at what's grabbed my attention, and in an instant the mood has changed like someone flicked a switch.

We don't say it out loud but we both know what those photos are going to look like. I place some money on the table.

"Come on. It's about time to go anyway."

We make our way back to where the Suburban is waiting. Our driver quickly folds up his newspaper and we drive away, leaving the sneaky photographer behind. By the time we get to the venue, our mood is light again. I always have an irrational fear that no one will show up to the shows, but I notice some pedestrians wearing *And Then* shirts which gives me some relief.

"The Warfield," our driver announces.

The security guard at the back entrance notices us right away and we are shown to the rehearsal room beneath the stage. The whole gang is there as well as the usual unfamiliar faces. A small drum kit is in the corner and amps line the wall.

The mood is festive and the volume in the room is high with shouting conversations. Lael walks in first and the small gang breaks into applause.

Her face turns a pretty shade of pink and she tries to play along, waving like she's a beauty queen. Little does she know, this is what the gang does every time you enter backstage.

I know this shtick, so I'm ready for it when I walk in behind Lael.

The weirdos go from loving applause to a resounding boo, pointing and hissing at me as I find my place in the room. Lael shakes her head, laughing at the bizarre welcomes.

"Hey, Lael," Calvi says, walking over to her with a suspicious grin.

"Hey, Calvi," she answers as she opens a beer.

"We were just playing a little game. Check it out. Hey, Switch. Show her how it's done," Calvi says. I know where this is going.

Switch springs into action. He rolls a magazine into a funnel and sticks it under his belt, then he puts a quarter on his forehead as he looks up. Tilting his head forward, he drops the quarter into the rolled up magazine tucked into the front of his pants and the room applauds.

"Looks easy enough," Lael says warily.

"Let's see you try it," Calvi says.

"You first."

Calvi watches her for a second and then tucks the magazine funnel into his pants and tilts his head way back, balancing the quarter on his forehead.

Lael then reaches over and pours most of her beer into the magazine funnel.

"Ahhhh!" Calvi screams as the crotch of his pants darkens. The room erupts into hysterics.

"Dude, seriously, that stupid prank is all over the internet," Lael says as she shakes the last few drops at Calvi. "You're going to have to try harder than that."

"This ain't over, newbie," Calvi growls at her before he stalks off toward the restroom.

After the immature, but expected, hijinks we spend the rest of the time mostly goofing around rather than rehearsing new songs. The interview with Rolling Stone goes as expected. Mostly they want to talk about the line-up change and how that's going to affect things. They also want some dirt on Nick and some soundbites on the chicken incident, but we play it as diplomatic as ever.

I have to say, I appreciate the tone the interviewer has with Lael. The world can sometimes feel like a boys' club and he doesn't make a note of her being an attractive young woman. Mostly, he and Lael speak about her unique sound. She really does have a unique aspect that's making our band sound different.

Better, even.

The meet and greet is standard—some quick conversations, a few pictures, signing a few things. There's slight tension between Calvi and Lael from the earlier incident, and I can tell Calvi has something up his sleeve for revenge. Lael is on guard when he's close.

"Okay, gang. Time flies, doesn't it? Let's do a quick sound check so we can go relax and have dinner," Arnie says, waving his arms as if to push us toward the stage.

The theater is empty save the crew, the Rolling Stone interviewer who is scribbling something, and a small group of VIP ticket holders. It's a strange feeling looking to those empty seats, but I take the time to always visualize things going well as I walk around the stage, strumming my guitar, making sure I can hear myself.

While we're making a racket tuning and adjusting, Lael is messing with the knobs on her teal pedal that I think will be the focal point of the Rolling Stone interview, the cause of her newly signature sound.

"Test one, two. Okay, let's play something," I say into the mic.

"Let's do 'FuzzFace,'" Calvi says.

I glance at my three bandmates and it looks like they're ready to go.

Lael starts the song off ringing out long, deep, rattling notes on her bass. Her eyes are closed and she hits the bass with the side of her fist. I can tell it's for the benefit of the Rolling Stone guy who is watching her closely.

Then, right on the beat where we all jump in, right at the moment when Lael theatrically throws her long hair forward and slams her foot down on her pedal, an extremely loud fart noise rumbles out of the main speakers.

My jaw drops open and I have to stifle a laugh. I did not see that coming.

Clearly, neither did Lael.

Calvi falls over with tears in his eyes, and Switch drops his sticks and hunches over laughing. Lael is in shock, frozen in a power stance with her foot on her fart pedal. The Rolling Stone guy is feverishly writing on his pad.

"You bastard," Lael yells, pointing to Calvi.

"Okay, so we're even now," Calvi says with a shrug.

From behind the drum kit Switch shouts, "Welcome to And Then!"

EIGHT

BRAD

We're in New Mexico and everything is lined up for total chaos. I have witnessed self-annihilation my entire life and do not have the capacity to put a romantic slant on drugs. We have the day off and Switch and Calvi keep on exchanging mischievous looks, which can only mean one thing. Arnie also feels what's in the air and makes an attempt to keep them busy, flipping through his iPad, looking for something to do in New Mexico.

"Aye, how about this," he says. "The Sandia Peak Tramway, or wait, a history museum. That could be interesting, aye boys?"

"What do you say, Calvi? Want to go to the museum today?" Switch asks sarcastically.

"Oh, that sounds just wonderful," Calvi answers, matching his sarcasm, then they both break out into laughter.

Arnie throws his iPad to the side and says, "Okay, ya

bastards. Do your own thing. Just remember tomorrow comes fast and we have a show to play."

Our bus stops at our hotel and Arnie hops out to get everything sorted at the front desk. Lael is reading a book in her little corner in the back, trying to ignore us. Every now and then she and I exchange a private glance and a smile, but at the moment she has all her focus on her book and her coffee.

To their credit, Switch and Calvi always seem to be able to dust themselves off and show up for work the next day, no matter what drugs they do or how much they drink. And it's not like they go on a tear every time we have a day off. Our schedule is too intense and expectations are too high. There's no way anyone could keep this pace up while getting wasted every other night.

But this isn't just any day off. We're in Santa Fe, New Mexico, Switch's home town. Strangely, *And Then* has never played Santa Fe so I haven't been here with Switch before. I have heard the stories, though.

In the past, it seemed to make things worse when I tried to stop Calvi and Switch from partying too hard. They would get defensive. Case in point, at this very moment, Calvi is looking my way, waiting to see how I'm going to react to the impending doom.

"Hey, man, it's none of my business, as long as you're ready to go tomorrow," I say, trying not to rile them up.

"Why don't you come along? Roar is going to pick us up and take us to the country," Switch says.

"Roar?"

"Yeah. Fucking Roar. You met him like ten times. The Norwegian guy with the beard," Switch replies. Testy, testy.

"Right-O, ladies and gentlemen. Here are the room

keys. The day is yours, so try to stay out of trouble," Arnie says as he hands out envelopes to each of us.

We're all getting our things together when a rather large Viking-type character steps into the bus. We all stop what we're doing and stare at the imposing figure.

"Roooooar!" Switch yells.

Roar responds with a Viking warrior yell, fists raised and clenched, his eyes wild.

"Oh, right. That Roar," I say to no one in particular.

The bus seems to get smaller as everyone moves around, greeting Roar. Arnie waits for the moment that Roar moves so he can get off the bus, muttering something under his breath as he goes.

"How have you been, old friend?" Switch asks.

"Good, man," Roar says.

"Still in the same place?"

"Yup. I thought we would head that way, have a barbe-cue…I have some new toys to play with."

"I'm sure you do," Switch says then gestures to Lael. "Roar, meet Lael, the newest member of And Then."

"Pleasure," he says with a polite nod that is at odds with his crazed appearance. He then addresses everyone else. "I hope you all will be coming along."

Silence follows. I don't want to go to the country with Roar to play with his new toys, whatever they are. As I'm trying to find the words to get out of this social corner, Lael breaks the silence. "All right. Let's do this thing."

I guess I can see how she would be intrigued, or per-haps she couldn't stand the silence and wanted to be polite. Either way, if she's going then so am I.

We pile into Roar's old Suburban with the roof cut off. It takes some effort to get the engine started, but once it gets going he revs it and turns his head back to look at us, laughing like a wild man. Then he looks at Switch in the passenger seat and they exchange more crazed laughter and a fist pump, a sort of primal communication that does not require modern language.

Roar fishtails out of the parking lot, creating a wall of smoke and dust behind us. Their laughter is getting louder, as if they're competing with the engine.

The journey is shorter than I thought it would be. We barely have time to listen to more than a couple songs of a Metallica album Roar has blazing. The song "Struggle Within," is playing when he pulls into the dirt driveway and kills the engine.

"Welcome," Roar says as he climbs out of the vehicle and is promptly greeted by a large Mastiff.

We all climb out except Lael who's struggling with her seatbelt. Before I do the gentlemanly thing of lending her a hand, I take advantage of her vulnerable state and tickle her.

She laughs, swatting my hands away and goes back to struggling.

"What kind of mess is this?" I think out loud. I press the rusty button but nothing happens.

Roar comes over, scratching his head, and says, "I didn't know I had seatbelts." He leans in to look closer and continues, "I mean, this is literally a couch I found that I tied down to the floor, so how the hell is this possible? Hang on. Hey, Switch, can you grab the knife in the shed?"

"Knife?" Lael asks with big eyes.

"The big one," Roar shouts to Switch.

"Okay…" Switch says, walking into the rickety shed.

Lael and I are looking at each other with equal parts

amusement and fear.

"Seriously, how did you manage to do that?" Switch asks, pulling down on the back of the couch and looking behind to where she could have possibly retrieved the old seatbelt.

I can feel my phone vibrating in my pocket, so I pull it out to see who's calling.

Ronald Ramsey flashes on my screen.

Oh boy, I say to myself, stepping away from Lael who is strapped to a death machine.

I answer. "Ronald."

"I thought I would check in to see how you're taking care of my daughter," he says, his voice just as brusque over the phone as it is in person.

"She's good, no problems at all," I say as Roar begins to lower a large machete to her seatbelt, Calvi and Switch standing over them as if they are in a surgery observatory.

"Look. I'm hearing things, bad things, some things I don't like," Ronald says.

"Well, I don't know, Ronald. You can't believe everything you hear." I try to sound as casual as possible while my mind flips through the Rolodex of all the things he could have heard.

"I heard Lael on the radio. Why is she doing press?" Ronald asks. Roar is violently sawing away at the seatbelt, putting his weight into it as he leans over Lael. Calvi and Switch adjust themselves to get a better view of what's happening.

"Oh, that. Right, fine, no more press. No problem, Ronald. Won't happen again," I answer as the seatbelt snaps and Roar and Lael fall over with the couch. I rush forward to see if she's okay but the sound of her laughing is the evidence I need, so I back off so Ronald can't hear the commotion.

"And the bus. This one amazes me. Seriously, Brad, if this is true…I'm hearing that her bus is traveling empty and she's traveling in *your* bus."

"What?" I answer, trying to sound innocent.

"Don't fuck around," he snarls. "This fucking tour is something she needs to do and I'm letting her do it so she gets it out of her system. Don't let her get carried away, got it? When this tour is done, she is done. I don't want her spending her life around people like you. No offense."

"Um," I say, slightly offended.

"Look, Brad, I'm thinking long-term, and for her, it's just not a good life. It's different for you," Ronald says.

Bang-bang-bang.

The deafening sound of a firearm rings through the air.

"What the fuck is that?" Ronald asks.

"Hold on," I tell him quickly, rushing around the corner of the shed to see Lael with a massive gun pressed against her shoulder.

Bang!

She fires and an old television falls over about a hundred feet away.

"Um," I say into the phone, "we're at the history museum. There is some war re-enactment thing, sorry about that."

"We? Is Lael with you?"

"No, no, she's back at the hotel. She said she wanted to stay in and read her book."

"Yeah, well, don't forget there are lots of young people that can play guitar and sing, but there aren't many who have the most successful record company in America supporting them. I support you, Brad. You know this. But…if something happens to Lael, I will drop you and make sure no else picks you up. From now on she rides in her own bus and she doesn't do press. Don't fuck around."

Ronald hangs up.

Lael turns to me and asks, "Who was that?"

I dive for cover because she is carelessly pointing the firearm directly at me.

"Whoa, easy there," everyone says at once. Roar takes the gun away before she can do any damage.

"No one," I tell her, not wanting to upset her in case that gun gets back into her hands.

Over the next few hours we hang out in the sunshine taking turns shooting televisions and beer cans, ripping around on Roar's homemade dune buggy, and just lying around being lazy. There is a large trough full of beer that everyone helps themselves to, everyone except me. Even at this stage of my life my own friends treat me like an alien when I'm not drinking.

Sometimes I feel like I don't drink now for the same reason I drank my face off in my teens and early twenties— rebellion. Whether it's a business meeting, a family function, or just watching a movie, if you don't have a drink in your hand people judge you. But I can't be feeling like a dirty dishcloth when I'm performing for a sold-out arena. I don't mind when the gang gets wasted—well, until I do. Today, anyway, at Roar's sunny little compound, I don't mind that my mates are letting loose. They work hard and they deserve it.

Lael is having a ball. I can barely see her face behind her large sunglasses, but she's clearly happy.

And always near.

She's only had a few drinks but when she talks to me her voice is at a slightly higher pitch and she's playing with her hair.

"Do you think I should cut my hair off?" she asks me, twirling a strand around her finger.

"No way," I answer.

"Why not?"

She's fishing for a compliment, I know it. "Well, you're young and hot so I'm sure—no, I *know*, you could get away with it if you really wanted to, but your hair is a part of your look. It's your signature."

Lael smiles at that, appeased. "Do you want to take a stroll?"

"Sure, I've been lazing around long enough," I say with a sigh.

We get up and head toward a trail opening as I yell back to the fellas, "We're heading back into the wilderness, don't shoot us if you can help it."

Roar has a rather large piece of land, and walking down this trail reveals its diversity. This little nature walk is doing me well. No buzzing amplifiers, no buses, no invasive fans. I can only hear our footsteps and the occasional bird.

And, of course, Lael. I've already discovered that she has the gift of gab and apparently when she has a few drinks in her, this is amplified. She's clutching my arm as we slowly make our way down the trail, the sandy path lined with sagebrush, the sky above a clear blue, while she chats away with little to no direction.

I enjoy spending time with Lael. She's just so easy to be with. She'll even take the liberty of answering her very own questions that she asks me. I walk, listen, smile.

And hold her hand.

She *was* holding my arm, but that seemed more of a way for her to keep her balance. This is different. I'm suddenly overwhelmed with a foreign feeling.

Lael has stopped talking and breathes in slowly while taking in her natural surroundings. If the handholding bothers her, she doesn't show it.

"So what is the deal with you and Lindsay?" she asks.

I shouldn't be surprised she's asking about that since we've talked about everything else, but I'm wondering if I detect a hint of jealousy in her voice.

"Lindsay? She's a friend," I answer.

"She's very pretty," she notes.

"Your father and his team like to make it look like we have a relationship for the press," I tell her. "That's all there is."

"I guess I knew that, I just thought maybe there was something there. Though I can imagine it would be tricky having a girlfriend with your lifestyle."

"I guess so," I say with a shrug. It's something I try not to think about.

"So, who was the last one?"

"The last what?"

"Girlfriend, silly. You're Brad Snyder. I'm sure you've had a few."

"Not really," I tell her, wanting to be completely honest. "I mean, I've had women in my life but never anything that serious. I'm constantly on the road, and you're right, it would be hard having a real, meaningful relationship with this life."

She stares at me for a moment, and I can feel her eyes searching me underneath her sunglasses. "Okay, who is she?" she asks wryly.

"What do you mean?" I say as I catch Lael from a little stumble over a rock.

"The bitch that broke your heart," she says.

I laugh and try to think of who that might be. The simple truth is I haven't let anyone get close to me. I'm surrounded by fans who are trying to get as close as possible, but I know better than to get caught up with one of them. I've had a few relationships with women that are in show business, but deep down they're all narcissistic socialites that inherently use people. I've learned the hard way to stay away from them.

But even though I laughed when Lael asked the question, I can't help but give it some thought. I keep thinking of my fans as one person, as if my relationship with them as one collective unit is a healthy meaningful relationship. Clearly that doesn't count. In my line of work, you have to protect yourself and that's what I've been doing my entire career. Before life with Ramsey Records I was basically a kid trying to survive. I don't think I'll ever stop doing that.

It's sobering walking along this trail with Lael, no press, no fans, only nature and the truth. I want to be open with her and answer her question, but I can't think of a defining moment, so I turn it around and ask her.

"How about you? Who broke your heart?"

She sighs, kicking a rock. "I dated the same guy through private school. We split up afterward but there were no tears when we said goodbye. He was a nice guy and all, but that's where it ended. You know how it goes."

We stop walking along the dusty trail and stand facing each other. There's a patch of brush beside us where birds sing and chirp, and we look at each other in a quiet standoff, our expressions natural, our breathing slow.

Lael glances at me over her glasses, looking inherently innocent.

"Who knows," she says softly. "Maybe you're the one who will break my heart."

Silence hangs in the air as I search for the words.

"Relax," she says, smirking. "I'm messing with you. Can you believe this place?" she asks and turns away from me to look at this little desert oasis we stumbled upon. Lael walks off the trail to explore the area, letting her open hand graze over the top of the grass.

"When do you stop?" she asks, glancing at a bird flying past.

"What do you mean?" I ask as I follow her meandering route.

"You're always on. You always seem to be Brad Snyder the rock star. When are you just Brad Snyder?" Lael pauses at an overlook that looks down over some rocky crevices.

I breathe in slowly and consider her question. "I don't know. If I seem that way it's because a lot of people are listening and I have to be careful."

"Yeah, and I'm the only one listening to you right now. There are no photographers, no microphones, and you're just a guy lucky enough to be here with me." Lael puts her hand on her hip in a display of sass. "Have you stopped now?"

"Yes," I tell her, though it's a tricky thing to figure out.

"Hmmm," she muses. "I don't know if you have. Lie down."

"Lie down?" I question.

"Do it!" she says, poking me in the ribs. "I want to try something. See if you can just be."

I put my arms up in submission. "Okay," I tell her, looking around until I see some flattened grass. We both get down until we're on our backs and we stare at the mid-day blue sky.

"I know it's hard to stop and just be in the moment, but we must. We're here and then we're gone," Lael says softly as she starts running her hand over my hair. I close my eyes.

"That's pretty deep for a nineteen-year-old," I tell her.

"Twenty-one," she corrects me.

I keep my eyes closed and ask her the same question. "What makes you stop? You know, being on. What makes you stop and be you, be in the moment?"

"I don't know. I love my dog," she says. "Maybe when I'm petting my dog I stop."

"Is that what you're doing right now?" I ask, referring to her running her hand through my hair.

She laughs and answers, "No, but I have to admit I'm very much in the moment right now."

"Me too."

"I believe you. It's good to feel good," Lael says, and nestles into me. We just lie there and say nothing for a while. My eyes are closed. Her scent is a mixture of whatever products she uses in her hair and fresh, dry air. I'm thinking of nothing, and I don't have a worry in the world. I run my hand up and down her arm and fight back some familiar primal feelings, as this isn't the time for that kind of intimacy. This is a sweet moment and I don't want to ruin it.

I'm calm, I'm happy, I'm in the moment. Everything stops and I fall asleep.

Pssst.

Pssssst.

I open my eyes to see the light has changed. I must have really dozed off. Lael is in my arms sleeping. It would be a peaceful moment, but it's Roar that woke me up. I look up at him and he motions for me to stay where I am.

"Don't. Move," he says in a concerned whisper.

Before I can question why, I hear the unmistakable sound of a rattlesnake.

I don't move a muscle.

Then Lael wakes and begins to make a stretching motion.

Roar swoops in with a stick and pins the snake down. It's dangerously close to us. I reach over and grab it near the head, making it impossible for its venomous fangs to make contact with my skin.

"Ahhh!" Lael screams and scrambles to her feet before scurrying away from the flailing snake in my hand.

Snap! Another snake strikes and misses Lael as she runs through the tall grass.

"This way, come on!" Roar shouts, running toward the trail as Lael follows.

"What do I do with this?" I ask, referring to the ravenous snake in my hand. I have no experience with reptiles and I've gotten myself into quite the situation here.

"Throw it!" Roar yells.

"Throw it?!" I would like to say I'm concerned for the snake's safety, but the truth is I don't see how it won't try and bite me the moment I relax my grip. "I have never handled a snake before!" I yell back, frozen in fear.

"Well, how the hell did you end up with one in your hand? You looked like a fucking professional when you grabbed the thing!" Roar shouts back.

"I don't know, man. I just reacted, and now I don't know what to do!" To say that I'm panicking would be an understatement.

"Throw it!" Roar shouts again.

"I can't!"

Roar mumbles something and heads back toward me.

"Look, just set it down, point it away from you, and let it go."

"Okay."

"Okay!"

I bend over, and to Roar's credit he's right beside me, speaking in a calming whisper. "Okay, you ready? Yeah? Now just let it go, man. Just let it go."

Snap! Another snake strikes from within the brush, and as quick as a wink Roar once again pins it down with his stick.

"Ahh, grab it, grab it!" His high-pitched Norwegian accent has the sound of genuine fear.

"What?" I question.

"Last time you grabbed it!"

"Are you fucking kidding me?" I ask. "I just said I don't know what I'm doing!"

"Oh my god, it's coming for my leg. The stick isn't working! Ahhhh!"

"Ahhh!" I join him and we yell cowardly together.

Without thinking, I grab the snake with my free hand.

"Thank you, thank you, Brad," Roar says, breathing hard, his eyes wide with fear and relief.

"Well, fucking hell," I say, trying to keep both snakes as far from my body as possible. "What the fuck do I do now?!"

"Let go of them. But let me get a head start," he says,

turning around and running back along the trail to his house.

"Oh fuck that! Coward!" I muster up some courage and run through the grass following him while both snakes slither and whip themselves back and forth, wrapping around my forearms.

I don't stop when I see Lael, I keep on running with my arms high in the air and snakes in hand. I run along the trail all the way back to the house with Roar and Lael close behind me.

When I get there I see there are at least twenty people hanging out in the back area.

"I could use a little help here!" I shout to the small crowd, showing them the angry snakes.

"That's Brad Snyder!" someone shouts.

"And he has rattlesnakes in his hands!" someone else yells.

Everyone *oooohs* and *ahhhs* as if I'm Alice Copper and this is my theatrical entrance. I try and quickly explain my situation without ruining my sudden mystique when a young bohemian girl steps out and gives me a dirty look.

"You're hurting them." She carefully takes them from me and walks far into the brush, disappearing. I don't get her name but that girl is my fucking hero.

Lael sidles up to me with wide eyes. I glance at her, my chest rising and falling from being out of breath, the adrenaline pumping through my veins. Better that than snake venom.

"Okay, I am totally in the moment now," I tell her.

She gives me a broad smile and a quick hug.

Roar comes in and hugs the two of us, then lets us go and says, "I have never seen that, my friend. I mean, first,

I have never seen someone take a nap in the middle of Rattlesnake Valley. Seriously, guys. There are like hundreds of snakes out there. Second, I have never seen a guy run full-tilt waving snakes around like a wild man. You really are a rock star, Snyder."

NINE

BRAD

A few hours have passed and we're sitting lazily next to a fire. The sun has almost disappeared behind Rattlesnake Valley. Twilight is my favorite time of day, so I relax and take it in. This eccentric group of people in this setting reminds me of a B movie. The budget film is in black and white, save for the fire that remains a vivid red. In fact, the color of the fire is so vibrant it causes arbitrary things to pop in contrast with the black and white setting. There is a group across from me playing music—a red guitar glows, a patterned shirt shines red. Behind the band, a young lady dances, and her red rimmed glasses glow as well.

Then dusk is gone, and it's night, and with it comes the demons. This film is a horror flick, of course, with young non-conformist types dancing around a fire. What monster is going to come from the shadows to interrupt their uninhibited joy? Could it be a madman wielding a chain saw, or maybe some vampires or zombies?

"What on earth is going on in your head?" Lael's voice brings me back to earth, sweet and soft as she touches my arm.

"Nothing," I answer, giving my head a shake.

I no longer have to dream up a villain for this movie—I'm in the moment and a real-life villain has presented itself.

Cocaine has taken over. The band is no longer playing, the girl with the red glasses isn't dancing, and the focus has shifted.

Things continue to change around the fire. Everyone is talking to hear their own voice, rolling their jaws, twitching, and doing line after line. Usually there is an attempt to keep it hidden, but with this group of misfits it's all hanging out. Someone spent a rather large amount of money on a rather large bag of coke, and it's safe to say that person is Calvi, judging by the fact everyone seems to be his best friend all of a sudden. The intensity is growing and my patience is dwindling.

Lael and I sit in our chairs and fight off drug-induced conversations with random people that zero in on us. They all want us to do a line, they sincerely feel it's in our best interest, and I have to swat them away like buzzards.

"Let's get out of here," I say to Lael.

"I don't think you can call a taxi from here," Lael says. She's handling things slightly better than I am—her voice is playful and calm. Her ambivalence concerns me, especially now, and the thought of her on blast makes me cringe.

"Come on." I get up and Lael follows. The crowd continues to grow—it's a wonder where they've all come from considering we're in such a remote location. I've also wondered the same thing about buzzards.

I lead Lael to Roar's shed. The desert wind has worn the wood down and the building is at the end of its life. There are large double doors that open up to the driveway, and I swing them open to see what Roar has hidden away.

"What the hell is that?" Lael asks.

The thing in question is some kind of homemade dune buggy that's taking up most of the realestate in the shed. It smells like rubber and gasoline, and looks like something a cartoon villain would drive. It's much larger than the one the fellas were playing around with earlier.

"This will work," I tell her.

"What do you mean, this will work?"

"This is our taxi. Hop in."

I take the first step and climb in the driver's side. There are two seatbelts and I quickly figure out how to strap myself into this death machine. Lael is close beside me trying to figure out her own. Obviously she hasn't had much luck with them lately.

It's not obvious how to start the engine, so I fumble for a while, but with some effort I'm able to wake the monster. It's far louder than our loudest concert. When I give it gas I can feel it rumble in my chest. I'm actually concerned it might shake the old barn to the ground.

I look at Lael, who's wearing some goggles that she found hanging in front of her. She appears like she's having second thoughts. Fuck that, we're doing this. I put it in gear and we tear out of the garage and down the driveway.

Roar yells at the top of his lungs in Norwegian, waving his arms and running behind us. I just smile and wave, pretending not to notice he doesn't want me to ride off with his toy.

Growing up in the city, I missed out of this sort of thing, so as I tear down the desert road, I regress deep into an adolescent dream and spin the tires around every corner. I turn to Lael, expecting her to tell me to tone it down but she is fumbling with the stereo. This demon machine has more horsepower than any God-fearing man should ever want or need, and the wattage of the stereo system matches the arrogance of the engine. I'm not sure how Lael manages but the new Metallica album is blaring (does Roar have it in every vehicle he owns?), shaking the metal frame around us.

With the engine screaming, the music blaring, and Lael shouting for joy, this is damn near perfect. I can't see her eyes because her goggles have a layer of dust on them, but the full moon lights her smile, a smile that makes me feel light and time stand still.

"Are we going to take this thing into town?" Lael shouts over the sound of the engine and music as the lights of the city approach.

I only answer with a devilish smile as I pull off the highway toward downtown Santa Fe. The new Metallica album is a long one and is still going strong as we roll into the center of town. We are getting honked at, yelled at, and maybe even laughed at. I know the moment we run into the police this will not end well.

I don't take my time. When traffic comes to a crawl, I feel like a sitting duck so I drive over medians and sidewalks. Lael holds on to the metal frame as we bounce over the obstacles. I sense this machine is capable of much more abuse.

I see a place that looks like a bar. I don't think there will be a ton of options and I know my luck will run out soon if I keep tearing around the city center on this insane-looking dune buggy, so I pull over and park, killing the motor and unbuckling my seatbelt.

"This place looks good," I say. Actually, the place looks too classy for us, but here we are. We climb out of our stolen machine and walk onto the patio of the white table-clothed restaurant.

"Welcome. Would you like to dine inside or outside?" the kind-looking waiter asks, seeming to not notice that we're covered in dust and Lael has goggles pushed back on her head, while our vehicle parked only meters away is totally illegal.

"Outside, please," I answer, playing it cool while the buzz of the journey hums through my veins.

We sit on the patio facing the street. Our stolen vehicle is parked crooked and looks painfully out of place in contrast to the nice surroundings.

We order a bottle of champagne and two steaks. We get lucky with the restaurant because everything is perfect.

Lael is perfect. She's become the focus of my attention since she picked me up from the airport all those weeks ago. I'm beginning to question why I'm so restrained with her, almost gentlemanly. That said, it's been an unusual day and I'm emotionally drained, my defenses are down, and I'm vulnerable. While Lael is watching some people gathering around the dune buggy, I'm watching Lael.

Why am I fighting this? Is it her father? Certainly, if I had an open relationship with Ronald Ramsey's daughter there would be consequences. I'm not sure it would be the complete end of my career, but Ronald would make good on his threat and try his best to ruin me. Even though I'm his cash cow, he would drop me if he thought I was trying to woo his daughter, the very person I'm supposed to protect.

Yet I'm not sure it's Ronald who's stopping me.

Lael is young. At first she seemed considerably younger because I could still see the kid I once knew, but since we've been spending time together I can't say I see that kid anymore. I see an attractive young woman instead. She is, in fact, so beautiful and sweet that I'm concerned I'm the wrong guy for her. She's a beautiful lake and I'm a barrel of oil floating around, harmless until opened. It's not Ronald, it's not that she's considerably younger…it's me.

There haven't been that many women in my life, but they all have something in common. My mother gave me away, Miss Sugar practically sold me to Ronald, and then there's Lindsay, who only wants to see me when I have a song in the top 40. It leaves me wondering, could it be me? Strip away my celebrity and fame—am I just a lost motherless loser with an oversized yellow t-shirt and shoes that are too big?

I drink the last of the champagne in my glass and feel myself going to a dark place.

"What's on your mind?" Lael asks.

"You."

"Good thoughts, I hope."

The waiter comes with our late dinner and puts it on the table, breaking our conversation before it can get too deep. Lael raises her fork and I instinctively hit it with mine.

"Let's eat," I tell her.

"Damn, this is good stuff," she says, savoring each bite with her eyes closed. Then, when she opens them, her attention goes to something over my shoulder.

"Umm, Brad," she says warily.

"What?" I start to turn around to see where she's looking.

"No!" she whispers harshly, leaning in. "Don't look now, it's the police, and they seem interested in our dune buggy."

I fight the urge to look and try and hide the smile on my face. I do my best to enjoy my steak while noticing our legs are touching under the table. Lael, meanwhile, looks like someone who's desperately trying to conceal their guilt. Shifting, twitching, and looking in every direction except where the police are apparently checking out our ride.

"Relax, it will be fine," I assure her.

Then, one of the police officers focuses his attention on us, stepping close to the patio fence. He clears his throat. "Did you folks happen to see who parked this vehicle here?"

I'm about to say no, but Lael pipes up before I can say anything. Lael, in a horribly fake and untraceable accent says, "Do you mean that silly one there? I didn't even notice it until now."

Silence hangs in the air as both the cop and I turn our heads toward the wild looking dune buggy that has the attention of everyone within a hundred feet.

"You didn't notice this vehicle until just now?" The cop questions.

"Oh, that one. Okay, yeah, I noticed that one. I thought you meant the one next to it, that Corolla there. No, yes, I noticed that one. Sure, yeah." Lael's strange accent sounds different than when she began.

I look at her in complete bewilderment.

"Where are you folks from?" the cop asks, sounding suspicious. I have to say I can't blame the guy.

"Australia. My name is Mildred and this is my husband…Tom," Lael replies in a very non-Australian accent.

"Sir, did you witness anything in regards to this vehicle?"

I clear my throat. "When *Mildred* was in the restroom I saw some teenagers park this vehicle here. I think they ran off in that direction. They seemed to be drinking." I try to match her crazy accent which has me sounding like both an Englishman and a Jamaican. Maybe with a bit of Norwegian thrown in. I'll blame Roar for that one.

"Could you describe them to me?"

"I'm afraid I cannot. They seemed pretty wild, and I didn't want to get their attention so I did my best not to look at them."

"Right," the cop says after a few long beats, looking us over. "All right, well, enjoy your dinner, folks. I hope you enjoy your stay here in Santa Fe." As wary as the cop seems, he thankfully puts his attention back on the dune buggy that is now being loaded onto a tow truck.

"What the hell was that?" I whisper to Lael. Her face is beet red and terrified. "Why the accent and fake names? Australia? That accent wasn't even close."

"I don't know, I don't know," she says, and doesn't blink as she downs a full glass of champagne.

"You're nuts," I say with a smile.

"I think I'm going to have a heart attack," she says.

"You're going to give *me* a heart attack," I chide her.

"I must tell you now, I'm not a very good liar."

"You don't say," I answer while laughing.

Lael covers her mouth, trying to hold back her

laughter. "Oh my god, I don't know. I got nervous."

"Alright, Mildred. I'm taking you home." I put some money on the table and we begin the short walk to our hotel. We walk arm-in-arm, breaking in and out of whatever accent Lael was performing earlier. Since it's rare that I drink, I'm definitely feeling the effects of the champagne.

In our hotel, riding up the elevator, Lael hugs my arm as if it were her pillow. My concern about what is right or wrong concerning Lael are all but gone as I look down at her.

Her teal hair over the tanned skin of her shoulders is a beautiful sight. I want to press her against the wall and kiss her. I'm finally *in* the moment and it's all I want, all I care about.

I don't give in, but I do hold her close, and I know she can feel my affection.

The elevator door opens and we step into the hall.

"I'm this way," I say, pointing down the hall.

"I'm this way." Lael points in the opposite direction.

Neither of us turn to walk away. We stand in the hall in silence holding eye contact. I know I'm going to kiss her, but I take my time. I like the way she's looking at me, and I can feel my lips curling into a smile. We haven't touched yet, but something has already begun and there's no turning back.

I reach out and hold both of her hands as she begins to run her fingers softly against my palms. I pull her in and she puts her hand on my chest. Our eyes are still locked on each other, and with every passing second the intensity increases.

I don't have to make an effort; rather I submit to the gravity pulling me into her. I grab the back of her head.

Her soft lips are open and we melt into each other. I'm becoming desperate to feel her skin on mine, our breaths are deepening, our hearts are racing, and our eyes are closed. Gently, I bite her bottom lip, and she responds by kissing me harder.

Ding.

The elevator door begins to open and we plummet back to reality. We take a step back from each other, trying not to make it obvious to Arnie who is standing there awkwardly with a pizza and a six-pack of beer.

"Don't stay up too late now. Big day tomorrow, aye?" Arnie says, his eyes darting around as he shifts his shoulders. He's clearly aware he interrupted something.

"Goodnight, Arnie," I say as he passes by. "Goodnight, Lael" I say to her more forcefully so that Arnie takes note.

I take in a slow, deep breath, trying to settle down. Arnie is fumbling with his room key only steps away and I try not to look at him.

"Goodnight, Brad," she says, one eyebrow raised. Arnie has the door open but he's struggling with the pizza, six-pack, and the self-closing door.

Lael struts down the hallway, swishing her hips side to side like she's performing a seductive dance. I watch her disappear around the corner—she never looks back.

Arnie's door finally snaps shut, and I'm alone. I've been wondering what kissing her would be like since the audition when she surprised me with her force and commitment. I can still feel her lips on mine. I want nothing more than to knock on her door and pick up where we left off. Whatever is happening between Lael and I is something new to me, and the way she kissed me has left me high. The image of her face is burned into my brain. I can still feel her lips and her touch. Her smell is still in the air, and her energy is inside me, running through my veins and exploding in my heart. I walk back to my room with a smile on my face.

I feel weightless.

TEN
LAEL

Holy fucking shit.

What the hell just happened?

I have barely any time to process the thoughts before I'm zombie walking across the hotel room and flopping over like dead weight onto the bed.

After the insane and ridiculous day I've had, I should be passing right out. I'm beyond exhausted and that kiss with Brad made my legs feel even weaker.

But I can't pass out. It's late and I can't sleep. I can't do anything but lie here and replay everything in my head, over and over again.

Never mind how the day started out. That crazy Norwegian fucker Roar showing up and then all of us piling into that SUV with the sawed-off roof and the seats that aren't actually seats but somehow a couch. Then being shuttled off to his compound in the desert where I fired a gun for the first time in my life.

Then the walk through the desert with Brad, which led to moments I'd only dreamed about, a closeness I've been craving. I know I've been bold with him, terribly bold, but it's the only way I know how to be. He just does something to me that brings it out, that makes me stop being afraid. I swear I could do anything to him, say anything (and from the way I was blabbering, I'm pretty sure I have) and it wouldn't matter. Brad can take what I'm giving.

And I can take what he's giving.

And I want more of it.

I'm a greedy little girl like that.

I sigh into my pillow and wish that my brazenness would carry me down the hallway to his room. But I could tell from the way that Arnie was looking at us that the time isn't right. In fact, I'm sure Brad kissing me was a big mistake. I know he's not supposed to lay a hand on me—I've heard the threats from my father.

And I know there's a lot at stake when it comes to Brad and his relationship with my dad.

It's just that I'm not afraid. I'm old enough to make my own decisions and the fact is, I like Brad. A lot. I mean, that's a given, it's always been a given. But this isn't a young teenager pining after a rock star. This is me, a young woman, getting to know this rock star on a very personal level. I'm falling for the real Brad Snyder, the man behind the mask, the man of few words and a damaged past. I'm getting to know him, and the more I get to know him and all his faults and flaws, along with everything that makes him magical, the more I like him.

And the braver I'm getting, for better or worse.

Fuck. That kiss. I can still feel it on my lips. The way he tasted, smelled, the feel of his hands in my hair, the way he bit my lower lip, tugging just so. I was so close to dragging him to my room.

I turn over and stare up at the ceiling, blowing a strand of hair off my face. I don't think I'll be sleeping for some time, and I feel like if I don't start talking to someone about all of this, I'll burst.

I bring out my phone from my bag and look at the time. It's almost midnight but Christy always burns the midnight oil when she's working. I've only texted her here and there, mainly checking on how Baby Groot is doing, but I could do with some female bonding. Though I've always been independent and never had many close female friends growing up, always preferring the company of boys except for my friend Shelby who moved to London after high school, being on the road can be lonely.

I decide to FaceTime her.

She answers on the third ring and I hold the phone high above me, my head back on the pillow, smiling at the sight of her face.

"Hey, am I bothering you?" I ask her, checking the small picture of me on the screen. I look all sorts of nuts with my hair spilling out around me, a crazed look in my eyes.

"Not at all," she says, bright-eyed, considering how late it is. "I was actually debating taking a break. I swear I'm going cross-eyed."

"What are you working on now?"

"Oh nothing. Nothing interesting compared to what you're doing. How is it? I caught your show in Phoenix! You did amazing!"

"It was on TV?"

"Well, I saw it on Youtube."

I'm touched that she looked it up.

"But," she says, "it was pretty amazing and really well shot. You were badass and the camera loved you. It kept focusing on either you or Brad. You are both fucking babes."

I swear I feel myself blushing.

"Well, thank you."

"So, tell me everything. I mean everything, the real things, not just the easy stuff that you can text."

"Are you sure? I don't want to keep you from work."

"Oh come on, you know it's fine. I've been working pretty much ever since you left. I'm in dire need of something exciting. Let me live vicariously through you. And please, please tell me you've gotten some action at some point."

I burst out laughing. "Did you think I was that hard up?"

She sticks her tongue out at me. "No, I didn't, but for the time we've been living together, I've never seen you go out on a single date."

"I work a lot."

"So? Work hard, play hard. And you're working now but don't you dare use that as an excuse."

"Okay, let me see Baby Groot first."

"He's right here," she says, and puts the phone down for a moment so I see a shot of the ceiling in her office. Then after some shuffling she aims the phone's camera back at her and Groot's little Chihuahua face is looking at me.

I swear I almost burst into tears. It's funny how attached you get to something even after a short time. It's not that I'm homesick, not at all, but seeing my little dog's face makes me realize how unstable everything really is for me right now.

And I can't blame that on anything but my feelings for Brad.

What I feel for Brad knocks me off balance.

Of course, Baby Groot doesn't know what's going on. He tries sniffing the screen and then licking Christy's face as she holds him close to her.

"Say something. Talk to him," she says, laughing.

"Hey, Baby, Baby," I coo to the screen, and he automatically starts looking around, trying to figure out where my voice is coming from. It seems kind of cruel to have such a disembodied sign of his owner around, but at least his tail is wagging. "I miss you so much."

"He misses you too," she says. "I've been letting him snuggle at the foot of the bed every night, and every morning I wake up with his butt practically in my face."

"Yeah, that sounds about right."

"So, don't change the subject. Who are you waking up with every morning?"

"Actually, no one."

"Not Brad?"

My heart can't help but skip a beat. "Why would you say that?"

"Because I saw that show. And I saw the way he kept looking at you while you were performing. He didn't give a rat's ass about anyone else in the band. His eyes were all for you."

I swallow hard. "Oh. Well."

"Come on, I know you're calling me because you have something juicy to say."

I sigh. "Okay, well. Nothing has really happened between us yet…we just kissed."

She closes her eyes and squeals, dancing in her seat

which makes Baby Groot jump off of her. "I knew it!"

"It just happened."

"What, tonight?"

"Like, ten minutes ago. Just outside his door."

"So what the hell are you doing here?"

"I don't know. Arnie, the manager, interrupted us. I didn't want to push it. I didn't want to get Brad into any more trouble."

"Why would he get in trouble? He's a grown man, ain't he?"

"He is, but…my father."

Christy exhales, rolling her eyes. "What now?"

"Well, you know how it was pretty much all him that got me this gig…"

"No, Lael. You got yourself this gig because you're one talented mofo. Fuck your father. Sorry, but…"

"No, don't apologize. Most people would say that. But Brad can't. He owes everything he has to my father. When he was fourteen he had nothing, was just bounced from foster home to foster home. Music was his only stability. And then Ronald Ramsey stepped in and gave him the world. Brad wouldn't dare mess that up."

"Yeah, but why would your father know? And why would he care?"

"Because he does. There's a reason he tried to get me to travel behind in that other damn bus."

"And he knows you're not the type to travel in your own bus."

"I don't think my father knows me at all, honestly. But he definitely doesn't want Brad touching me, that much is for certain."

"So your father doesn't have to know."

"There are snitches everywhere," I tell her, lowering my voice as if my hotel room is bugged. "Besides, Arnie just caught us."

"Aren't you kinda friendly with Arnie? You told me before you left he was the only one really on your side of things."

"Yeah. I don't think he'll say anything but this industry, man, you never know where allegiances lie. Everyone is either lying or blowing smoke up your ass, and everyone is trying to get the last dollar out of you. I don't trust a single soul here. Not Arnie, definitely not the other guys in the band. Brad is the only guy I trust."

"Are the other guys treating you fairly?"

"I don't know," I tell her. "I guess. I can tell they don't like me though. It's just subtle things. Switch is okay, though he seems to have a small-man complex, as I guess all drummers do. Calvi definitely isn't my fan. He's always glaring at me."

"Is that the Italian dude? He looks like he's glaring on every album cover I've seen."

"Nah, it's more than that. He's judging me. He thinks I'm not cut out for it."

"Well, you know it's bullshit. Take it from Christy here, you fucking wail on that bass. If anything, those dudes are just jealous because you're a young woman and you're holding your own with them. No, not even holding your own, you're blowing them out of the water."

"Right. Well, I guess that reminds me I should probably tone it down a bit."

"Fuck that. Don't tone it down. Why, cuz you play bass? So what? Who says that bassists have to keep their head down? Don't sell yourself short. That's not like you.

Think of what Brad would say if he heard you speak that way."

I find myself smiling dreamily. "He would say I'm being silly. Oh man. What am I even doing, Christy?"

"With what?"

"I don't know. I like him. I really do."

"Everyone knows that." She laughs softly.

"No, I mean...I think I might be falling for him."

"Everyone knows that too."

"In a real way."

"Well, that happens. It's either you find out that your idol isn't the man you thought they were or they turn out to be exactly what you thought."

"Or better. Brad is better than I thought. He's caring, you know. He's so quiet, and yet when he's with me, his attention is only on me. It's like he never has to say a word for me to know what he's feeling. And he's like...he just wants what's best for the band. He doesn't drink much, doesn't do drugs, he believes in the music and being the best version of himself. I don't know, I guess before I knew him, I figured with his tragic upbringing he would be a bit of a downer and secretly do drugs or some shit like that. It would make sense. But he's not like that at all. He's just..."

"Perfect?"

"Perfectly imperfect. And every moment we have, we end up spending it together. Like gravity is pulling us into each other's orbit and there's no choice but to either collide or keep rotating around each other."

"That's some deep shit, Lael," she says dryly.

"I know." I run my hand over my face. "It's late. I should let you go."

"So, what are you going to do? Just pretend the kiss

never happened?"

"No. I can't pretend it didn't happen. It's seared into my brain, in my soul. His kiss branded me as his. For now. Forever. Who knows." I hear her laugh because I'm being so dramatic. "But I can't just move on from that. And I don't want to."

"So go back in his room and continue where you left off. Go get some hot rock star ass."

I chuckle. "I think he's probably sleeping by now. We had a long, crazy day. At one point he was running around with two rattlesnakes in his hands. Man, it was the scariest, funniest thing I've seen in a long time."

"Dude. Rock stars really do know how to party."

"Then we stole a souped-up dune buggy and took it into town. The police ended up towing it away—luckily they didn't know it belonged to us. It belonged to this crazy Viking guy named Roar."

"See, this is what I'm talking about. This is the part where I get to live vicariously through you." She pauses. "Just promise me one thing before you go, okay?"

"Sure."

"Next time you get an opportunity to be alone with him? To kiss him? You take that damn opportunity, you hear? You use it. You do the crazy shit you've always wanted to do. Be brave and bold and jump his bones."

I burst into giggles. "I'll see."

"No, I'm telling you. Doesn't mean you have to broadcast it to the world, but this is a dream come true for you, and very few people are lucky enough to have this happen. You need to exploit it. Make it worth your while. These are the memories that you'll reflect on one day and tell your children."

"I'm going to tell my future children about the time I screwed a rock star?"

"I dunno," she says with a tired shrug. "Maybe that rock star ends up being your future husband. Just gotta play your cards right. Seize this opportunity by the horns."

"I'll seize it by something," I mutter under my breath. "Okay, I better go. I'm starting to fade."

"Me too. Please text me when you've gotten somewhere."

"Will do, miss nosy."

"Hey. *You* called *me*."

"And I'm glad I did."

I hang up and slide the phone over onto the nightstand. I'm too damn tired now to wash up and get undressed.

I lie back and stare up at the ceiling for a few moments, going over what Christy said about Brad being my husband one day. It was a totally glib remark, meant to be a joke, but it has me wondering—if what I'm feeling for Brad is genuine, then what really is next? And where can it go?

There's no doubt that it could stall and go nowhere, even if I do end up grabbing the situation by the horns, so to speak.

But what if it doesn't?

What if there's so much more to this, to us?

What if…

My eyes close.

I fall asleep.

ELEVEN

BRAD

"Your old pal is on the bill tonight," Arnie says with a taunting smile.

"My old pal?" I question.

"Jean *Maaaaaaarc*," Arnie says in a long, drawn-out French accent.

The whole crew begins to laugh at Arnie's little performance. When he sees I don't find it as funny as everyone else, he pats me on the back.

"I'm just having fun with ya," Arnie says with a chuckle, drinking what's left of his morning Bloody Mary.

Switch, Calvi, Arnie, Lael, and I are all having breakfast at Café Du Monde. The humid air is warm and the sounds of tourists letting loose are all around us. There is something carefree about how they walk, how they sit in their chairs, how they smile. Music filled with horns, drums, and guitar is coming from a block away, and the thick air carries the sounds and smooths the edges, making the perfect soundtrack for my morning coffee in New Orleans.

There's a scruffy dog under the table next to me that I'm having a stare down with as I sip my strong coffee. I put my mug back on the table, and my eyes meet Lael's. She's been watching my pleasant exchange with the little mutt, and we share an easy smile. There must be something in the way we look at each another because the rest of the table shifts uncomfortably in their seats, looking away like they've witnessed an intimate moment.

"Who is Jean Marc?" Lael does her best French accent to match Arnie's.

"He's the lead singer of Satellite of Mars," Calvi says with his mouth full of food.

"I love that band!" Lael exclaims.

I know my bandmates love that she said that. But I hate it. Jean Marc is one of those oversexed, cliché rock stars. He never seems to turn off the act, and he sees me as his American counterpart. He's constantly belittling in this bizarre French mojo kind of way. His Parisian crew seem to love it when he talks down to me, and my crew are often too bowled over with laughter that they can't stand up for me. To be fair, my mates are usually laughing at how ridiculous Jean Marc is, his cartoonish delivery, and at his lack of humility. The fact that he doesn't realize how silly he comes across makes for a hilarious situation.

There's also a cultural difference between us that makes everything dreadfully awkward. He's constantly trying to dominate me and I'm constantly trying to get away from him. My bandmates and manager have a habit of inviting him to my trailer for shits and giggles.

Lael starts singing a Satellite of Mars song quietly to herself, just loud enough for us to hear, and the boys exchange looks of sheer joy in response. Arnie chokes back some laughter and tries to shift gears.

"All right all right, it's only for one show. It's not like we're touring with them," Arnie says as he stands up and puts money on the table, his rather large belly sticking out as he puts his rather large wallet into his back pocket. Arnie always makes it seem like he's paying with his hard-earned money when he takes care of the bill, which is definitely not the case.

"Don't be late for sound check, boys. We are one of four bands playing tonight so it'll be a tight schedule." Arnie notices the little dog and gives him a wave on his way out.

Calvi and Switch also stand up. Switch pulls out a comb and pushes his hair back while Calvi somehow contorts and puts his blazer on without looking away from his phone.

"What are you guys up to?" I ask.

"We're meeting up with some people from our Facebook group," Calvi absently answers, still looking at his phone.

"Who is she?" I tease.

Calvi finally looks up at me. "I'm doing this for us, Brad. You have to stay connected. I'm almost offended."

Switch is still shamelessly combing back his hair, looking at his reflection in an ornamental mirror on the restaurant wall.

"Who is she?" I ask again.

Calvi puts his phone in his pocket and walks toward the exit.

"Not she. There's more than one. Courtney and Karen, and they happen to be twins," Calvi says smugly over his shoulder.

Switch reluctantly puts his comb away and follows Calvi out the door.

Lael and I share a laugh. I sit back in my chair feeling more relaxed now that I'm solely in Lael's company. A smartly-dressed server refills my empty coffee cup and I thank her.

"Are you going to eat that?" Lael refers to the bacon on my plate. I was, but I lie and tell her no. She stabs it with her fork and relocates it to her plate.

It's refreshing how she doesn't seem to show any signs of awkwardness or regret about last night.

I carefully sip my scalding coffee and watch her devour what's left on her plate. I want to spend the day with her, naked on a hotel bed, with an open window letting in the warm New Orleans air and the sounds of the French Quarter.

Lael looks up and seems startled by my primal gaze.

I make an attempt at a joke to lighten the moment.

"Have you ever noticed eating a Caesar salad is like a game called find the bacon?"

She chuckles and sits back in her chair. With a deep breath she pans the restaurant and peers out the large French doors that open to a courtyard.

"I love it here," she says, half to herself and half to me. Her eyes are thoughtful as she takes in her surroundings.

It's interesting how oftentimes people are beautiful because of how they see the world rather than how the world sees them. I watch her take in the morning air and I can almost feel the calmness in her heart. With Lael, it's like she can pick and choose the smallest, most beautiful things in a room, gather them all, and hold them inside her. She finds the beauty in everything, and in turn she becomes beautiful. From where I sit, I can't see what she's looking at but I can feel what she feels. Through her eyes, the French Quarter has never been so perfect.

"I love it too. You know, my father was born here. He made a living playing the trumpet and working odd jobs," I tell her.

"Really? Very cool," she says, shifting her attention to me. "I don't think you've ever spoken about your dad."

"Well, I can barely remember him. I was quite young when he went to prison."

"Oh, sorry."

"No, don't be. It is what it is."

We sit in silence, and her sympathetic eyes stay on me as she leans forward and delicately puts her elbows on the table. Her movements are slow and feminine—everything about her seems caring and thoughtful. She covers my hands with hers, her eyes narrowing conspiratorially.

"Let's make a deal," Lael suggests.

"A deal?" I question with a suspicious smile.

"I won't talk about your father and you won't talk about mine."

"Your father wouldn't be happy if he knew what was happening between us."

"And what is happening between us, Brad Snyder?" Lael asks with a raised eyebrow.

I feel heat build in my chest like I just took a perfect drug. I boldly hold her gaze, neither of us looking away.

Lael doesn't wait for my answer and breaks the brief silence. "You know…I hate to be so blunt and presumptuous but…whatever you want, I want. If it's just a physical thing, then that's fine. But if it's deeper…"

"It's deeper," I tell her, and my confession sends

endorphins from deep in my heart to the surface of my skin, making the hairs on my arm stand on end.

Lael's intense gaze softens into a smile.

I can't help it. I lean over the table and kiss her.

Her hands are still on mine and I can feel them tighten as our kiss deepens. Our mouths are closed, but there is an easy passion. I feel her smile and breathe in the subtle scent of her shampoo.

Lael eases back into her chair and pans the room. Her body language says she likes it here but she's ready to move on. I silently agree.

"I think I prefer it during the day—the French Quarter," Lael says as we walk down iconic Bourbon Street.

"Too many drunk tourists at night?" I ask.

"Something like that."

I don't get recognized everywhere I go. I try to dress down and blend in, and learned long ago not to invite attention when I'm in public. Today I have Lael by my side, and she does *not* blend in.

She's wearing skin tight black jeans that stretch around her curves with tears and rips that contrast with the smooth skin on her thighs. Her thick, wavy teal hair falls over her bare shoulders, and her mirrored aviator sunglasses leave only her mouth to convey any expression. This would be enough to steal the attention of passerby, but it's how she's strutting that demands attention. I notice a middle-aged lady elbow her cigar-smoking husband when she catches him staring.

"I can't believe we have sound check in two hours," she laments.

"You're not burning out already, are ya?" I ask.

"Oh, come on."

"Well, what do you want to do?"

"I know a great way to burn an hour," she teases. "Your room or mine?"

I know it's a joke but I consider the question. She *is* particularly radiant today.

"No, I'm kidding!" Lael says as she puts hand under my shirt in a playful way. I flex my muscles and hope she doesn't notice.

"Ha ha, you flexed."

I guess she did notice.

"What?"

"What is it with guys doing that?"

"I didn't flex…"

"Ha ha, sure. I bet you're not even capable of me touching you without having to flex your muscles."

"Whatever."

"Okay then, let's see."

We stop walking and face each other, smiling like children, her a taunting bully and me, a defiant rebel. We're on a street just off Bourbon that's considerably less busy; in fact, for the moment, we are the only ones on the block. We can see Bourbon Street, the people flowing like technicolored water. The sun is shining on us between two old Victorian buildings.

"What are you doing?" I ask as Lael holds eye contact, an impish smile on her lips as she puts a hand under my shirt. Her touch makes me feel light. Lael's face relaxes and so does mine, and I kiss her slowly. I run my hand up her back and down to her ass, hooking my thumbs under her tight jeans. I pull her in, pressing her against me, letting her feel everything. Her hands slide around me, clasping behind my neck as I slide a hand up her back. We are perfectly tangled, trying to make contact with as much of our bodies as possible.

Her room or mine? It doesn't matter.

We kiss. Our tongues wrestle as we push into each other as much as possible. My eyes are closed and I am lost in the moment. Lael is hanging off me, so I put one hand on the cold brick wall to balance myself.

Lael pulls away and gives me a questioning look.

"What?" I ask, breathless already.

"I can tell you hold back with me."

"What do you mean?" I ask, trying not to sound impatient.

"It's because I'm younger or something."

"Hold back?" I repeat.

"The way you handle me is too gentle. You know you won't break me, Brad."

"Too gentle? Jesus, that's one I haven't heard before."

"You don't have to be like that with me. Sometimes sweet is nice, but not always," Lael says.

I smile at her, enjoying this conversation. "Okay, so what do you want right now?" I kiss her again.

"Come on." Lael pulls me into an alley. We walk past fire escapes and some crates, then the narrow alley takes a hard turn to the right and comes to a dead end. We are surrounded by brick walls and there are a network of pipes in front of us.

I know what game she's playing, and I'm more than willing to join in. Though she does seem to be taking off her clothes which is something that's taking me by surprise. I assumed in a situation like this, high noon in an alleyway, we would keep on as much clothing as possible. I would unzip and she would shimmy her jeans down, and we would make quick work of it. But this girl is standing in front of me completely naked on top of her pile of discarded clothing.

She's completely exposed.

She's completely stunning.

In the severity of clear daylight, her body seems hyper-real, and it takes me a good few moments to realize what's going on.

I'm the fucking luckiest guy in the world.

"Hard," Lael says as she turns around and grabs hold of a pipe to keep herself steady.

Even though I'm slack-jawed at how naked she is in front of me, I'm more than ready to take her. I kiss her neck as I unzip. Slowly, effortlessly, I fall into her. Lael takes my hands that are on her breasts and puts them on her hips.

"You can't hurt me, remember?" she says, her voice throaty. "Hold me tight. Fuck me. This is all I've ever wanted."

I hold tight and put her young body to the test. If sex is music, this is punk rock—fast, explosive, to the point… and less than two minutes long. Her body is beautiful and perfect in the contrast of this dingy alley. A narrow ray of sunshine shines in through the buildings, highlighting beads of sweat on her chest. If sex is a car race, this is a drag race, pedal to the floor and getting to the finish line as fast as possible.

I'm close, and she can feel it. She pushes into me with a moan, and we briefly make eye contact, her expression primal, wild.

"Come inside me," she says, her heavy eyes still on mine.

Her words take me to the edge. I hold tight and

somehow I'm able to move faster and harder.

My race car crosses the finish line. The punk rock song comes to an end.

"Fucking hell," she swears, but I barely hear her. My heart is pounding too loudly in my head.

But I can't stay inside her forever, not here, so I zip up.

"I've always wanted to do that," she says with a smile as she quickly slips her clothes back on. "Especially with you."

I'm trying to catch my breath. Reality is sinking in, and I'm amazed at what just happened. I can hear the sounds of the city funneling into the alley where we are.

"Ew, look at my hands." She holds them up to show how dirty they are from hanging on to the pipes. "Okay, back to the hotel to clean up." She marches past me as if what just happened was totally run of the mill for her. I take one last look at the scene of the crime before I follow her back to civilization.

The hotel is only a few short blocks away and so it's not long before we're in my hotel room. Lael is in the shower while I drink a coffee by the window, lost in my thoughts. They're a bit scattered, considering what just happened in the alley, but they keep coming back to one thing: I like my life with Lael in it. Even though it's been a short time since the day she picked me up from the airport, I'm having a hard time imagining life without her in it.

"Get in here, Snyder!" Lael shouts from the bathroom.

I put down my coffee, undress, and join her in the shower.

"C'mon in, dirty boy," she says, wagging her finger at me seductively.

She looks beautiful. All her makeup is washed off, and her wet hair is pushed back off her face, her smile genuine.

"Let's see those hands, you dirty girl," I tell her, playing along.

Lael holds up her clean hands for inspection and gives me a childish, proud smile.

"I bet you like it when I'm a dirty girl," she says playfully.

Damn. This is something else. It's a sunny day in the French Quarter, and here I am with this stunning young woman, smiling and laughing in the shower.

I'm happy.

I'm actually happy.

"Can you go again?" she asks, mimicking her early position, only this time her hands are on the clean pipes of the fancy shower.

I don't answer. I turn her so her bum is pressing into me, and I show her I can.

When shower time is over, I wrap her in a towel.

"You realize we were supposed to be at sound check ten minutes ago," I tell her.

"Oh shit," Lael says, putting her hands to her face.

"Don't worry about it. It'll be fine," I assure her. I don't want her to regret anything we just did.

Bang, bang.

The door practically rattles off the hinges.

"That doesn't sound like housekeeping," I say warily as I walk out of the bathroom and across the room.

Bang, bang.

The door rattles with each hit.

I look though the peephole and turn to Lael.

"It's your dad."

TWELVE

BRAD

Lael is standing as still as a deer caught in headlights and ready to run at any moment. I look through the peep-hole again and see Ronald's ugly, distorted face.

"He's still there!" I whisper to her. "Hide!"

Lael scurries into action like an animal seeking escape and heads into the bathroom.

"No, under the bed," I say as I lift the sheet only to find no space at all. I glance up to see Lael climbing out the window to the fire escape in her robe with a towel on her head.

"Are you nuts?" I protest and investigate what she's stepping out onto. The fire escape is small, high up, and like many things in the French Quarter, old and rusty.

Bang-bang-bang..

"I know you're in there. Open the door!" Ronald shouts.

With her dancer's grace, Lael steps out onto the landing with ease and ducks out of view.

I close the curtains and walk to the door, taking in a deep breath and exhaling slowly with my hand on the deadbolt.

Click.

I unlock it.

"Ronald, what brings you to New Orleans?" I ask as surprised and casual as possible.

He doesn't answer. With a bunch of papers in hand, Ronald walks right past me into my room, two henchmen following. He looks around the corner to where the bed is, opens the closet door, and then checks the bathroom.

"Where is she?" he finally asks, turning around.

"Who?" I answer.

Ronald takes a step closer to me, invading my space, letting me know he doesn't like my answer.

"I just got back from the venue. I thought I would find you there for sound check. I thought I would find Lael too. Funny how both of you are taking the day off. I gave you specific instructions, Brad. *Very* specific. Don't tell me you're crossing the line with my daughter, so help me god."

"I don't know what you're talking about."

Ronald slams a fistful of magazines on the table. They fan out, and I can see Lael and myself on the covers of all of them. One of the pictures is framed in the shape of a heart. I'm amazed how fast they went to print.

"That looks worse than it is, Ronald. You know how they can manipulate things," I tell him. He of all people should know this.

"I said no press for Lael, and I find out she's going to be on the cover of Rolling Stone next month. You see, Brad, this is supposed to be temporary, and what is happening here is that you are taking advantage of a young and impressionable girl that looks up to you."

Ronald points his finger in my face.

I try to speak but Ronald cuts me off. "*You* are putting me in a position here. This is something *you* have created. I'm left with no choice." Ronald lets his words hang in the air, my attention shifting to the security guards in matching suits behind him.

Holy shit. Am I about to be roughed up?

"Look, Brad, people disappear all the time," he says slowly, his voice remaining casual even though I know his intention is anything but. "If something happened to you, my god, could you imagine? It would be horrible. I mean, your album sales would probably enable me to retire, but what a loss it would be. Those magazines would have full page stories on you. Lael would be devastated, I'm sure. But then you know what would happen, Brad? Time would pass. How long do you think it would take for you to be forgotten—to truly disappear? Faster then you think, my friend. Within weeks it would be like you never existed and I would buy a fucking boat."

He's speaking so calmly, so coolly, that I know I have to take him seriously.

"Are you threatening me?" I ask.

"You should know better than anyone that the world is not safe, that people are not good. I'm a very dangerous man, Brad. The truth is, I don't like you. You were a street kid when I met you, and you still are. I can see it in your eyes—what you really are. I don't want you to be with my daughter, and I don't want my daughter to be in your band. Whatever is going on with you and Lael stops now. If it wasn't for the press having an interest in Lael playing in the band, I would pull her out right now. But, as it is, she'll have to finish the tour."

Ronald walks to the window, and I can feel my heart rate increase. He continues to speak to me even though I'm looking at his back.

"You do have something in common with her. You know what that is, Brad? I created both of you. Think about it. The last ten years of your life, there's nothing that hasn't happened because of me. I know what's best for her, and what happens in the next ten years of her life will be because of me too. Only she can't know that. So I need to let nonsense like this tour happen sometimes so she feels like she has some control, even though nothing could be further from the truth. And you, Brad, you are not a part of the plan."

Ronald turns to face me and smiles like a salesman, opening his arms with innocence and changing his tone.

"All right, kid. Are you feeling ready for the big show tonight?"

"What?" I'm completely baffled. He's gone from mob boss to little league coach faster than I can blink.

"I have some business to take care of so I'll see you there. Break a leg." Ronald points to my leg, which kind of takes away from the figurative nature of the expression.

He walks to the door and one of his security guards opens it for him. Before leaving, he winks at me and says, "I'm sure you'll do what's right and we can get past this."

Ronald leaves the room and his thugs follow. I turn to the window, expecting to see Lael climbing back into the room, but the curtain is waving in the breeze and she's not there. Leaning out the window, I see her sitting on the platform with her back against the wall.

"Hey," I say, resting on the window's ledge.

"I've never heard him talk like that about me before," she says, looking pensively to the sky.

I don't know what to say. We both need time to process, but she should be inside.

"Come on in," I tell her.

"I can ruin everything for you. I think I already have," she says, ignoring my suggestion.

"You know that's not true." I hate hearing this from her.

"I think it is true," she says, shaking her head then climbing through the window. Once she's inside, she looks up at me, her eyes full of emotion and frustration. "He has the next ten years of my life planned out. What's that all about?" She sighs heavily. "Look, maybe I should walk away from all of this, you, the band, my father, everything," Lael says with an air of defeat.

Something inside me is expecting her to leave. I've been falling for her carelessly and now I'll pay the price. History is repeating itself. I try to imagine her walking out the door and never seeing her again, and I can't bear the thought.

I reach out and grab her, needing her now more than ever.

"Don't do that," I whisper to her, trying to meet her eye. "I need you. I need you tonight on stage, I need you for this tour…"

She doesn't respond. Instead, she begins to get dressed and I sit down. I'm not afraid of Ronald, but I will never underestimate him. He owns the rights to all my work. I've been told that even if I leave he'll profit off anything I do in the future. I don't own my property, I don't own my cars.

My life is a house of cards.

Ronald was right about one thing, though—I'm still

the same street kid he met a decade ago. Even after all these years I have not lost the sense of who I am. I don't need these luxuries, and try as he might, I'll always have a fanbase and a career. I'm afraid of nothing, except one thing: Lael walking away.

"You must regret messing with the boss's daughter now," Lael says, standing in front of me with her hands tucked into the pockets of the sexy leather pants she's put on for the show.

"I regret nothing," I tell her, standing up. "And I'm not afraid of your father. You got that? So—let's make this a show to remember."

"All right, all right," she says, her head hanging for a moment. Then she looks up at me, fire in her eyes. "Let's do it."

Backstage is a beehive of activity. A show with multiple acts like this one always is. Lael and I fight through the narrow halls, trying to find someone from our crew to guide us. Even though many of the people lining the hall greet me as a friend, I don't recognize them. Finally, I see just the man I'm looking for.

"Arnie!" I shout to get his attention.

"You two twits nearly gave me a heart attack," Arnie answers then looks at his watch. "You're on next. You literally have ten minutes before you hit the bloody stage. Let's go. The other lads are waiting for ya."

I look back at Lael, and we exchange smiles as if we are mischievous children. There is no band playing at the moment, only the rumbling sound of thousands of people.

The smell of leather jackets, cigarettes, pot, and smoke machines lingers in the air.

I live for these moments. I feel like I belong. The air is electric and it lights me up when it fills my lungs. Arnie leads us to a corner where Switch and Calvi are waiting. It's normal to not have a proper dressing room for this type of gig.

"Look who decides to show up," Calvi says, shaking his head in disapproval.

"Boys," I say, greeting them casually.

Switch is artfully combing back his hair seemingly unconcerned by our late arrival, but his eyes look past me with concern, which causes me to turn around and see who has his attention.

Ronald is walking toward us with another tall, grey-haired man in a suit. Ronald stops and stands with his back to me in a disrespecting way.

"John, I want you to meet my daughter Lael," Ronald says, pointing to her like she's a piece of meat on the menu. "You're going to do great tonight, sweetheart."

Lael gives a peculiar smile and puts her attention on our guitar tech.

Ronald doesn't take notice of her dismissiveness and moves on with his acquaintance.

I try not to let him bother me. I can see my guitar on the rack, and I can see the route to the stage from where I stand, so for me the show has already begun. I have learned when to change, when to become selfish and be that other version of myself that takes over for the show. It can't happen too early—there are too many people ready to make judgments. If I ignore someone's smiley hello, it could have repercussions—for all I know they could have millions of followers and my dismissive reaction could turn into a long article of how awful I have become. Then their millions of followers would copy and paste to others who would copy and paste, comment, and destroy.

I know better, and I've learned a trick or two. When I'm in a large room full of people who want to talk to me and it's impossible to connect with each of them, I make sure to connect with only a few. Not in a fake way—there are always interesting people to talk to. I look into one person's eyes and ignore the rest of the room. I don't try to make eye contact with everyone, only who I'm speaking to. I know the rest of the room is watching my every move, secretly wanting me to mess up so they can have a story to tell. As long as I treat who I'm speaking to with respect, it's noticed by everyone else in the room.

It's a part of the job, it's a balancing act. When to turn off, switch gears, when it's too soon. I used to start the show, in my head, hours before. I couldn't blame people for not understanding, really—the opening act hadn't hit the stage yet and I was a pacing wild man who couldn't be reached. The larger the venue, the larger the crowd, the further from reality I go.

Now, at this moment, I'm gone.

There is no sound, everything and everyone around me is blurred out—they don't exist. I can see the route to the stage, my bandmates, and nothing else. I can hear Arnie's voice but I don't see him. I don't need to see him. I'm selfish and only take what I need.

Someone hands me my guitar, and I strap in for the ride. We're using a wireless system tonight so I make sure the guitar doesn't make a sound that will rocket out of the main speaker to the crowd.

"All right, boys!" Arnie shouts.

The lights go dark and a faceless man with a flashlight guides Switch, Calvi, and Lael along the route to the darkened stage. I always go last.

I don't hear the crowd. I can hear Arnie's voice but it seems like he's miles away, and I don't care what he's saying. I follow the flashlight, floating along the route, someone slapping my back along the way. I begin to hear the crowd, I feel the strings of my guitar, the breath in my lungs, the electricity in my heart firing bolts of lightning to my limbs, preparing them for battle.

It's not so dark that I'm not recognized, and the crowd begins to roar. My soul has been a few steps behind, but it has caught up to me now and steps in.

I have my first thought since I left my body backstage.

Turn on your guitar volume. Wait for Switch.

I've had problems in the past getting too lost in the moment and forgetting to turn on my volume. I assume the voice in my head is me, or maybe it's Mr. Robson.

Click, click, click, click.

My heart stops and I hold my breath when I hear Switch bang his sticks together.

Then it begins.

I hit the opening note and the lights explode on cue. My guitar thuds and shakes the stage when I hit the strings. It takes only a moment before Calvi, Lael, Switch, and I have the motor running. The piston is firing up and down, and the motor shakes and roars.

The crowd looks like a surging sea coming toward me. They are a part of this machine, and they're doing their job well. The fake smoke and colored lights make everything seem like a dream. I sing the first line of the opening song and the crowd sings along too.

This is a short set, so we hit the ground running, When I turn to face Switch, I see he's already a sweaty mess. Calvi, normally calm, cool, and casual, is standing on a monitor wedge thrashing his body around, windmilling his arm with each note he hits on his gold-top guitar. It almost feels like the four of us are trying to one-up each other.

Even Lael is performing differently than I have ever seen her. I like it. I think everyone does.

Time passes too fast with these short sets, and we only have a couple songs left. Lael is under a single light, and to my surprise she's taken off her shirt. There she stands in her leather pants, bra, and little else. She begins the song "FuzzFace" moving her hips from side to side seductively and has the attention of every person in the venue.

As always, she has my attention.

Lael's background as a dancer is showing right now. Myself and the rest of the band take a step back and let her have the stage, and she uses every inch. The end of this particular song is purposely unstructured so we can improvise, and it's at this moment that Lael takes the bottle of whisky from her amp and begins to chug it while still keeping the rhythm happening with her right hand on the bass. The crowd adores it.

That's when I see Ronald to the side of the stage. He must have been there the whole time.

I'm starting to have a new perspective on things.

Lael passes me the bottle of whisky, upside down, while it's still pouring out on the floor. I hold it, unsure of what she has in mind. She goes to her knees and begins playing her bass wildly, letting the whisky pour down her throat. The guitar tech must have hit her special teal pedal because I hear the familiar tone kick in at that moment.

The crowd reacts wildly. The front row has half their bodies on the stage, fists in the air, screaming for the moment to continue. Lael lets most of the whisky fall down her neck and stomach, drenched.

On her knees, she gyrates her hips up and down and plays with a mix of skill and ruthless improvisation. Myself, Calvi, and Switch have the good sense to let her take the lead. It's rare to have such control over a large mixed crowd like this, and Lael has them eating out of the palm of her hand.

The song has already gone on longer than it ever has before, and now Lael is climbing the PA speakers. I already know we won't have time to do our closing tune on the set list. Honestly, there's really nowhere to go from here, so it's just as well.

Lael climbs higher and higher, and the light man follows her the whole way. I've been using the whisky bottle as a slide, and I take a shot of what's left in it, but when I do my mouth is filled with only pure unsweetened iced tea.

I can't help but smile. I look up at Lael dancing in the rafters and wonder what else she has up her sleeve.

THIRTEEN

LAEL

Well, that was a fucking doozy, I think as I walk off the darkened stage with shaky legs, my clothes absolutely soaked with all the iced tea I poured all over myself.

"That was unreal," Brad says, walking beside me with a giant grin stretched across his face. "I'm in awe of you right now."

As tired and as wired as I feel, I match his smile. After everything that happened between us earlier, I'm more connected to him than ever and all the adrenaline and lust is coursing through me. I feel like I might explode, and I'm wondering if the backstage area is the place to do it.

But before I can say anything to Brad—suggest we go off somewhere for a drink, or just find an empty room— my father looms in the distance, arms folded across his chest. After what I witnessed in the hotel room, he's the last person I want to see, and I know he feels the same way about seeing Brad and me together.

I step away from Brad, putting distance between us, and keep my eyes forward. I don't even think I can talk to my father at the moment. All those horrible things he said were ringing in my ears for most of the show. That's partly why I did the whole act with the whisky bottle, to piss him off.

The other reason is because I really wanted to show what I'm made of. I'm not just some replacement on bass. I'm Lael Ramsey, and I bring a whole new deck of cards to the table. I wanted the mouths of every last fan to be open. I wanted the band to look at me with respect. I wanted my father to see that I'm far more uncontrollable than he thought.

I wanted so much.

I think I got it.

"Lael," my father says. His eyes are warm but his voice is hard. I have to remind myself that he has my entire life planned, that he thinks he controls every last piece of me.

"Hey," I say to him, trying to keep my voice light as I hand my bass to a guitar tech and wipe the sweat off my face with my arm. I notice his eyes don't leave mine, not even to glance at Brad who is walking away from the both of us.

"I had to see your show. I had to know," he says. "You did good, real good. Not sure I like that whole bit with the alcohol, but the crowd loved it. They loved it. Look, we need to talk."

"What about?"

He looks around to see if anyone is nearby listening. Backstage, everyone is bustling to and fro but no one pays us much attention, and if they do, they're subtle about it.

"Everything, Lael. You've been on the road for some time now. It's about time we catch up. How about we grab a drink at the hotel bar?"

I sigh internally. That's the last thing I want. I can't possibly pretend that everything is fine, that I didn't hear him earlier, that Brad and I aren't sleeping together, but I know I'm going to have to.

Luckily my father loves to hear the sound of his own voice. I probably won't be able to get two words in, even if I wanted to.

"Sure," I tell him, plastering a fake smile on my face. "Let me get washed up though."

"I'll have the driver take us to the hotel," he says.

This way there is no escape.

I nod. "Let me just get my purse from the dressing room."

I turn and quickly hurry over to the dressing rooms down the hall, needing some last-minute courage from Brad.

But when I burst inside, it's empty save for Arnie.

"Where is everyone?" I ask him.

"They've gone to a bar, love," he says.

"Without me?"

He smirks. "Seems like they knew you would have some business with your father."

I hate the fact that I'm going to be missing out on a fun night. I wonder if I can join them afterward. It would all depend on my father and how closely he's watching me.

I just nod and turn around as Arnie calls out after me, "Don't ruin anything for Brad, Lael. He's doing his best."

I give him a dirty look. Like I would do anything to jeopardize that.

It's not long before I've shimmied out of my sweaty leather pants and taken a nice hot shower and I'm joining my father at the hotel bar.

It's quiet here, which is probably why my father picked it. Everyone else is out on Bourbon Street or other places in the Quarter. He has a booth in the corner, and I slide on in, expecting a lecture.

Surprisingly, my father doesn't lecture me much. Not at first. I sip on a hurricane while he has a glass of cognac and talks about the music industry.

By the time I'm done with my drink and have ordered another, he starts.

He folds his hands in front of him and gives me a stern and loaded look.

"Lael," he says. "You know I do a lot for you, don't you? Do a lot to keep you happy. And I know we've lost touch a bit when you left to go backpacking. But I do my best to do right by you. I hope you know that."

I nod, wishing the server would hurry. I need that second drink, stat.

"But I'm hearing some rumors and I'm concerned," he adds.

"What about?" I ask carefully, trying to look innocent.

"For one, I know you're not traveling in the other bus."

"That was better for band morale. I play better when I bond with the guys."

"And that brings me to the other shit. Bonding. I don't want that, you hear? You don't need that. Especially with Brad Snyder."

"Brad and I are just friends. Co-workers, even," I tell him, smiling gratefully at the waiter who drops off my hurricane.

"That's not what I'm hearing."

I eye him suspiciously. "What are you hearing?"

"Lael, please. I have eyes and ears everywhere. I understand that he was your crush. I get it. A musical idol, even, I don't know. But you can't…involve yourself with that boy."

"Brad is twenty-seven," I remind him. "He's hardly a boy, and he's someone capable of making his own choices."

"Brad started from nothing. He would be nothing without me. I'm like a father to him. Do you know how much responsibility lies in our relationship? I overlook and oversee everything he does. I made him, Lael. I did that. I made him what he is. And sometimes he seems ungrateful. Someone who was truly grateful wouldn't be breaking my wishes like this. You don't bite the hand that feeds you."

I don't say anything to that. No matter what I say, my father is going to throw something back at me. Everyone always owes something to Ronald Ramsey, including me. It's never the other way around.

"Look, princess, I'm looking out for you." His tone is sweeter now as if he's trying a new approach, but even his sweet tone is off-putting. "I just want the best for you. That's why I do everything for you. I only have your best interests in mind. You know, the Ramsey name is a legacy. Something to hold on to, to be proud of. It's a brand you represent."

I suck back my drink, hoping it goes straight to my head. Oh, I get it. It's not about what's best for me, it's about what's best for him and the Ramsey name.

"You know the media is already talking that you got the gig because of who I am…"

Actually, every interview I've done has only reflected on me favorably, but I don't bother bringing that up.

"And I don't want them to think that," he continues, swirling his cognac around his glass. "What's worse is if you hook up with Brad. That's not good. Not good at all. The media will turn it around and say you're in the band because of him. You don't want that. You don't, Lael. You want to say you're here because you're talented."

I meet his eyes. "Do you think I'm talented?"

"Of course I do."

"I've never heard you say it."

"Look, do you think I would have let you have a chance at this if you were just going to make a fool of me?"

What about making a fool of myself? I think.

"You've got talent. You've got the chops. I see it. Everyone does. Now do the right thing for everyone and preserve it. Don't lower yourself to Brad's standards, don't become part of the rumor mill. Keep your head up."

"Or else?" I say.

He glowers at me. "Or else there will be problems."

Problems like making Brad disappear? I know it was probably just an idle threat, but still.

"You know he was last with Lindsay Lyons. That relationship, as fake as it was, helped her career. He's going to be with someone else next, someone else from Ramsey Records. You don't want to mess that up, believe me. You don't."

I swallow hard.

"I have to go, Lael," he says suddenly, getting up. He leans across the table, looking me dead in the eye. "Remember what we talked about. We don't want any problems. You don't want any problems. Brad doesn't want any problems." Then he straightens up. "I'll be off in the morning, going to New York. I'll see if I can drop in again soon. You're doing good, kid."

Then he leaves as abruptly as he showed up.

I sigh and try to get the attention of the waiter for another drink. When I don't see him, I decide to mosey up to the bar and get it there. Quicker service anyway, and no one likes to sit at a booth alone.

But when I grab a seat on the stool, I notice I'm sitting right next to Jean Marc. The French musician I love and the guy Brad seems to hate for some reason.

"Hey," I say to him.

He turns and looks me up and down. "You are Lael Ramsey," he says in his accent.

"You know who I am," I say brightly.

"I do. How can I not? Look at your hair, it's so bright. And you play so well."

It's funny, back in the day I would have been overjoyed to have Jean Marc sitting next to me, but now that we've played the show and I'm exhausted, plus the fact that I slept with Brad, I don't feel that same pull.

Still, he seems like a nice guy, if not a bit pretentious. I mean, who wears a silk neck scarf and a fedora?

"Thank you for the compliment," I tell him. "I heard you put on a great show tonight."

"You didn't see it?"

I smile to myself. Brad would be so happy that Jean Marc knows we didn't catch his show.

"No, we got to the venue late," I tell him.

"Such a shame. Well, I caught your show. I have to say, I've never seen two players with such chemistry before."

"Are you talking about Calvi and Brad?" I ask him.

He grins at me and takes a sip of his drink. "No. Those two secretly despise each other. I can tell. I mean you and Brad. You are sleeping together, no?"

I burst out laughing, feeling my face go red. "I don't know what you're talking about."

"Oh, you can lie, but I know. I know. I've been there myself."

"Oh really? Who were you sleeping with?"

"A true man never kisses and tells," he says. "But I can give you some advice."

"I'm not sure I need advice," I tell him.

"Everyone needs advice, mon Cherie," he says. "Especially someone as young as you. You live in a beautiful, idealistic world."

"And you're here to ruin it?"

"No, no, no. I am not like that. Have some faith, Lael Ramsey." He leans in closer. "My advice is the opposite. My advice is to never lose that beautiful, idealistic world, the one that lives deep within you. This industry makes people hard. It turns them into shells. The world does it to everyone, but playing music like this will do it the most. Hold on to that purity inside you. The goodness in your heart. Where your youth comes from and stays. Make it eternal. View the world through the rose-colored glasses. It's much prettier that way. And believe in love and changes for the better. Believe it with everything you've got."

I can't believe this Frenchman is getting so deep with me. But in a way I can. I just never expected to hear him be so non-cynical toward love.

He shrugs. "You can take it with a grain of salt, but know it's the truth. Don't let the world corrupt you. Stay good. If you love this man, this Brad Snyder, don't ever let anyone tell you it's wrong or it doesn't mean anything. Love means everything. It's why we sing about it, yes?"

I nod. "Yes."

Absolutely, yes.

FOURTEEN

BRAD

"Yoko. There, I said it," Calvi says as he stands up and takes a step back from the bar as if he'd just lit a stick of dynamite with a short fuse.

Switch takes a shot of whatever it is he's drinking and keeps his eyes forward. I can tell this is something they discussed between them more than once. I can also tell Calvi wants Switch to back him up and is frustrated that he's on his own confronting me about this.

Calvi sits back down, and the three of us stare forward and say nothing. Switch waves his empty glass to the elderly barman.

"A round for the three of us," Switch says.

I take in a slow breath and prepare myself. I don't want to drink, but all things considered, I'll play along. There's mutiny in the air and I need to bond with my mates. I need to get Calvi to knock this shit off right now, comparing Lael to Yoko Ono. I also try to not think about tomorrow's hangover, but I do.

Sure, I'll feel like a dirty dishcloth for the next couple of days so I can make you happy, I think. The barman lines them up and the three of us shoot them back.

"Why do you guys even care? She's awesome, and you know I won't let you down," I say, still wincing from the shot. God, it burns.

"The truth is, if we auditioned one hundred more people we wouldn't find a better bass player," Calvi says, not looking at me. "But it's not about that. It's about who her father is, man. Don't bite the hand that feeds you. AKA, don't fuck this up. For all of us. She's young and she's hot and you're getting carried away."

"Another round," I say, snapping my fingers.

That's the problem, you see. I'm a guy who doesn't like to drink a lot until I have a drink. Then I'm a guy who likes to drink a lot.

"I like her," Switch says, twirling his empty shot glass.

"You mind taking this out of my back?" Calvi says, referring to the imaginary knife Switch has stabbed him with.

"Cal is right," Switch says, changing his tune. "You're getting carried away with her. Maybe it's time for you to back off. If the label drops us and Ronald puts a team of lawyers on us to keep us down, it's all of our careers, not just yours."

I shoot the whisky back and think about his words as it perfectly burns my throat. I've been with these guys for almost a decade. They've let me lead them, and they have had my back the entire journey. They've never been a part of negotiations with Ramsey Records. I have always been the liaison between the company and the band. I would come back from a meeting and tell them what happened, and they have always put a great deal of trust in me. If I fall, we all fall, I get that.

"Brad, look, think about it. How can this end well? Explain to me one possible outcome where your little affair with Lael will not have an awful ending." Calvi's speaking to me closer than I would like, and I can smell the whisky on his breath. "There are no secrets. You know Ronald will find out everything that happens on this tour."

I'm happy Calvi brought this up because Ronald does seem to be getting a play-by-play and I've been wanting to know who's been feeding him the information. I've suspected it was Arnie, but Calvi is quickly becoming suspect number one. I can tell he knows I'm suspicious of him by the way I'm looking at him, and his body language becomes defensive, which makes me even more suspicious.

"Don't you find it strange how Ronald always knows what's going on?" I ask him, eyes narrowing. "I wonder who's feeding him information. Who's the rat?"

"What are you saying? You think I've been telling Ronald about you and Lael?" Calvi says, clearly offended.

"Well it sure as fuck isn't me," I answer.

Calvi stands and I stand too. We face each other, staring each other down. My barstool is knocked over by Switch, wedging himself between us.

"Relax, fellas, have a drink," Switch says, pushing us apart. Three more shots are on the table, and after a tense moment we all take whatever glass is closest and shoot it back. Calvi and I are still staring at each other, and we both slam our glasses down without breaking the exchange.

"So you three kiddies are And Then?"

Calvi and I break our standoff and put our attention

on the man speaking to us.

I recognize him. His name is Gregg something or other, and he plays drums in a band called B.S.R. He's an older guy with a reputation for causing trouble. If half of the rumours I've heard about him and his band are true…and this man is clearly looking for trouble.

Feeling that whisky course through me, I take his challenge and square off with him.

"Hey fellas, come take a look. It's Ronald Ramsey's boy band."

Gregg is talking to two ominous looking characters sitting at a table behind him. I'm surprised I didn't notice until now that all three members of B.S.R are sitting only steps away from us.

I used to love hearing the stories about them from the guys that worked at the theater with Mr. Robson. Folklore legends, rock and roll's most dark and obscure band is right here, calling us down to their level. They famously turned down Ronald Ramsey and every other offer, and remain independent to this day, for better or worse. I'd actually say worse, since a critical acclaim and a tiny cult-like following only gets you so far. Especially now that they're looking down their noses at us.

I don't like this attack, especially coming from these guys, these *too cool* old know-it-all rockers. Calvi and I aim our aggression at the drunken bully. No one dares to call us a fucking boy band and lives to tell about it.

We take a step toward him and Switch follows suit. I feel like we are three wolves, hackles raised, snarling and growling at this intruder.

The other two members of B.S.R stand up. The six of us stand off and ready ourselves for battle. Just as tension reaches that critical point where fists begin to fly, the bar room door flies open and an old friend barges in—Roar.

He looks like he had to run through a battle to get here, out of breath and full of hate as he makes his way to us. He kicks chairs out of the way to clear a path, and has the walk of a fighter ready for war. A Viking.

I feel a smile begin to form on my face because our team has suddenly become stronger in this fight. I look at Gregg with a little more confidence and bravado, but my smile quickly disappears. Roar does not seem to notice he has just walked in on the beginnings of a brawl—he is focused on me.

Oh right, I think to myself, remembering I stole his vehicle and it got taken away by the cops. That was back in New Mexico, but it doesn't surprise me that Roar is a few days behind. Nor does it surprise me that he's here for my blood.

As if in slow motion, I see Roar's huge fist come toward my face. It gets bigger and bigger, then slams into my nose with a crushing force.

I fall back into the bar, and for a moment I feel like I'm floating. I'm floating because my feet are not touching the ground—Roar is literally throwing my nearly limp body over the bar.

I'm half in a dream and feel very little, and when I crash land on the other side of the bar I sense the beating is over. My vision is clouded from being punched in the face, but I can see the old barman polishing a glass, seemingly unaware of the full-scale brawl that is happening before him. I can hear the chaos of punches and chairs being broken, but the sounds slowly fade away and the old barman disappears behind the curtain of my eyelids as I slip into the black.

"Wake up."

The words sound like they're far away. There's a small part of me that knows I'm lying on the bar floor, but I'm trapped in space and unable to respond.

"Wake up, man." I recognize the voice and I'm pulled back to reality. Calvi is shaking me. He has a black eye, a bleeding lip, and his face is red with fatigue.

"Did we get 'em?" I ask, referring to the brawl that I obviously missed.

Calvi waves his hand back and forth indicating it was a wash. "Those old guys are pretty tough. Roar almost had them all beat, but that fucking bartender jumped in and beat the hell out of all of us."

I must still be dreaming because that old-timer could barely lift a glass.

I stand up and take in the mayhem left behind. It looks like a bomb has exploded. And there's the old barman, slowly picking up a chair from the wooden floor. The neon lights in the window flicker, and the music coming from the speaker is very low. The room is nearly empty, making the sound of the chair on the wooden floor echo.

My head is still foggy; in fact I feel like hell, and I'm slow to compute my surroundings. I feel like I've exhausted my visit behind the bar by the way the barman is looking at me. My broken brain finds the exit, and I stumble through the narrow opening, bracing myself on the sticky surface.

My mind is slowly beginning to clear but a sharp headache is causing me to wince. I feel like a ghost in a dive bar trying to understand how I've ended up here. Also because the fellas standing only feet away from me don't seem to notice me. The barman does, but I assume he's able to see ghosts, just like that barman in *The Shining*. Or was it the other way around?

Getting knocked out, it's no damn good.

I'm standing next to Switch, Calvi, and three members of B.S.R. Switch and one of the guys share a hug. Calvi and another are sharing a laugh.

What the hell did I miss?

"Some help you were," Switch says to me sarcastically.

The other guys laugh. Roar walks out of the bathroom looking like a Viking that was at the losing end of a battle.

"I think it's time to roll," says Jack Willow, the band's lead singer. He's looking at the barman who's staring at Roar with cold, cold eyes. Roar is visibly fearful of the old barman and leads the pack out the door.

The dark city street is cold, all humidity from earlier gone. The few people around look like a mix of nocturnal drug addicts and drunk college students en route to Bourbon Street. There's not much life around, save a glowing light coming from an English-looking tavern up the street.

The newly formed gang is standing in a circle on the sidewalk apologizing to each other. It looks like the beginnings of some very unhealthy friendships.

Meanwhile, Roar is ignoring the chit-chat and is focused on me. My heart sinks. I'm weak, and I fear another whack from him will be the end of me. He doesn't blink and takes three heavy steps toward me. I close my eyes and prepare to meet my maker.

"I'll forgive you, snake man," he says into my ear as he gives me a bear hug, lifting me off the ground. "You owe me some money first, then I forgive you," he adds.

"I can start by buying you a beer," I answer, looking up to Roar towering over me.

I can't tell if this is the entertainment district or the warehouse district, but we all start heading toward the light of the tavern like a moth to a flame. We walk in the middle of the broken concrete road, limping, strutting, gliding along in the afterglow of adrenaline. I'm still not feeling like myself, but the high energy of this crew of misfits is giving me a lift.

B.S.R are indie darlings who have kept their dark mystique as they have aged. They are the complete opposite of *And Then*. We're considered mainstream, basically created by the record company. We're in celebrity magazines with our starlet girlfriends. People don't go to vinyl shops and ask for our records, but they certainly would buy B.S.R. records with pride.

Jack Willow is wearing a loose-fitting brown blazer that smells of cigar smoke, wise-guy leather boots, and the collar of his dated shirt is half sticking out. He walks next to me and I wait for him to talk.

"You know, kid. I don't know how you do it," he says as he lights a half-smoked cigar.

"Do what?" I ask.

"Work for Ronald Ramsey. Can't be easy."

"I don't work for Ronald Ramsey." I know what I sound like and immediately regret it. Jack laughs out a cloud of smoke.

"He works for you, right? Look, you are deep in the machine and it hasn't seemed to break you. You're a smooth kid."

"Thanks?" I say as I run my hand through my hair. I can't tell if he's being sincere or not. Jack is zeroed in on me and senses my defensiveness.

"You write your own shit, right?" he asks.

"Yeah," I answer.

"I like that limousine song," Jack says as if the compliment was some kind of offering.

"Thanks."

Jack wraps his arm around me as we approach the entrance of the pub. The place is called Moby's as stated by the flickering neon light in the window. There's a chalk board next to the entrance with the words *Open Mic Tonight* scratched in large letters. The distinctive shaky vocals of an open mic performer are pouring out of the entrance. The bouncer is staring at me in disbelief, and I can tell this will not be an evening that I'll go unnoticed.

"Here you go, brother. For me and my son here." Jack still has me under his arm and pulls me in closer as he talks to the bouncer. He gives the speechless guy a twenty and struts into the bar, finally releasing me from his hold. He makes a direct route to the bartender, lit cigar in one hand and a fist full of cash in the other. He hands the barman the cash and leans over the bar to exchange a few words.

Our crew pours into the room almost drowning out the nervous performer on stage. The lady is strumming a ukulele and singing sweetly, then her song ends and we give her a loud round of applause.

A heavy empty glass is put in my hand—the barkeep and Jack are handing glasses out to everyone in the joint.

The host of the open mic thanks the lady and asks if there is anyone else who would like to play.

"Brad wants to play!" Jack shouts as he pours what looks like whisky into my glass. He continues around the room filling glasses as if his feet never touch the ground.

"No thanks, I'm good," I respond, waving my hand dismissively.

I back away to the edge of the room. I consider joining Calvi and Switch, but they're sitting at a table with a couple of gals and I don't see a place.

"All right, well, I'm the host of open stage tonight, so if anyone wants to come up and play let me know. My name is Vince Stark and this song is called "Would" by Alice in Chains."

The host begins to play a very quiet, stripped down version of the famous song. We all shout and cheer in support, our cheers softened by his gentle playing. The energy in the room is electric—I don't know if it's just the whisky, but I'm truly having a good time. My headache is long gone and I take in the positive energy that's swirling around the room.

I wish Lael was here.

The bassist and drummer from B.S.R hop on stage. All the equipment was there waiting, asking to be played. Mr. Stark looks very pleased to have the famous rhythm section joining him. I'm surrounded by people who are trying to buddy up to me or have their picture taken with me. I point to the stage, indicating that's where their attention should be.

The bassist, Gregg, gives the signal to keep the same riff going so they can get into it. The sound gets bigger, and the room cheers as the drums and bass fill out the sound. Switch, Calvi, and their new lady friends begin to dance.

"So, where is the girl?" Jack asks as he tops up my glass.

"The girl?" I question.

"Your new bass player, who I assume is your new girlfriend," Jack adds.

"She's Ramsey's daughter, you know," I say.

"I know," Jack says through a smile. A silence lingers, and Jack takes a drink from the bottle, continuing on. "The boss's young daughter and your mates think she's gong to ruin the band…just make sure it's worth it."

"Worth what?"

"Everything?"

"Without question," I answer. The words fall from my lips and I hold eye contact without blinking.

Jack matches my intensity and says, "Life is too short, man. Trust me, it goes fast. You'll be just fine starting over without Ronald Ramsey. If you're in love with this young lady, jump in, take her, and never look back."

I look at Jack very suspiciously. He seems to know more details than he should. Just intuition, perhaps.

"Come on." Jack again takes me under his arm and walks me to the stage. The room begins to explode as we step up. Jack hands me a mic, but I wave it away and motion for him to begin the verse.

He complies. The host and Jack both sing the verse while I size up the guitar and amp in the corner. I sling the guitar around my neck and test it out to see if it's in tune.

Close enough for this kind of night, I think.

Jack places the mic stand in front of me and puts the mic to my lips for the chorus. I strum along and belt out the words. Jack lip syncs and works the crowd with the bottle of whisky still in hand.

At the end of the tune, the entire room shouts the final words so loud it rivals a stadium crowd: "IF I WOULD, COULD YOU?"

FIFTEEN

LAEL

I hear Brad's door close.

I probably should have been asleep. Lord knows I wanted to text him at every moment, but I don't want to be *that* girl. Friend, bassist, something more…whatever I am to Brad, I don't want to push it.

But I do want more of him.

So much more.

I get up off my bed, wearing just a long, threadbare Anthrax t-shirt that I've had forever. It barely covers my butt but I'm not going far.

I swipe my key off the coffee table and make my way to the door, pausing by the mirror to look at myself. My makeup is washed off, my hair is a mess, and yet I don't care. Brad has seen a million different versions of me, including the one earlier—stark naked in an alley and getting fucked while hanging on to dirty pipes. I never thought I had that in me, but this man is making me do all sorts of crazy things.

Including sneaking across the hall to his room, when I know for sure there are spies everywhere. I know what Arnie said to me, and I know what my father threatened, but I can't seem to stay away from him.

Maybe I'm a fool. Maybe all my hormones are awakening for the first time in my life. Maybe I'm being driven mad by lust and years of obsession over him. Who knows.

But I want him. I need him. And no one else will do.

I open the door and quietly close it behind me before shuffling across the hallway to his room. I knock on it softly and wait.

I hear him walking around in there but nothing else happens.

"Brad," I whisper, knocking again.

The footsteps get closer. The door opens.

He's standing on the other side looking sexy as fuck.

And drunk as a skunk. He might even be swaying a bit on his feet.

His eyes widen at the sight of me and he cries out, "La–!"

But I quickly shove my finger to his lips to shut him up and make him walk backward into his room until I'm shutting the door behind us, flipping over the lock just in case.

"What are you doing here?" he asks, but he's grinning. He's happy to see me.

"I don't know," I tell him, putting one hand on my hip. "How drunk are you?"

"Pretty drunk. I've had a hell of a night."

I walk toward him, grabbing the hem of his shirt as I inspect his face. His eyes are glazed, his smile crooked.

And his nose is swollen. Purple is spreading to his eyes.

"Brad, did you get in a fight?!" I exclaim, dragging him over to the lamp and flicking it on. I gasp when I can see him clearer.

"It was Roar," he says.

"Roar? How the fuck was it Roar? Where did he come from? Why did he hit you?"

Brad shrugs, still smiling. "I don't know. Vikings do these things."

"Brad…"

"Oh, right. He was mad that we stole his dune buggy and got it towed. He was stuck with the bill."

"Oh shit. I never even thought of that."

"Neither did I," he says. "Usually when I get into shit, someone is there to fix my problems just like that."

"Someone like my father."

He doesn't say anything, his smile fading slightly.

"Anyway, Jesus. Are you okay?" I ask.

"I'm fine. He knocked me out clear over the bar and then there was this brawl. But it all happened while I was under. But we all made up after."

I shake my head. "You guys are nuts, you know that?"

"No, you're nuts," he says, looking me up and down. "What are you doing tempting fate like this? The moment I saw you talking to your father, I could have sworn you were done with me."

"Done with you?" I ask. "Brad, I'm just getting started."

He chews on his lip, his eyes becoming heavy with lust. "Oh really? He didn't scare you off?"

"Did he scare you earlier?"

"Baby, nothing is going to keep me away from you. Not your father, not the band. If it's a risk, I don't fucking care. You are worth it."

That's exactly what I've been dying to hear.

"Get on the bed," I tell him.

He raises his brow. "Oh?"

"Do it. You're drunk and I'd like to take advantage of you."

"I would love it if you did. I'll give you a helping hand though." He starts to undress himself, and he has to lean against the dresser briefly so he doesn't fall over while taking off his pants.

My god, he's a gorgeous man. Just enough chest hair, just enough muscle, just enough of a tan. He looks like he works out, but not too much. He's lean and sculpted and naked, here for me to ogle and admire.

And then there's his dick. I barely got a look at it earlier in the alley, but now it's here, large and in charge and in all its glory.

I really lucked out with this man. Brad Snyder is turning out to be everything I thought he would be and more. Much, much more.

"Are you done admiring me?" he asks with a cocky smile. Normally I would cut him down and say he doesn't have a right to look so pleased with himself, but honestly, he can be as pleased as he wants. The man is perfect.

"No," I tell him and lift my shirt over my head while sliding off my underwear. It's funny how I feel zero shame or self-consciousness when I'm naked in front him. It just feels natural. Right.

Hell, maybe it means I'm cocky too.

"Do you have any idea how gorgeous you look?" he says, his voice in a low whisper. He's looking me over in awe.

"I could say the same to you. Now get on the bed."

I pause, remembering earlier. "Oh wait, do you have a condom?"

"Maybe?" he says. "We didn't use one earlier…is that going to be a problem?"

"It shouldn't be," I tell him. "I'm on the pill."

I just haven't been taking it very regularly since we've been on the road. I don't want to risk it again.

He walks off to the bathroom and I get on the bed. When he comes back, he has one in his hand.

"Lie back," he says to me.

"Now you're in charge?"

"You bet I am. Lie back."

I'm okay with this.

I lie back on the bed and watch eagerly as he opens the packet and slides the condom on. Call me weird, but I've always found the sight to be strangely erotic. Or maybe it's just that I like to see a guy handle himself like that.

He keeps his eyes on mine, burning with new lust that seems to be born from fire. Meanwhile, I'm so turned on already that I'm wet, the heat building between my legs.

He crawls on top of me, his dick bobbing out between us, grinning at me like we're sharing a secret. I guess we are.

His hand slips between my thighs, parting them slightly as his fingers find my clit. I let out a small, anxious gasp as he teases it, his eyes never breaking from mine. "I've been thinking about this all day. Even during the show."

"So have I," I admit, feeling strangely shy for just a moment.

Something smolders in Brad's eyes and he grabs my hips, parting my legs further.

He reaches for his dick and runs the crown of it up and

down my clit, pausing to dip it briefly inside before bringing it back up.

My eyes close, and I surrender myself to his teasing. I never want him to stop and yet I want him inside me more than ever. He's not pushing in—it's just a slow slide, back and forth, but I feel myself opening for him anyway, my body hungry, then becoming wildly desperate for more, just like I was earlier in the alley. I swear this man turns me into a wild thing. I'm both languid and tense, surrendering and spurring him on as he rubs against me over and over again.

I swallow hard, making a whimpering noise that sounds like begging. My heart is starting to pound in my head, my skin is hot and tight, and my nipples are hardened pebbles in the room's air conditioning.

"I want you inside me," I tell him. "This is torture."

"But it's the best kind," he whispers.

With a slow exhale, not breaking eye contact, he leans on his elbows and pushes himself in.

Slowly.

Inch by inch.

It feels good, then it feels like too much, then I don't even know what I feel because all I feel is him.

This isn't a crazed quickie out in a dirty alley. This is him and me, in this bed, soft and gentle and slow. It's right. It's so damn right.

I stretch around him, decadently full, taking the time to enjoy and worship each other's bodies, to see how we fit, to see how good we can make each other feel.

I'm soaking in every part of him.

This man.

My rock god.

My everything.

"Does it feel okay?" he asks, groaning through the words.

"It's more than okay," I say, licking my lips. I look at him, caught in the heated vibrancy of his stare. "God, you feel so good."

He nods and watches me intently as he pushes in further. His lips part as he sucks in his breath, and his forehead creases in lust and awe, like he can't believe this is happening, can't believe how good it feels.

"Lael," he moans, his hands sliding to my breasts where he pinches my hardened nipples. "I hate that I didn't find you earlier."

Something in my heart swells.

"But you've found me now," I tell him, my voice breaking into a breathless groan.

He's watching me, watching himself, watching *us,* where he sinks into me, disappearing. He's entranced by the sight, the slow push in, the slow pull out.

How can this man be all of this and more?

Each rock of my hips, each thrust of his, pushes him in deeper, makes us connect like magnets, the space between us buzzing with adrenaline and lust and this energy that we share. We're like power generators, creating electricity, atoms shifting in the air. It affects everything, the way his abs clench as he pushes inside, the tiny beads of sweat that gather in the creases, the dampness of his brow. I reach around and tug his firm ass toward me, wanting more, and he drives in so deep that the air leaves my lungs.

"Oh, Brad," I groan, feeling the emotions swirl inside me as the energy builds and builds, threatening to overtake me.

My head drops back against the sheets, my eyes closing in shock as I surrender. He's in me, in so deep, and I don't ever want him to leave.

This is better than any fucking show that ever will be.

It sets off something deep inside, a jolt of power that hums and buzzes and builds as it slowly increases, spreading, heating up. It's going to take over, it's going to pull me under and apart, and I've never wanted to come so badly in my life.

I've never wanted to feel so absolutely undone.

"Deeper," I whisper hoarsely.

He responds instantly.

With a rough growl he starts thrusting deeper, one hand making a fist in my hair. He leans down, pressing his damp chest against mine, and kisses me, quick and hot, tasting like sweat. My mouth is ravenous against his, the need inside me building and building. Our teeth clash—it's messy and wild.

And then we find our rhythm, our bodies coming together in synchronicity. He's pounding and pounding and pounding me, the headboard moving against the wall.

I can't keep my eyes off of him, his eyes, his body. The muscles in his neck are strained as the sweat rolls off of him, and his eyes are lost in a primal haze. The sounds that come out of his mouth with each thrust are so real and raw that they threaten to undo me.

I'm barely holding on.

The bed slams back against the wall again and again and the sheets are pulled loose, my breasts jostling. The energy inside me is a live wire, and I have seconds to keep in control.

I surrender.

"I'm coming," I cry out, my voice raw and raspy and drowning with desire, trying to hold his gaze. He holds mine back, his eyes burning in victory.

Then I'm twisting as the orgasm washes over me. My body jolts and shudders and I'm high above this world, made of a million universes. Only warmth and joy remain as I come down, floating, feeling as light as a balloon.

"Fuck," Brad grunts, his fist in my hair growing tighter. His growling, animalistic noises, the slap of his sweat-soaked skin against mine, the creak of the bed, all fill the room.

Then he lets out a long, raw moan, shoulders shaking as he comes.

The pumping slows. His grip in my hair loosens.

He collapses against me, his hair damp and dark and sticking to his brow. His eyes take me in, his breath heavy and hard.

We don't say anything for a few moments. There's nothing to say. We just catch our breath, our chests rising and falling against each other. Slowly, very slowly, everything comes back into focus.

We're in Brad's hotel room in New Orleans and I've slept with Brad for the second time today.

And even though we're still at that stage where we could chalk it up to hormones and being two ridiculously good-looking people, I know that isn't the case. I was prepared to walk, prepared to just let it be this lustful physical thing, but it's more than that.

And I think it is for him, too.

"Do you want to spend the night?" he asks me as he pulls out and rolls off of me. He gets rid of the condom and climbs back on the bed, pulling back the covers and motioning for me to get under them.

"I shouldn't," I tell him. "I don't want us to get caught. Lord knows my father is probably going to show up on the fire escape at any moment and look in here."

"That's extremely creepy," Brad says, "and I wouldn't put it past him. Look, just get under the covers for a little bit."

I give him a wry glance. "I didn't peg you for such a cuddler, Brad Snyder."

"Don't tell anyone. The fan sites would have a field day."

I laugh and join him under the covers as he wraps his arms around me, holding me tight. I have to fight against sleep. I've never felt more peaceful and relaxed in all my life.

"You know, you were really something tonight," he says to me.

"So I've heard."

"I mean it. You're full of surprises."

"All the better to keep you on your toes."

He runs his fingers down my cheek and then pushes my hair behind my ears. "So tell me what your father talked to you about. Or do I want to know?"

"It's nothing you don't already know. The same old warning. Doesn't want me getting too attached to my role in the band and he doesn't want me to be corrupted by you."

I feel Brad stiffen beneath me. I can tell that it bothers him, what my father thinks. I don't think there's any love lost between them, but I think it pains Brad that my father still thinks he's that hopeless kid he first discovered. That he's trash and nothing more. I want Brad to know he's better than my father will ever know.

"I'm surprised you're still here," he says softly.

"I'm not going anywhere, Brad. You know I'm not afraid of him. The only thing I'm afraid of is not being with you."

"Then we share the same fears."

As luck has it though, I fall asleep. When I wake up, the alarm clock is glowing four a.m.

I know we could get in big shit for this, so I get out of bed, careful at first not to wake Brad, but he's nearly lifeless and snoring like a bear.

Then I sneak out of his hotel room, making sure no one sees me leave, and head back into mine.

You'd think I would have fallen right back asleep again, but the truth is, my thoughts swirl around Brad like a hurricane.

How can something that feels so right be considered to be so wrong?

And when is everything going to stop being so complicated?

If I'm being honest with myself though, I know it's only going to get more complicated going forward.

SIXTEEN

LAEL

It's been one month on the road since Brad and I started sleeping together.

Things officially can't be any more complicated than they are.

The only bonus to everything is that my father hasn't showed up yet and I haven't heard anything from him about Brad and I either. I've also never seen anything about us mentioned in the media and on gossip and fan sites, which makes me think that we're epically good at sneaking around.

That said...things aren't exactly perfect at the moment.

It's nothing to do with Brad.

It's more that the weather has turned sour, blizzards are everywhere on the east coast making us late for more than a few shows. Sometimes I think it would be so much easier to just hop on a plane but flying in these storms seems just as dangerous as driving.

And there's something else going on right now.

I'm not feeling quite myself.

In fact, I'm feeling awfully sick every afternoon.

I'm trying really hard not to think about it.

"Penny for your thoughts?" Brad asks as he grabs my hand and leads me toward the bus.

We're just inside the compound of the stadium in Detroit and snow is falling steadily. The rest of the band and Arnie has gone off to have dinner somewhere but Brad and I have opted to stay behind. I'm sure Calvi has a feeling of what's going on since he gave me the stinkeye before he left, but no one can prove anything.

God, I hope they don't have hidden cameras on the bus.

"My thoughts are worth gold," I tell him as the bus door opens with a hydraulic hiss, "because they're only of you."

"Such a charmer," he says to me, helping me up the stairs and then closing the door behind us.

Maybe it's because I'm trying not to think about certain things, but the moment we're sealed in the bus and I'm alone with him, I practically jump him.

Well, I try to.

He makes the first move.

He moves, fast, and his lips are on mine, crushing and soft. Pure velvet lust that turns sweetly violent.

His hand is at the back of my neck, his other fingers are pressing at my jaw and cheek as his tongue assaults me with such rolling passion I can feel it all the way in my toes. He's in complete control and I surrender. I surrender completely. I want him to take me, take me over, devour me, annihilate me. I want him to erase my fears. I want him closer than ever.

What if? The thought snakes into my head.

But it's fleeting. I push it away and concentrate on Brad, on this very moment in this tour bus where he's unravelling me to the core, stripping me of all defenses, making me more vulnerable than I ever have before.

He's a wild animal, voracious as his mouth sinks into the valley between my neck and my shoulder, biting with hunger and lust.

I groan loudly and one of his hands slips low along my hips, hiking up the hem of my dress. Every nerve ending on my body dances with anticipation.

I want him to take me away, I need him to.

His hand slides inside my underwear and down, down to where I'm absolutely soaked.

"Shit," he murmurs against me. "You're going to be the death of me one day."

Likewise, I think. His thick rough finger slides along my clit and my body immediately melts into his hand, needing more, wanting more. I'd never had the need to get off strike me like this before, like a match. My emotions and hormones are in for a hell of a ride. All this sneaking around, all this worry, it all melts away the moment he touches me and everything I'm feeling right now is intensified more than normal.

I grab hold of the back of his neck, his skin hot to touch, my body hungry for him. His fingers play gently along my clit, teasing like fluttery wings, before the they plunge up inside me.

A gasp escapes my mouth.

"Oh god," Brad says thickly, bringing his lips back to mine. "I can't control myself when you make sounds like that."

"Then don't control yourself."

"You're playing with fire," he says before he's lowering his head to my breast, pulling the neckline of my dress to the side until my nipple is exposed and hardening in the air. His lips gently suck at the tip before he draws it into his mouth in one long, hard pull.

My back is arching for more and breathless groans are coaxed out of me. We're still standing in the middle of the tour bus and I'm not sure how much more I can take like this. I mean, where do we even go? We won't be able to have sex on the bunks, there's no room.

He pinches my nipple between his teeth, distracting me, and, as he does so, plunges his fingers back inside me, three of them this time. I expand around him, needing more. Every inch of my skin is on fire for him and only he can put out the flames.

Before I know what's happening, he's pushing me back down the aisle. "Get on the floor," he says, his voice husky and rich, dripping with need.

I drop down to my knees on the rug, staring up at him while he quickly yanks down his jeans. His dick bobs free and I'm breathless once again.

Since I'm already on my knees and I'm salivating for the taste of him, I grab his ass with one hand, my finger-nails digging in as I tug him toward me. With my other hand I grasp his dick at the base, making a ring around it. He's so goddamn hard, it's like velvet steel, and silky to touch. I can feel the hot blood rushing underneath, the way his shaft ticks with each beat of his heart.

I close my eyes and tentatively slide my tongue along the sensitive underside before circling his crown. His hand goes into my hair, pulling lightly, and he groans as I try and take him all into my mouth.

"Easy now," Brad says through a groan. "Keep it up and there won't be much left of me. Turn around."

My heart is pumping hard in anticipation as I pivot around on the buses harsh carpet so I'm on all fours, my ass raised in the air. He drops to his knees behind me and I hold my breath, waiting for his touch.

Swiftly he lifts up my dress until it's bunched around my waist and slides my under down. Then he grabs my ass, squeezing hard so I stay in place. I flinch, the pressure from his fingertips is firm and yet the moment he yields, I want it even more.

He pulls me toward him as he positions himself and with one swift jerk, pushes into me. The air is expelled from my chest as he fills me, a gasp broken on my lips.

"Are you okay?" he asks, shuddering the words as he pushes himself fully inside.

I can't speak. I can't think. I can only feel, every single inch of his dick as I squeeze around him. I try and nod, get my breath.

"Does that sound good?" he asks, his voice thicker now. "Can you handle that?" He pauses, slowly pulling out in such a teasing, languid way that it's torturous. I feel empty, aching for him, I want him to fill me up and up and up, like a balloon ready to burst.

"I feel everything," I tell him.

He hisses, "Yes," and then he's pounding into me, fast and deep and relentless. Over and over and over again, this breakneck pace that has me trying to hang on to the rug for dear life, my breasts jiggling with each quick, hard thrust.

His pumps become quicker, deeper, and messy, like

he's losing control and going over the edge and taking me with him. I've never had a man in so deep like this, not just inside me but inside my head. He's everything I've ever wanted and everything I shouldn't have and he's fucking me like we might lose everything tomorrow.

He has no idea, no idea…

The same urgency that's running through him is running through me. I drop onto one elbow, and with my other hand reach for my clit, the pressure building to unbearable heights as he fucks that sweet spot inside me. He grabs the back of my hair until it's gathered in his hand and pushes forward until my cheek is pressed into the carpet and he's holding me down, grunting hard with each thrust.

I'm so wet, slick and ready for him, it doesn't take long for him to push me to the edge. I feel just as I do when I'm on stage, that moment when the roar of the crowd raises you higher and higher and you swear that you'll never come down.

But you do.

And in this case, right now, it's a beautiful come down.

Brad is merciless, groaning hard with each thrust, this rough, animalistic noise that gets louder and louder the closer he gets to coming.

I don't even have time to tell him I'm coming. It just happens, quick and swift, and I'm swept away, tumbling and turning, like I'm crowd-surfing above millions of adoring hands. My body quakes and shudders from head to toe as I pulse around him. I am light and heavy and my heart has wings. I never want to feel anything but this, never want anyone else but him.

"Lael," he groans out my name and then I feel him as he comes, the pressure in my hair, the slamming of his hips into my ass. The sounds coming out of his mouth are blistering and raw and I'd give anything to watch his face as he empties into me.

Then his thrusts slow down, his hand in my hair slowly letting go, releasing the pressure from my head. He's breathing hard, his toned body hovering over me. Drops of sweat fall onto my back, making me shudder.

"First time on a tour bus," he says to me, pulling out. I immediately feel bereft without him.

"Oh shit," he says.

"What?" I say, slowly flipping around so I'm on my back and staring up at him. "Is it my knees?" I ask, noting how red and raw they are from where the carpet rubbed me.

"No, I forgot to use a condom," he says. "Sorry, I was so carried away, I just had to have you. I didn't even think."

I clear my throat. Yeah, about that, I think.

But I don't say it.

"It's fine," I tell him. "Don't worry about it."

"Are you sure?" His brow is creased with worry which feels like a fist to my gut.

"I'm sure," I tell him.

"We have been pretty good about it," he says.

I don't want to talk about it anymore. I quickly get to my feet and pull up my underwear, smoothing my dress back down. "We should probably get out of here. Who knows if people saw us come in here. We know people talk."

"Though to be fair, we've been pretty good at the sneaking thing." He pulls me toward me and grins at me before placing a sweet kiss on my lips. "It's almost fun to pull one over your father and not get caught."

I manage a stiff smile.

What happens when the thrill runs out?

We can't do this forever?

What happens if…

"Hey are you okay?" he asks me, tipping my chin up to meet his gaze.

Maybe?

Maybe not.

"I'm fine," I tell him. "Let's go get something to eat. I'm fucking starving."

"That's my girl."

We walk off the bus and back to the stadium.

I knew.

I fucking knew it.

I'm staring down at a pregnancy test in my hand, the third pregnancy test in a row I've used. I'm so fucking tired of peeing and seeing the same result.

Positive.

Positive!

Holy fucking fuck.

I'm pregnant.

Pregnant with none other than Brad Snyder's baby.

This can't be happening. It just can't be.

But it can, I tell myself, tossing the stick into the trash with the rest of them. And you know it.

It's true. Normally I wouldn't think much about getting pregnant while on the pill, but it must have been that first time we did it in the alley. There was no condom and at that point I wasn't as regular with taking my pills as usual.

Being on the road every single day really messed that up for a bit, even when I had an alarm set to remind me when to take them.

Then there's the fact that for the last while I haven't been feeling like myself. Then I missed my period.

It happened a few days before Brad and I had sex on the tour bus. I was kind of hoping that sex would bring it on, as much of an oxymoron as that seems.

I was in denial. I didn't want to face facts.

Brad knew something was up and I played that show in Detroit feeling less enthused and more distant than normal. But I didn't want to tell him. Not until I knew.

Well, now I know.

It's as clear as day.

Those lines on all those tests, all different brands, they don't lie. Not to mention feeling sick and missing period. Everything is swirling together to create a not-so-perfect storm.

Shit.

What the hell do I do?

I'm only twenty-one and pregnant by the man I'm not supposed to be with.

If I have this baby, my father will disown me.

I might just ruin my entire relationship with him, let alone my life.

And Brad, Brad didn't sign up for this. We're together now but we're sneaking around. Having a baby would tie him to me forever and that might not be something that he wants.

We haven't even discussed what we are to each other.

We haven't even exchanged I love yous.

I mean, I've barely had time to figure out how I feel

about him.

Okay, that's a complete lie.

The truth is, I do love him.

I'm in love with him.

And I always have been.

Only this time, it's for real.

It's not a fantasy, it's far from it.

It's raw and it's messy and it's beautiful.

And it's mine.

No matter how Brad feels about me, he can't take away the fact that what I feel for him is true. He can't stop me from loving him.

Every single moment of this tour for the last couple of months, I've been falling deeper and deeper, head over bass, until I'm rocked by it, by my very love for him.

In some ways, this baby is a product of that love and that feeling alone is probably why I'm not even contemplating an abortion. I'm absolutely respect a woman's right to choose, but getting rid of this baby doesn't seem like an option. It represents my love for Brad. It represents how wonderful he is with me.

And, to be honest, this is something I've always wanted. A family of my own, a product of love. I've always had dreams of being a mom, I just figured it would happen the normal way. You know. Fall in love…with someone who isn't a famous rock star and doesn't have a complicated relationship with your father and isn't completely forbidden. Followed by a proposal, marriage, and then kids.

Not like this. I could have never predicted this.

You're getting ahead of yourself, I remind myself, leaning against the hotel bathroom sink and staring at my reflection in the mirror. I'm not glowing yet.

And yes, I am getting ahead of myself. For all I know, Brad won't want anything to do with the baby or me.

Then again, I can't imagine Brad being like that. I might scare him off and he might have never planned to be with me beyond all this sneaking around on the tour, but he's not the type of guy to just leave a woman when she's pregnant. He's had that growing up – he will do the right thing.

But there's a huge difference between the right thing and the thing that I want.

And the thing that I want is Brad.

And the baby.

I shake my head, trying to come to terms with how quickly my life has changed.

Thank god I'm pretty good at swinging with the punches.

SEVENTEEN

BRAD

It's rare I see snow and I can't remember ever seeing it fall so heavily. The wind is blowing sideways and I can feel it push against the side of the bus. I know George can feel the wind because he is wrestling with the steering wheel and leaning in close to the windshield. I don't understand how ol' George can see the road; from where I sit it looks completely black. The high-beams make the falling snow look like stars and comets whizzing by as we fly through space. We aren't flying through space, we are on a highway in the middle of nowhere, en-route to Chicago, and we're all terrified.

No one is saying a word. Everyone's eyes are forward and we collectively brace ourselves when the large bus swerves and shakes. Everyone is in their usual spots. Lael's in her seat at the front of the bus on the right, near the exit. Seeing her visibly afraid awakens something in me. I want to protect her. I have no idea how I might do that if the bus rolls off the highway, but foolishly I feel I could. I sit up tall and square my shoulders. I don't care what my bandmates think as I make my way over to sit next to her. I wrap my arm around her and I smile.

We've all heard how fear is contagious. The truth is *all* emotions are contagious. I've made my living on that principle. Even at this point of my career there are times when I walk out on stage and the crowd is off. There is a funny frequency in the room that everyone has caught. There's no telling how it started, and it doesn't matter. If you don't like what is being said, change the conversation. It's my job to do just that and I do it well. Sometimes it takes a carrot, sometimes a stick and there are times where it's best to not say a word and just wait for the right moment. Like a bear standing in a glassy pond watching the fish below, building trust, waiting.

I'm waiting for her. I can feel her and all of her emotions everywhere our bodies are touching.

"You do realize it's safer to fly than take a bus around the country," Lael points out with a chuckle.

This is another thing about fear, people are quick to pass blame. Although she's right, I'm the reason we have to take the bus everywhere rather than fly.

"We're fine," I reply with a reassuring tone that is slightly forced.

As I answer her we pass flashing lights and sirens and can barely make out the overturned vehicles. Lael tenses up and pushes into me.

"Don't let fear win," I say as I pull her in tight.

I can feel her slightly relax. Partly because she's amused by my cliché advice, but mostly because we are pulling off the highway. I assume we are being diverted due to an accident.

"So I guess you've been in a few blizzards on a tour bus in your day?" Lael asks.

"Actually, almost all of our tours are in the summer. Though there was a time in Norway where we had some close calls on windy cliffside roads."

"Why are we doing a tour in the winter?" Lael asks.

"I don't know," I answer truthfully. "Someone has to."

As I take a moment to silently question why we are doing a winter tour, Lael notices my confused contemplation and we share a laugh.

"Lael?"

"Yes Brad?"

"When this tour wraps up, will you come with me to one of those tropical vacation places where the sand is white and the water is blue? Like, Tahiti or somewhere like that?" I ask her, as if I was thinking out loud.

"What?" she questions.

"Last day of the tour we fly to a beach that looks like a postcard," I say.

"Okaaaay …?" Lael's simple one-word response drags out and her pitch dips and dives.

The bus stops with a thud.

George unbuckles his seat belt and stands up to address the gang. He's expressionless as always, and he straightens his ill-fitting blazer before talking.

"The highway is blocked and we can't go any further. I am sorry to say you will not make it to Chicago on time. We are parked in front of the only motel; I assume it will fill up quickly, if it isn't already. I am old, so I get priority for a room. If there are not enough rooms available, there is enough fuel to keep the generator going so the bus will be warm. Good night."

With that, George puts on his grey hat and opens the door. The wind whistles, and blows in snow.

"We are going to miss Chicago, this sucks!" I can hear Calvi from the back.

"Alright lads, chin up, these things do happen. Everything from here to Chicago has been canceled due to the storm," Arnie says, while attempting to write an email on his phone.

"Well let's try to get some rooms while we can," Switch says as he zips up his tight leather jacket.

"Right, right, I will look into it." Arnie gets up and makes his way out of the bus, forcing the door open against the wind.

I stealthily hold Lael's hand for a moment and squeeze it tight to let her know I'm going to get up.

She pulls me in.

"I need to talk to you," she whispers.

"Okay, alright," I answer.

"Alone, later."

"Everything okay?"

"I'm not staying on the damn bus, we have been on this thing for eight hours!" Switch shouts.

"I don't mind staying on the bus; it's probably better than that fleabag motel," Calvi says.

This moment is not private and whatever Lael has to say will have to wait.

"Fuck it, I'm not waiting here," Switch says as he stomps off the bus and into the blizzard.

"I am going to see what's going on," I say to Lael.

I push open the door and step outside. The wind is so cold it's like a million tiny shards of ice stabbing your skin.

I rush to the yellow light coming from the lobby entrance. When I step in, I'm overwhelmed with the smell of cats, cigarette smoke and dusty electric heat.

"Madame, we need five rooms, are you sure you only have two?" Arnie asks the lady behind the desk.

The lady has big blank eyes that refuse to blink and thin brown hair that falls past her shoulders.

"Yeppers," she says slowly. The cigarette smoke falls out of her mouth.

Arnie steps away from the desk and turns to Switch and I.

"So," Arnie says.

"So," I add.

"So I'm taking one of the rooms," Switch says.

I roll my eyes. That's Switch, always looking out for number one.

"The other room goes to the lady," I conclude.

We can see several people through the window making their way to the lobby. Arnie quickly turns his attention to the lady behind the desk.

"Very well, we'll take your last two rooms," Arnie says as he pulls out his wallet.

"Five hundred," she replies, then takes a long, slow pull from her half-burned cigarette.

"Five hundred, are you serious?" Arnie asks.

"Yeppers," the lady says and again lets the smoke fall from her mouth.

The lobby begins to fill so Arnie gives her the cash and takes the keys. Switch grabs one and leaves without a word.

"Shall we then?" Arnie motions to the door and the two of us make our way back to the bus. Neither of us were concerned about spending the night on the bus—we have many times, it's actually quite comfortable. After a long eight-hour drive with the same people it does get small fast, but there's plenty of room for Calvi, Arnie and myself to be comfortable.

"No, I think you should take it, Arnie," Lael says politely.

"What am I, chopped liver?" Calvi pipes up with a little laugh.

"Enough of that my dear, here's the key. It's surely not a fancy hotel, but it has a hot shower, privacy, and a bed." Arnie insists and hands her the key.

Lael gets a few things together, gives me a look that I well understand and leaves the bus.

"Alright lads, how about some scotch?" Arnie suggests.

"No thanks, I'm exhausted. I think I'm going to lie down," I answer.

"Can I take my portion to bed with me?" Calvi asks Arnie, who is already pouring a glass.

Arnie hands him a glass and gives him a disappointed look. After playing with some electric breakers, he disappears to the back of the bus. I am left as alone as I can be and lie down on the couch with a heavy blanket.

Sometimes, when I am lying here, getting ready to sleep the night away, I'm hit with a wave of loneliness. I think about how I'm without family, that all of my relationships are really business associates.

I'm alone.

Then I ask myself, why? It's obvious it's my fault. But why have I never allowed someone to be close to me? I've never let my guard down and let love in, without a care of what might happen.

Love—it's a drug I've never tried because I've seen it

kill so many others. Maybe I am the drug and deep down I know I'm no good. What kind of man needs this life I'm living? What kind of man wants to stand on stage and have tens of thousands people scream for him? There is so much fakeness I have lost myself in and I'm so completely selfish.

No, I'm not protecting myself, I'm protecting whoever wants to be close to me. I'm no good and I know it. My own mother knew it.

I feel sleep beginning to come.

This is my internal process; I beat myself to sleep every night.

My phone vibrates.

I am pulled out of my sleepy thoughts and see that Lael is texting me.

This is a big bed for just me…;)

I close my eyes and smile. If ever there was someone I should protect from my silly life, it's her. When the rock star thing wears off, I'm afraid of what she'll see. I don't want to fall in love with her then lose her; the people I love tend to disappear. It really is a drug, and I'm afraid I've already let it in my veins, it's flowing through my heart.

I am high thinking about sneaking into her room. I am high thinking about taking her on a sunny beach vacation.

I reply: *Room number?*

213

I grab a few things and make my way over. I don't feel the cold because my blood is running hot. Room 213. I knock quietly and the door opens almost immediately; she is waiting for me.

Lael is wrapped in a towel, her face has no make-up, it's natural and beautiful. The room smells like her shampoo.

"Hurry up, let's get under the covers, it's freezing," she

says playfully.

Lael takes me by the hand to the bed. I'm overwhelmed by her. Her silky skin, bright eyes, her soft lips that seem to want to smile. The heat in the room is cranked and there is still steam coming from the bathroom. It's not freezing at all.

"C'mon, take it all off Mr. Snyder," she says, as she pulls at my leather jacket. I pull in and kiss her, her mouth is soft and we melt together perfectly. My tongue wrestles with hers for a moment then she pushes me away.

"Your jacket is wet and cold, take it off, all of it," she demands. Lael climbs onto the bed and kneels.

I begin to undress.

Lael playfully takes off her towel. I don't think I've ever met someone more comfortable being completely naked. She seems more at ease than when she's clothed. I'm not bashful but I almost feel silly standing there naked. I'm more than ready for her, though, and she notices.

"You're perfect," she says, as she crawls over to the edge of the bed. With her hands on my naked ass she pulls me in, she takes me in her mouth passionately, but only for a moment. She sits up so we are face to face.

"Come to bed baby, aren't you cold?" Lael says in a voice I've not heard from her. Her hand is running up and down my length, still commanding my attention, never breaking eye contact.

I kiss her, moving so I kneel on the bed and we hold each other tight. Running our hands over each other's skin. Even in this position, our bodies are trying to find the other. I am trying to find her, and she is trying to accept me. I lay her down and our bodies know where to go. Her legs wrap around me, my arms go around her. Kissing passionately, we make love. Rolling around, taking turns, simply letting go.

I want to make her feel good. I want her to love me. My hands do everything they can to push her over the edge while I am just moments away. We untangle and she opens her soul to me. I push in as deep as I can, overwhelmed with passion but I'm still careful to be gentle.

When it's over, I ease off and she puts her hand on my chest.

"Where did you come from?" she asks.

We lie together, face to face, kissing softly. We let our lips graze each other, she tugs my ear lightly. I pull the blankets over us. She is smiling so beautifully, we stare at each other and let a wonderful energy pass back and forth. At the same time, we laugh at our prolonged staring contest.

"What was it you wanted to tell me?" I ask.

The air in the room changes instantly. Her smile melts away. Lael lies on her back and pulls the covers to her chin.

"Brad, god, I don't know," Lael says, looking at the ceiling rather than me.

I feel it coming. I had let my guard down ever so slightly and now she wants out. This is where it ends. This is where she says it's been fun but that's a wrap. Time to call it quits, we're done. I'm disappointed in myself, how could I have been so careless?

I prop myself up and prepare to be dumped. I practice my casual reaction in my head, I don't want to lose dignity here.

"Brad," she says in a whisper.

"What's up?"

Lael turns to face me. I can't read her expression but the way she looks at me makes my heart quicken.

"I'm pregnant."

I feel nothing. I hear nothing. My heart has stopped and I have forgotten how to breathe. There is a microscopic version of myself living in my head that is desperately trying to bring me back to life. Pulling levers, yelling at computer screens, trying to help me react to this news.

Slowly, very slowly, I'm beginning to feel something, I hear the hum of the room again and I see her face. I have the same feeling as when I saw her scared on the bus during the blizzard. I want to protect her. I want to let her know she is not alone, but unfortunately I'm not yet able to speak, so I just stare at her. I feel like I've been letting it hang for hours, but I know it has only been seconds. Lael always seems so confident, I think this is the first time I've seen this much fear on her face.

I exhale and can feel the muscles in my face relax, feel myself become more present. We both put our heads on the pillow, letting the last of the fireworks in our chests burn out.

I smile.

She smiles back and I can see a flood of emotion in her eyes.

There's a small part of me that has never felt more like a child, immature and unprepared in every way. There is another part of me that has never felt like more of a man and with every passing moment that feeling gets stronger. I look at this beautiful young woman, and I know, deep down, this is the beginning of the rest of my life. Deep down I know this is good.

I can speak again. My expression must be telling her how I feel because she's already reacting to words I have not yet spoken.

I hold her hand and can feel her emotion in the tightness of her grip. I can tell she feels alone.

"I know this is crazy, but the truth is, I'm happy," I say, as if I'm thinking out loud.

I consider for a moment that maybe she did not want to go through with it, and this was going to be a very different conversation.

"I mean, we're in this together. You are not alone."

A tear falls from her glassy eyes.

"I'm scared," she says, fear obvious in her voice.

"You can't let the fear win." I repeat my words from earlier on the bus.

She smiles. It's a cheesy thing to say and she's almost rolling her eyes, but it has the effect I was hoping. Lael is starting to relax, I'm starting to relax.

"Whatever you want to do, I'm with you, but I want to let you know I'm not going anywhere," I say, trying to be delicate. I lean in and kiss her. "We can do this," I whisper.

Lael wipes her eyes.

"I keep picturing myself barefoot living in the suburbs; this was not in the plans," she says.

"It doesn't have to be like that. Why? We can set up a little baby station on the side stage. Arnie can be a babysitter, we can get little baby headphones and a tiny little And Then shirt. You can be a world-traveling rock star, kill it on stage every night, and still be a mom. Moms work all the time, you'll just have a cooler job than most." I'm getting excited and speaking quickly.

Lael still looks slightly overwhelmed, but at least she's smiling.

"Look," I explain, "we are writing our own story, we are in control. I don't care about the band, or the company.

I care about you."

Lael's hand is still in mine and I can feel it relax for the first time since she told me the news.

"Are we alright?" I feel electricity in my chest when I ask that question.

Lael smiles, leans over, and turns off the light. She tucks into me and I hold her close. The room is dark and the sound of the blizzard outside rattles the window.

"Yes, we are. Are you going to sneak back to the bus?" she asks.

"That got old a while ago. We are done sneaking around. I want to tell the world," I whisper.

We make love until we fall asleep.

Knock, Knock, Knock.

"Time to get up." I wake up to the sound of Arnie's voice.

The morning light coming from the window looks like heaven, the blizzard is over and there is a blanket of white snow reflecting the sunlight in a shadowless glow. Through the paperthin walls I can hear Arnie knocking on Switch's door a couple rooms down.

"Morning sunshine," I say to Lael, who is slowly waking up too.

I get dressed and look for the coffee maker, but this no-tell motel doesn't seem to have one.

"I'll get the coffee going on the bus, meet ya there," I say, then kiss her on the forehead.

As I step out into this winter wonderland and close the door behind me, I see Switch stepping out of his room. He gives me a loaded look. I give him a smile that speaks volumes and I don't look away. He walks my way and passes close by.

"Something you want to get off your chest?" I ask him, daring him to say something.

He doesn't answer. I have been more than patient with both his and Calvi's concerns and it feels good to give him a clear message: my patience has run out and the conversation is over. Anyone else that has a problem with my relationship with Lael will quickly realize I don't care what they think.

I walk to the bus with new confidence I've never felt. I feel like no one can hurt me, I'm in control, I'm a man.

I step onto the bus and smell coffee already brewing. George is reading his paper with the ease of a man in his own home. Switch is pouring an obscene amount of sugar into his coffee and Arnie is finishing a conversation on his phone. It can't be easy for Arnie, taking care of this rag-tag operation.

"I have good news and I have bad news," Arnie says as he tucks his phone into his pocket.

"Good news first," I say, as I walk by him to the coffee maker and pour two cups.

"Good news is we will make it to Denver in time for the show," Arnie says with a smile.

"And the bad news?" asks Switch.

"Well…" Arnie is interrupted by Lael opening the door.

I pass her the coffee I was planning to bring to her room.

"The bad news is we have to take a charter plane from an airport a few miles from here." Arnie tries not to make eye contact with me as he speaks.

Of course, this is only bad news for me because of my fear of flying.

"George will have plenty of time to get the bus to Denver so we can continue the tour as scheduled." Arnie sits next to George and they begin to make some plans.

I slowly sit down and try to process the news, but I'm jolted off of the couch by Calvi, who is still sleeping, concealed under blankets.

"Ahhh!" Calvi shouts.

"Ahhh!" I shout back. "How in god's name can you sleep there with all of us here talking, you weirdo?"

"What did I miss?" Calvi asks.

"Aliens have taken over the world and we are the last survivors," Switch says with a smirk.

"We are flying to Denver on a charter," Lael chimes in.

"Oh." Calvi scratches his messy hair and takes a coffee cup Lael poured for him.

"Okay, off we go then," Arnie says, while George fires up the engine.

We arrive at the airport, which is really nothing more than a runway and a hanger. There is a snow plow that just finished with clearing the runway, that pulls up close to us. The snow plow guy gets out and walks toward us, smiling with a cigar clenched in his teeth.

"You Arnie?" he asks, after taking out the large cigar.

"I am," Arnie answers.

We are all standing abreast in front to the bus.

"Great. Chuck. I will be taking you to Denver this morning. Right this way," Chuck says, motioning toward a small airplane.

"Right-o, come on lads," Arnie responds, then waves

bye to George.

The bus pulls away. I feel like I'm in an ocean and I'm watching my life raft float away. I can feel sweat build beneath my clothes, despite the cold air.

"It's okay, it will be a short flight," Lael says to me while we watch the rest of the crew walk toward the plane.

"I'm fine," I say.

I am not fine. But I don't want Lael to see me like this. I try my best to conceal my anxiety and walk in the snowy footsteps my bandmates made.

It's not long before we are all strapped into our tiny seats on the tiny plane. There is not a seat left, Arnie is in the co-pilot seat wearing a headset.

Chuck gets in and slams the door. The cigar has gone out, but it's still in his mouth.

"It will be a rough ride. Denver is the worst, stay strapped in tight," Chuck shouts at us over his shoulder.

He pulls levers and switches and the plane shakes to life. It takes almost no time before we are racing down the runway and in the air. My eyes are closed and I concentrate on breathing. I don't want to have a meltdown in front of Lael. I try to imagine landing safely in Denver.

After some time in the air, the turbulence begins. It feels like we fall twenty feet and then snap back up. We are moving side to side, up and down.

I feel like this is the end. I'm twenty-seven-years-old, I'm a rock star, and I'm going to die in a charter plane with my pregnant lover. It's almost poetic. Except that I can't feel my limbs, my hands are in tight fists and my eyes are closed tight.

I'm having a panic attack. I have lost reason. I have lost control.

"Brad, honey?" I can hear her voice but it seems like she's miles away. "Brad," she's closer, she's holding me and stroking my hair. "Don't let the fear win," she says, in my ear.

I think about last night when I told her the same words. I want to be strong for her, I want to be strong for our future family. Family—I'm going to have a family.

I get my breathing under control. My heart is still racing but I have to focus. I focus on her.

We touch down and I'm myself again. I smile at Lael and she smiles back. She just saw me at my weakest and I can tell by how she's looking at me that I haven't lost her. She calmed me down. I feel like we can take on the world together.

Chuck turns to face us and with a black-toothed grin says, "Welcome to Denver."

EIGHTEEN

LAEL

"Lael," my father's voice booms from behind me.

I nearly jump right out of my skin. Shit. I've been extra jumpy since the damn plane landed in Denver, the last person I expected or needed to see was my father.

But there is he, the devil himself in the flesh, standing in the lobby of the Kimpton Monaco hotel.

He's smiling too.

I don't trust that smile.

I look around for the rest of the band. I'm a bit early. I said I would meet them down here before we went out for dinner. They wanted the complimentary happy hour that the hotel provides.

"Looking for the guys?" my father asks. "I sent them on their way. I need to talk to you about something in private."

My heart thuds against my chest.

Shit.

He knows. Oh, he has to know.

I don't know how but he knows I'm pregnant.

He knows Brad and I have been a thing.

He knows all.

That's why I don't trust that smile.

It's the cat that swallowed the canary.

"Whatever you have to talk to me about, we can talk about it here," I gesture to the lobby.

"I'm afraid not. You might make a scene."

Oh, god.

"I can tell you're already getting riled up," he says, placing his hand on my shoulder.

I shrug him off. "You tell me here. Whether I make a scene or not, that's up to me."

I know it bothers him that so many guests are mingling in the lobby, trying to soak up the free booze. So many guests that probably recognize him. But I don't care. He wants to control me? He can't control me now.

"Fine," he says, eyes turning hard. "You want it this way, fine. I don't care. It's you who will suffer, not me." He lowers his voice. "I know you disobeyed my orders. I know you're sleeping with Brad."

"And how would you know that?" I ask him, wondering what else he knows.

"I have eyes and ears everywhere."

"Who told you that? How do you know you can trust him?"

"Because I can," he says. "And it's Marc Calvi. He's seen you with him on more than one occasion so don't even pretend."

Calvi. I knew it. I'm going to fucking murder him.

Then Brad's going to want to murder him right after. A double-murder and no regrets.

"Look, Calvi is just looking out for the band. As am I. Your dalliances with Brad have been disrupting everything."

"No they haven't!" I cry out, attracting the attention of a few people nearby. I lower my voice, knowing I'm completely hormonal lately. "The band has been just fine, we're performing better than ever. I mean, the tour is almost over, dad. Just let it be."

"So you don't deny it."

"No, I don't deny it."

"Then you're not the smart girl I thought you were."

"I beg your pardon? Not smart? For the last couple of months I've been navigating the dirty, two-faced scene of live music. I've been dealing with the media, I've been dealing with expectations, I've been dealing with everything in order to ensure that every night I give it my all and give it my best. And I do. I'm consistent. I work hard and it pays off. And the only person I don't have to deal with, who gets me, who understands me and helps me, is Brad."

My father shakes his head, looking ever so disappointed. "You're young, Lael. Young and confused. Too young to be a musician, too easily corrupted to be with this band. I should have known but I thought I was doing what was best for you."

"I am doing what's best for me," I tell him, jabbing my thumb into my chest. "This was never up to you. I have control over my life, you don't."

"That's where you're wrong Lael. I have control over everything you do. And I can make it end for everyone in a second. For you. And for Brad."

My heart starts to speed up, my face feeling hot. "What are you saying?"

"I'm saying that it's over."

"Over?"

He raises his palm dismissively. "I'm not going to even give you a second chance because I gave you that already and you let me down. You let me down, kid. And that hurts. It hurts. You'll never know a father's pain, what I'm feeling."

"Oh, bullshit."

"It's over. Either you leave this band and make tonight your last show or Brad does. There's no way both of you will be part of this band ever again. So make your choice."

"You can't do that."

"I can. I own Brad. You know this. And he owes me. I'll pull him from the band."

"He is the band!"

He shrugs. "Then there are no more shows. I've made enough money from this tour, it doesn't really matter if you do the last shows or not. Who cares? If it all ends, who cares? I'll build up another band with someone who respects me."

"You're a monster," I seethe. "You're not a father at all."

It has no effect on him. "You're not a parent, you'll never understand the sacrifices."

I can't control what I say next. It just roars out of me, like a volcano. "I will be a parent!"

"Yeah, one day."

"No," I tell him, gathering my courage. "Now. In nine months. Dad. I'm pregnant."

He stares at me completely calm and cool. He doesn't even blink.

"You're what?"

"I'm pregnant," I tell him. "I'm going to have the baby. And Brad is the father."

Everything happens in slow motion. My father goes pale, his skin almost matching his blonde hair, and he starts to sway a bit like he's going to faint. His mouth drops open. He's in shock.

"I'm sorry," I blurt out. "I didn't want you to find out this way but it's true. I'm going to have Brad's baby, and there's nothing you can do about it."

I have to admit, I'm totally expecting my father to blow up right there and then but he manages to hold it together. I'm pretty sure he's having a stroke on the inside but on the outside he looks as blank-faced and impassive as ever.

"You really know how to hurt me, don't you Lael."

"Don't be like that."

"I'll be like whatever I want. Obviously I can't stop you. But I can stop this band from going forward. What I said earlier sticks. Either Brad leaves the band or you do. Make tonight your last show, you hear me? You or him, make up your mind."

"Who the hell is going to play bass?"

"I have Bruce Ross on call," he says, giving me a satisfied smirk. "I had a feeling something like this would happen. He auditioned for them and will make a great fit. Better than you did."

"No one will do a better job than me," I say, shoving my finger in his face.

He just stares down at me with cold eyes. "Don't kid yourself, Lael. I let you do this as a favor. The fantasy is over. Back to reality with you. You and your *baby*. Good luck trying to get Brad to be a part of it."

Then he turns, grabs a glass of wine off the table and strolls out of the hotel with it in hand, as if he owns the place.

I'm left simmering in the lobby, my heart thumping, my limbs feeling numb.

How dare he?

I mean, I wasn't expecting hugs and kisses when I told him I was pregnant, but I also wasn't expecting him to just walk away like that, like he didn't care at all.

And I certainly didn't think tonight would be my last show.

Shit.

I mean, it's the right thing to do. I can walk, it's harder for Brad. I am just a replacement in the end, Brad is everything to do with the band. And I know that if I tell Brad what just happened, everything that just went down, that he'll be the one to quit.

This is his life. I can't let him do that.

I'll just have to lie to him.

It won't be easy though.

I'll have to make something up. Tell him that I'm just not feeling it anymore, that I want to go home and start being a mom. I've been feeling great, maybe a bit tired lately, but I can always use the pregnancy as an excuse. He can't question that.

But of course, no matter how I swing it, this is going to be my last show.

The end.

How on earth am I going to come to terms with that? How am I going to say goodbye to the band? How am I going to say goodbye to the beauty and joy it brings me? The sense of purpose?

I guess in some ways I would have to anyway. After tonight, there's only three more shows. My father was right, the fantasy would be over and soon. But even so, I needed time to prepare, time to grieve. I didn't want it to be like this, being given the boot because everything good that happens to me comes with a mountain of complications.

I feel bereft. I want to go into my room, crawl into bed, and cry. Maybe it's the altitude here, but I feel like I could sleep forever and then maybe wake up and have it be a bad dream.

But I won't do that.

I can't.

If this is my last show, then it's my last show.

I'm going to pull up my big girl panties and give it everything I have.

Every last inch of my heart and soul.

I'm going to rock, pregnant and all, like I've never rocked before.

But first…

I'm going to find Calvi and punch him right in his god damn face.

NINETEEN

BRAD

I never watch the opening band. I know I should, out of respect, but I can't. The moments before the show are mine, I go to that other place I need to be to be able to perform in front of a sold-out arena of screaming fans.

I hate the trend of music these days, it's too casual. It's fashionable to walk on stage eating an apple, dressed like it's laundry day. I'm not like them. I take it very seriously. When I told Lael to show the crowd no respect, I hope she knew what I meant. I have immense respect for the audience, but I do not fear them. What I was talking about is that bad energy in the room that can happen sometimes. You shouldn't respect that.

I never concern myself whether I look humble and modest, I don't overthink. When I step on to the stage I demand respect. People want to be led, when the energy in the room turns into a confused sea, don't jump into the water. Show up with a pirate ship and make them beg to come aboard.

There's still plenty of time before the show, but I feel it's one of those damn nights. I can feel it from my dressing room, the rumbles from the opening band, and the reaction of the crowd rumbles through the walls and into the room where I sit, alone. I need to be alone today, busy building a pirate ship in my mind.

Calvi and Switch always watch the opening bands. I think they do it not because they are down to earth good guys, but more because they want to be seen that way. I'm happy they take that role, it takes the pressure off me. Lael usually finds a quiet place to play her bass, and dolls herself up. She has been scarce today. I know Ronald showed up unexpectedly and I haven't seen her since. I wouldn't usually think anything of it but emotions are running high for various reasons.

I've had some time to processes the fact that Lael and I are going to have a child. I think I've felt every emotion on the spectrum of emotions. I've been full of life since she told me the news; it's given me perspective. I wonder if in some deep way I wanted Lael to get pregnant. I've always been so careful in the past, all these years and I've never slipped one past the goalie.

When she told me the news, I felt fear, but there was a deep immediate acceptance. I can't imagine what I would have felt if someone from my past told me the same news. I probably would have felt an instant dread when I consider being tied to some woman for the rest of my life.

But with Lael, that couldn't be further from the truth. When Lael told me, I almost felt…relieved. She's a ray of sunshine; I am creating life with the sun.

I'm lucid and letting my mind wander. I let it go

anywhere it wants as long as it doesn't go into the confused sea just outside these walls.

Time passes and the opening act is done. The walls are no longer rumbling; the volume of the crowd turns down and sounds like a busy night-time freeway.

Lael walks in, she doesn't say a word and doesn't look at me. I've noticed she has an impeccable tuning fork. I've never spoken to her about my pre-show rituals, she's just picked up on things and finds a space for herself to fill. She has that ability musically, too.

Lael also lets herself go to another place before the show like I do. I like how she takes it so seriously. So when she says my name, I am surprised she's talking at all.

"Brad," Lael says.

I take a moment, turn my head to her. She's sitting on the couch, slumped over in defeat. She looks nothing like she usually does before show time. Something is terribly wrong.

"This can't be good," I say.

"It's not," she says.

I get off the chair in front of the vanity mirror where I sit and join her on the couch.

"Lay it on me," I tell her.

Arnie pokes his head in. "Five minutes," he says quickly, then disappears.

"Sorry, I don't want talk before the show, but I thought you might want to know," Lael says pushing her hair back behind her ears.

"Lael. It's okay, I know it's scary stuff, but everything is going to be fine," I assure her.

I'm not bothered by her preshow chat in the least. The pirate ship in my mind is built, it is fierce, and I am ready.

I'm ready for whatever she has to say to me, and I'm ready to have an amazing show.

But Lael is struggling to find the words.

"What's wrong?" I ask.

"I'm sorry but I can't finish the tour with you. I'm so sorry, but I'm afraid this will be my last show."

I hear her words but they're not sinking in. I have a good tuning fork too, and it's vibrating out of control.

"What? Why? There are only a couple show left. Are you okay?" I ask. "Is…is the baby?"

"I'm fine," she says, not meeting my eyes. "The baby too."

"Are we okay?" I ask with concern.

"Yes, baby, yes, we are better than okay." She finally meets my eyes. "It's a girl thing. It's a pregnant thing. I need to be at home right now. I should be seeing a doctor, I need to shift gears a little." She holds my hand as she speaks emotionally.

When I consider that I have no idea about pregnancy, I begin to feel selfish. I haven't considered maybe she should be under the care of a doctor, maybe she should be in the hospital right now. Is she in pain? I'm overwhelmed by the sudden awareness of my own ignorance.

"Are you in pain? You don't have to play tonight; I don't care about that. I care about you. I will take you home right now." I'm speaking nervously and quickly, concerned I have put her in danger.

Lael's body language tells me to turn down my intensity. I realize I'm on my knees in front of her and holding her hands like she's dying soldier.

I get myself together and sit beside her again.

"Relax, I'm fine. The baby is fine. We are fine. I just

need to do this, and I need you to be understanding," she says this with so much conviction.

I feel guilty that she's now the one calming me down.

Outside, the volume of the crowd spikes up, I imagine the house lights went down. Our five minutes are up. This has been the best tour of my life. I know there will be other tours but this one is special.

And the reason it's so special is leaving.

I take a moment to let this reality sink in.

The crowd starts chanting. They sound like an angry mob but at least they are unified, that makes my job easier.

And Then... And Then... And Then...

"I want you to sing the first song," I say to her.

"Fuzzface? Why?" she asks, seeming embarrassed by the idea.

"It's yours, you've made it your own. I want this memory, please, for me," I say.

The crowd begin to stamp their feet on each syllable, the light fixtures above us begin to rattle and swing.

And I can see on her face that she's willing and ready.

Calvi walks into the room, his nose looking bruised and puffy.

"What happened to you?" I ask pointing to his wounded face.

"It's getting crazy out there, we have to go on stage now," He says ignoring my question. I notice he doesn't look at Lael at all and she's glaring at him like I've never seen her glare before. There's also a touch of smugness in her face.

"Okay man, sounds good, we're not far behind," I answer.

Calvi disappears. My attention is back on her. If this is

the last show with Lael on this tour, I want to remember every moment. I want her to have an amazing experience that she can draw upon for years to come.

We stand up. I don't say a word, we hold eye contact and let the energy rise. Every cell in my body is vibrating and I know she feels the same.

"I am going to miss you," I say.

"I am not gone yet."

"Then let's do this thing," I tell her.

We walk to the wing of the stage. We look at each other one last time before we both disappear to the place we need to be.

Lael walks on stage and the crowd stops it's chanting and roars instead. She struts to her bass and I know there is not a woman in the room that doesn't wish they had a fraction of her confidence.

I try not to think about what the men are thinking.

I wait from the wing of the stage and watch for a few moments.

A single spot light shines on her.

She takes a few steps to the edge of the stage and just stands there in the spotlight and lets a tension build.

Every eye in the room is on her.

As if she's in slow motion she hits her bass with the side of her fist. The whole area shakes. The note rings out and echoes. Her eyes stay up and I imagine every single person in the arena feels like she's looking them dead in the eye. She hits her bass again, still her eyes are up, stoic and in control.

Beautiful.

On the third hit she hits her famous pedal. It was loud before but it's now violent. She's on her knees, her technicolor hair over her face.

On the fourth hit the light man makes the entire stage glow teal.

I walk out and the entire band begin the slow, heavy, seductive riff. She whips her hair around and commands the stage, commands everything.

I stay back, beside the drums and watch her as if I were her biggest fan.

Perhaps I am.

She steps up to the mic and begins the verse;

Combing back my hair
Thinking of you, late night phone calls
Lead us to our end

I join her on the chorus, the crowd are perfectly unified, Switch and Calvi are in the pocket. We sing together:

An emptiness, I need a companion
In the dead of the night I can find reasons too
And there is something in you that turns me on

The way Lael says the last few words makes me wish I could record the song again. She makes the song sexier, she makes the band sound better. When the song ends the crowd tells her she did a good job. It's a challenge to keep that energy up for the rest of the show. If we ever do that again we would close with it rather than open.

Lael is a tough act to follow.

But we manage.

We blow the crowd out of the water with each and every song.

It's one hell of an amazing show.

When it's over, we leave the stage and the crowd thanks us with a roaring applause that lasts longer than usual. I feel like they know it's a special night.

Wow, that was a good one, mates!" Arnie says to us. "Let's get the VIP stuff out of the way so we can celebrate."

Lately we've been doing all the meet and greets after the show. I prefer it that way. I can't say I ever feel like doing it after the show but it's a hell of a lot better than before when it takes me out of the zone. And sometimes the fans can really vibe you out.

Arnie guides us to where the radio winners and big spenders wait. We round a corner and I'm not only surprised by the amount of people waiting, I'm surprised at how many of them are teenage girls with teal hair.

I think we're all taken aback.

"Look at all the mini-Laels," I say to her.

I can tell she's both flattered and embarrassed but she takes on the role well. I can't think of a better mentor for these young girls to have. To me Lael is strength, she uses her feminine energy in a beautiful way that empowers her. It looks like she has some followers that feel empowered by her, too.

We all stand abreast as usual, the teal-haired young ladies skip right past Calvi, Switch, and I to meet Lael.

They look up to her with wide eyes. Lael becomes a slightly different version of herself when she greets the young ladies. She seems tougher in a way and I feel like she knows her manners are going to be emulated by these girls and she only has a moment with them.

I like her message; the world treats you like you let it, be tough.

I'm beyond proud. I'm not happy this is the last show with Lael for this tour but I couldn't ask for a better send-off.

Lael takes pictures with all of them. There is a nice moment when a teal-haired young teen does a little princess pose for the camera and Lael shows her the rock and roll symbol with hand and demonstrating how to scowl. That little girl is still a princess when she leaves, but instead of a wand in her hand she carries a sword.

I'm high from the show in the best way. But what goes up must come down and when Lael gives me the look that she is leaving, I come down hard.

I crash.

"Alright partner, I will see you in a week," Lael says with half a smile.

"Now, you're leaving now?" I question.

"Come on, walk me out," she says.

She exchanges hugs and goodbyes with Switch and Calvi. Her hug with Calvi was awkward and hard to watch. She laughs it off and we head down the hall, and we stop at a metal door that leads to the loading area.

"I have a ride waiting for me," she says.

"So this is goodbye."

"For a week," she assures me. "Actually less than a week. You better come straight to my place when you get back to LA." Her voice is soft and caring. "And text and call me whenever you can. I'll update you with any baby news."

"I'm going to miss you" I say. I am trying not to be over the top, I don't want to freak her out.

But the truth is, it breaks my heart that she's leaving.

Somehow, though, I keep it together to save face. I wish I could find the words but they're just not there.

She opens the door and I hold it while she goes outside.

There's a black limousine waiting.

Fuck. This is all happening so fast.

"Don't forget about me Snyder," she says as she struts away.

"Hate to see you go but I love to watch you leave," I call out to her.

She turns her head and laughs.

We're both grinning at each other.

It would be as good a send-off as I could ask for but then it happens.

This limousine door opens and Ronald steps out.

He's wearing a long black trench coat and his lips are in a closed grin.

My smile disappears when we briefly make eye contact.

Lael doesn't look back at me, she gets into the shiny black limousine and Ronald follows her.

As I lean against a post in the dark loading area and watch the limo drive away, I think about a song I released on an old album called Spaceship Limousine. It's about a young limousine driver that modifies his limousine so it can fly to space in order to impress a woman.

It's a song that wasn't well received but it's still one of my favorites. When you are in love with a gal, you will do anything to impress her. I'm in love with Lael and I will fly to the moon for her.

This is going to be the slowest, longest week of my life.

TWENTY

BRAD

"Thank you! We are And Then, you can buy our albums wherever you buy music. This is the last show of an amazing tour, so this is a special night. I hope we made you feel good. This last song is called 'Shut the door, have a seat,'" I shout into the mic, addressing the sold-out crowd. The audience is a sloppy bunch; Vegas is always an interesting show. The people eat too much at the free buffets and drink more than they ever normally would. They are mostly all fans, but you will always find a handful folks that are just looking for some entertainment. They could have seen a magician or Celine Dion, but they came here.

I don't hate playing in Vegas, but it does feel more like work sometimes. The crowd is there to be entertained, unlike somewhere like Portland where the crowd is there to participate and create an experience.

I make it through our last song. We politely wave and

leave the stage. Bruce Ross doesn't have a fraction of the energy that Lael brings to the music, but he is a pro and I appreciate him helping us out. I put my guitar on its stand next to a smiling Arnie.

"This was a hell of a tour my friend!" Arnie says to me.

"Yes, it was," I answer. I raise my arms and give Arnie a hug. "Until the next time," I say, then quickly add, "But next time no charter planes."

We share a laugh and part ways. I make my way down the steps to the backstage area. Everyone is trying to make eye contact. There is a certain pressure—all of these folks will tell the story of what you were like. I smile and say hello, but I keep on walking and remind myself that the show isn't really over until you close your hotel room door. It's just a different act.

I round a corner and see that this act of the show will have a challenge. Ronald Ramsey is sitting in a chair speaking to a small group. He waves his arms expressively and takes up more space than he should. The group is all nodding in a yes motion like a bunch of bobble heads.

"There's the man!" Ronald shouts and motions to me.

"Ronald." I address him with respect, but without reverence. "What brings you to Vegas?" I ask.

"I came to see the last show of the tour. Sold-out, very impressive. The numbers from this tour have been great, truly fantastic." Ronald speaks directly to me, the crowd around him beginning to thin out, with only the suits that work with him remaining. Ronald flattens his tie and presses on. "I think about that kid I found in that alley, and boy look at you now. Hasn't he come a long way?" Ronald asks his henchmen, but doesn't wait for an answer. Switch walks in and takes a seat.

"Steve, good to see ya." I never can tell if Ronald really can't remember Switch's name, or if it's some form of dominance.

Switch raises his glass and dips his head, but doesn't say a word.

"So, the tour's over. After a little break let's get back in the studio. Let's keep the energy up, now is not the time to start slowing down," Ronald's voice fills the room, even though he's looking in the vanity mirror as he speaks.

I consider telling him his days of controlling my career are over, that he can sue me all he wants, but I'm leaving and I'm taking his daughter with me. I smile at the thought, but I don't want to be careless, this is Lael's father after all. For now, I will play my cards safely.

"This is what we do," I answer casually.

"Good, I look forward to hearing some demos. I have some other business." Ronald swings his chair around and stands as gracefully as an old, tall round man can.

"I'm glad we can have a working relationship like this Brad, really. I mean it's truly the best thing for both of us. To think how close we were to ending it all in Denver. It's much better this way. When I gave Lael the ultimatum to leave the band or I would end you, she made the right decision." Ronald's words hang in the air, he is smiling a devilish grin.

She lied to me. I know she was trying to protect me but I'm still angered, I'm hurt, I feel betrayed. I fight to keep my emotions under control, but my hatred for Ronald is almost impossible to conceal. Thankfully, he takes it upon himself to leave.

"Really Brad, going from a homeless orphan to leading one of the most successful touring bands in the world….

I've done a terrific job with you." Ronald walks by me and slaps me on the back. "You don't have to thank me, just hold up your end of the deal and we're fine." Ronald leans in close, so only I can hear his words. "Lael won't keep it, she will make the right decision." He leaves, and his minions follow.

I can feel my blood boil. He's talking about my unborn child. Why didn't Lael tell me he knew? Why didn't Lael tell me about this ultimatum? My relationship with Ronald is going to change forever now and I'm looking forward to it.

"Why can that man never get my name right?" Switch asks.

I sit next to Switch on the opposite end of the couch, trying to shake off finding out that Lael lied to me about why she left the tour. Calvi walks in.

"Who died?" Calvi asks.

"You just missed Ronald, he gave our marching orders to head back into the studio," I answer.

"Oh goodie," Calvi says, then takes a sip of from a large tiki mug with smoke billowing out.

I push myself to the edge of the couch and speak soberly, "You know fellas, I want you to know that no matter what happens you are my brothers. One day we will be free of Ramsey Records; I don't know when that will happen, but that day won't be the end, that will be the beginning."

I stand up and give Calvi a one-armed hug. I can hear his drink sizzling.

"Take care man, talk soon." I pat him on the back and then look at Switch, who is standing up.

"Come here ya son of a bitch," I pull Switch in and we hug it out.

"I know you're only looking out for the band, but I need you to relax with the whole Lael thing. She makes me happy," I say to both of them.

"You sure you know what you are doing man?" Calvi asks with an odd tone to his voice.

"I am, I want her in my life and I need you fellas to be okay with that."

Silence hangs in the air.

"I've never seen you like this man, I am happy you found someone. It would be better if she wasn't Ronald's daughter, but what are ya going to do? I wish you the best," Calvi says though I can't tell if it's sincere or not.

I look at Switch for a reaction.

"What he said," Switch says, and points to Calvi.

"Well alright then. I will love ya and leave ya. And if you don't mind, I'm stealing the bus," I say as I walk toward the exit.

Switch leans in and inspects Calvi's strange cocktail, then says, "Take it, I'm sick of that damn bus."

"Take care fellas." I wave as I walk out the door.

I'm in the back parking lot and see ol' George, drunk as a skunk and wearing one of those visor hats gamblers wear.

"Hey George, looks like you're heading back to the tables, I was hoping for a lift to LA," I tell him, knowing damn well he won't be driving me anywhere.

"My shift is over son, here's the keys, take good care of her," George replies in a drunken voice as he tosses me the keys.

That was easy.

I catch them and look at the massive bus. I don't even drive a car. George doesn't wait for a response and heads back to the casino. I look at the busy Vegas street I have to reverse into and my heart sinks.

"Oh boy," I say out loud to myself.

I step into the bus and close the door. After some fumbling I get the engine started. It occurs to me I have no idea what Lael's address is, so I pull out my phone and send a text.

I've stolen the bus, I'm driving it to your place, address please ☺

She responds right away:

What!? Stop stealing vehicles, you're going to kill yourself. Take a taxi!

I smile and text back:

Too late—on my way

She texts:

Please don't get into an accident. 150 Nagle Ave, Sherman Oaks

I begin backing up. I lay on the horn and don't let go. I'm being yelled at and drinks are being thrown at the bus, but I don't care. At least I'm not running over anyone.

After a twelve-point turn, a hundred cars honking at me, and a serious traffic jam, I'm finally pointed in the right direction and on my way. I'm smiling like a mad man driving down the strip in a bus, on my way to see Lael. God I miss her, I can't wait to see the look on her face when I pull up with this thing.

I fumble with my phone, getting the G.P.S. going. I struggle to keep my energy up when I see my E.T.A. It looks like I'll be arriving at six a.m. Obviously I could have planned this better, but I'm on my way and I'm not turning back. I turn on the radio and the Allman Brothers are playing. Perfect, I can't think of a better sound track.

I pull onto the freeway and my back wheels driving over the curb cause the bus to bounce around violently, almost knocking me out of my seat. I turn down the radio and buckle up.

After a long boring ride on the highway, I managed to stay awake and make it to LA and the G.P.S. says I'm close. There's a yellow warning light, indicating I have low fuel, that I have a sincere conversation with. I beg and plead to not run out of gas.

I'm *so* close, just a little longer, come on baby.

The G.P.S. gives me my commands:

Turn left

Turn Right

Destination is on your right

And then I'm here, I made it, I'm exhausted.

I park as close to the curb as I can and turn off the engine. The bus is dreadfully out of place on this quiet residential street. I feel drugged; I played to a sold-out crowd, then drove through the night to get here, and now it's morning and everything feels completely surreal.

There she is, I can see her one house down from where I stopped. She's stepping out of the front door and closing it behind her.

I take in a deep breath – I can't wait to hold her – and feel a second wind wash over me. I put on my jacket, only to try and look cool. I drink some water from a bottle to try to remedy my dry mouth. I'm nervous, I hope she hasn't changed her mind about how she feels about me.

She's walking this way. I prepare to get off the bus as gallantly as possible, like a knight dismounting his horse, like a captain from his ship, like…

I miss a step and fall flat on my face.

"Brad! Oh my god are you okay?" Lael shouts and runs over.

"That was a longer drive than I thought," I answer, rolling to my back.

Lael lies on the grass with me. She holds my face and kisses me softly. "I can't believe you did that. I've been up all night, worried. I wanted to call or text but I imagined you reaching for the phone and crashing. Do you even have a license?"

"No," I answer.

"Brad!" Lael scolds me.

"I. Missed. You. So. Much." I kiss her between each word.

"C'mon, we're lying on my neighbors' lawn." Lael pulls at the cuffs of my jacket.

I stand up and we face each other, her teal hair is tied up and she's wearing a long tee shirt and comfy pants. The air smells like flowers, the morning sun makes her tired eyes squint. She looks like home and I would have driven that bus around the world to see her.

"Lael."

"Yes, Brad?"

"I am in love with you."

She leans in and kisses my bottom lip softly. Her face is completely relaxed, and she looks at me with the most caring eyes I've ever seen. She tilts her head and as she kisses me again, I can feel her giving me her trust; so completely vulnerable and perfect.

"Inside," Lael commands, her voice soft.

She holds my hand with a soft grip and walks me to her front door. She takes me down a short hall and into her room.

"You must be so tired, baby," she says, pulling at my shirt.

She undresses me completely. I would have at least kept my boxers on, but I forgot who I was dealing with here. She slips out of her clothes and is completely naked. I get the impression this is how she always sleeps.

We get into her perfectly soft bed and tangle our naked bodies together.

"And I'm in love with you," she whispers in my ear.

I fall asleep in the morning light with a smile that lasts for as long as I'm asleep.

There's a *thud* and *crash* that wakes me. I don't know what time it is, but the room looks considerably different with the blinds closed.

The door opens and a young black woman walks in. Lael wakes up when the woman opens the blinds.

"Oh, sorry, I didn't know you had company," the woman exclaims, surprised to see us. "It's eleven a.m., you must have had a hell of a night." She struts right over to the bed and sits down cross-legged facing me.

"I'm Christy." She introduces herself to me and shakes my hand.

"Brad," I reply groggily.

"I know," she laughs.

"Christy…" Lael interjects.

Then a little Chihuahua scurries into the room and jumps onto the bed.

"This is Little Groot," Lael says, introducing me to the dog who gives me the side eye. "Ok, now that we all know each other, how about a little privacy?"

"Fine. It's nice to meet you Brad," Christy says with a smile and struts out of the room.

"The door!" Lael shouts.

Christy raises an eyebrow then closes it slowly.

"Does she always come in here like this?"

"I tend to oversleep these days," Lael says. "It's her gentle way of waking me up. Apparently I can be prickly if she tries to force me awake. How did you sleep?"

"Like a baby, this bed is amazing, how do you ever get anything done?"

"I figure you spend a good chunk of your life in your bed, best to get a good one."

"Look, I want to talk about something," I tell her. "It's about the events that led to you bowing out of the last shows of the tour. I know what really happened."

Lael closes her eyes and puts her head back on her pillow. I wait for her to say something, but silence hangs in the air too long so I continue.

"I'm not mad, I just want you to know we don't have to tip-toe around. Your father won't have any control over me very soon. I'm tired of this fake business and I want to start something new. I don't need to take over the world, I just want to do something great. I want to create something with you. A new life. The three of us."

Lael smiles and pulls the covers over her face for a moment, then pulls the covers away. We laugh like children playing.

"What are you thinking?" Lael asks.

I swing around and lie on top of her, pinning her down. I hold the back of her head and look at her with intensity.

"I have no idea," I answer.

We laugh again. Lael adds, "Sounds like fun, count me in."

We spend most of the rest of the day naked in her

amazing bed. She orders food, we watch Netflix, we are perfectly at ease. Beyond the borders of this bed the world does not exist. I know I have to take care of a few things and can't stay here forever. The bus, for one. I do have a condo I should check on, and there is the issue of the rest of my life I have to figure out. But I know exactly where I need to go.

After some time, I kiss her goodbye and promise to return tomorrow.

I have a car come and take me to the old theater, the only place I seem to be able to get perspective.

It's a little late in the day for me to have the theater to myself. Surely there will be a band doing sound check. That's fine. Sometimes I can't think if it's too quiet.

I step out of the car and stand under the marquee of the old beautiful theater. I know every crack on the sidewalk here, I know what the rain sounds like when it hits the roof. I swing open the door and step into the foyer. The heavy door closes behind me and it's like someone turned the volume knob of the city all the way down.

It's sacred. I spend some time in the foyer, breathing in the smells, beginning the process of forgetting—remembering. I can hear the familiar sounds of a band setting up. I head up the winding red carpeted steps to find a spot on the balcony. There is something about that moment, when you step into a cavernous theater from a dark hall, something inside you wakes up.

I watch the band and their crew set up, laugh, and horse around. Behind me there is a spot above the spotlight I used to climb up to where I could watch what was happening. I have countless memories here, some are good, some are bad. I think of myself as a child and how I carried feelings of guilt and shame with me. Of course the irony is I was an innocent child and no reason to feel any shame.

A child. Lael is going to have my child. There will be someone that doesn't know me as Brad, they will call by my new name; Dad.

I'm going to be a father. I've never had a family, have grown to accept that. I always felt that was so final, that I don't have a family and I'm alone in the world. It never once occurred to me that it could change, I could start my own family.

I wish I had someone I could share this news with; I can imagine what Mr. Robson would say. Surely he would be a proud grandfather.

When Lael told me she was pregnant, there was a part of me that was a scared kid, but those feeling are gone. It made me see the child that I am and I know what I must face. I did what I had to do to get here, but it's time for me to take control of my life. It's time to become a man.

If Ronald wasn't her father, I would simply walk. I would tear up the contract and walk away. He could do his best, but I know I would be fine. Even though I hate the man, he *is* her father. So I'll give him a chance to do what's right. He's made threats, I have to consider that he may be dangerous. I could be worth more to him dead than alive—but I don't believe it. I'm not concerned about that, deep down I know my safety is not in jeopardy.

"Did you come to say goodbye?" I'm startled by her voice. Ms. Sugar steps onto the balcony, an older version of the women I knew, but it is unquestionably her.

"Say goodbye?" I question.

Sugar takes the seat next to me.

"How are ya kid?" she asks.

"I'm doing my best," I answer.

"Well, I guess that's all you can ask for," she says with a chuckle.

"Are you going somewhere?" I ask.

"Oh, you don't even know. It's the theater sweetheart, it's being turned into condos. In a couple months this will be a construction site. Money talks I guess." Sugar's words hit hard.

She delicately opens a flask and takes a hit, then offers it to me.

"No thanks," I say, waving my hand.

I can't find the words, so I don't reply. I look around the theater and feel like I'm looking at a dying friend. I take in a slow deep breath to calm my emotions.

"I'm going to be a father," I tell her casually.

"Fantastic, good for you, the kid is having a kid, what do ya know?" She sounds drunk. She tries to take another drink but the flask is empty.

"I have an eight-year-old son, ya know," she says.

"I didn't know that, what's his name?"

"Kevin."

We share a moment. I have a hard time imaging Sugar as a mom, but then again I'm sure she has hard time seeing me as a father.

"How much did they sell the theater for?" I ask.

"I don't know, I don't even know the owners. I have a business card here, a realtor left it around and I grabbed it." She rifles through her leopard-print bag. "Here it is." She hands me the card. "I am sure I'll see ya around kid, congratulations on being a father, that's real swell."

Sugar gets up with a fraction of the grace she once had,

and leaves the way she came. I look at the card, Mary Cade is the name. Her picture is on the card. I always wondered why realtors put their head-shots on everything.

Mary Cade, I think we need to have a conversation.

But first I have some business to deal with at Ramsey Records.

TWENTY-ONE

BRAD

I'm in my condo waiting for him.

His name Carlos Cortez.

Carlos is a lawyer.

I've had too many coffees and my heart is racing. I don't love this condo but I love the view, and because of that I'll miss it. I'm standing by the window looking out, admiring the skyline as if it were a painting. The coffee mug in my hand begins to shake, so I put it down. It took me over an hour to find the heavy stack of papers that are my contracts with Ramsey Records and they're sitting on the coffee table waiting for Carlos to look them over.

I feel embarrassed at how unorganized I am. I've been so grateful to be able to be able to work and live as a musician that I haven't dared question anything. I felt like if I started asking questions the spell would be broken and I would return back to the alley Ronald had found me in. A decade has passed since that day, and I have more than earned my keep.

I've never looked at these papers, I've never had an agent, I've never had a lawyer. I had to think long and hard to find someone not tied to the company. I really don't have any contacts outside of Ramsey Records. The only lawyer I could think of is the guy from the billboards and the ads on park benches. He's everywhere. I didn't even have to google him, his number and his tag line are etched in my brain. *Call Carlos!* Bright yellow ads with a picture of him giving a thumbs up. I'm happy he's able to come on such short notice.

Ring.

When my phone rings I feel like it's an alarm, it's almost never good when someone's calling. Who calls anymore? Friends text unless someone has died. This time it's the doorman announcing Carlos. I forgot to let them know I had a guest coming, I don't think I've ever remembered to do that.

"Carlos, thanks for coming on such short notice." I shake his hand aggressively, my speech rushed.

"Not a problem," Carlos answers.

"Please sit down," I say to him.

Over the next few hours I tell him everything, perhaps even more than he needed to know. I was in a very rare mood where I needed to talk. I began with my first show, on my birthday at the old theater. I told him how I first met Ronald, how I went from the streets to where I am now. I told him about how I've fallen in love with Lael, I told him about the baby. Finally, I told how I want out of Ramsey Records and I need him to help me.

"So, this is all you have?" Carlos asks, referencing the large folder on the table in front of him.

"This is it," I answer.

Carlos leans over and rifles through the stack of paper.

"Well Brad, it's amazing what you can fix when you throw money at it. I assume you have an impressive bank account, you can probably buy yourself out of a contract. I will need some time to go through all of this," he says.

"I've never had a bank account, I don't have a penny, I own nothing," I say with a tinge of shame in my voice.

"What do you mean, how do you get paid? How do you pay for things?" Carlos asks.

"I have these, I just use them as I need them," I say, showing him my credit cards that all say Ramsey Records.

"The condo?" Carlos asks.

"Not mine," I answer.

Carlos shakes his head in disbelief. "Okay Brad, I'm going to need time to process this. There's a ton of information here." He stands up and walks to the door.

"So, what do you think, can I get out of this?" I ask.

"I haven't a clue," he answers honestly.

When Carlos leaves, the condo feels empty. I want to see Lael.

I text her and ask if I can take her to dinner. There is a great restaurant called The Bellwether close to where she lives. Unfortunately, she is having a girl's night with Christy, so we make plans for tomorrow evening. I tell her I love her and wish her a good night.

My bed feels awful, Lael's bed is much more comfortable. I fall asleep and dream deeply, I dream about her.

⌒

Ring.

It's morning and my phone is making that awful sound again. It's a siren warning me another human wants to talk to me and it's never good. I wake up but don't make an effort to answer it.

Ring.

This must be serious, I think to myself. No voicemail and an immediate call back equals some serious stuff. I reach over to see who is so eager this morning.

Carlos Cortez is written on the screen.

I sit up and answer the call. "Carlos! What's up?"

"Brad! Okay, so if I understand you correctly, you are a weird child-star that has never had a bank account, so obviously you never cashed a check. Right?"

I take a moment to shake off the lack of respect, then answer, "Right."

"Okay. I've been up all night with this. I think we have something," he says with some excitement.

"Great, what's up?" I ask.

"Well, the bad news is I think you have the worst deal ever made in rock and roll history. I mean, this should be criminal, but your signature is everywhere and it's as legal as it gets," Carlos says.

"Okay and the good news?" I ask.

"Well, you have never been paid, like—ever. You have been treated more like a product then a person. I can guarantee almost everything you have purchased with those credit cards has been written off as a business expense." Carlos is speaking with excitement, but I'm not sure I'm grasping the good news yet.

"Right…?"

"Right! So even though you have the shittiest deal I

have ever seen, you still have never been paid your tiny percentage owed to you."

"How much?" I ask.

"Two percent," he answers.

"So how much is that?" I ask.

"I dunno, two percent of what ever And Then has made in the past ten years."

Shit.

"Let's go to the office now!"

"What? No, Brad, this stuff will take time. We'll have to go through his lawyers. Best case scenario is we settle out of court, but even then this will be a long battle," Carlos says.

"I'm putting on my jacket," I tell him.

"Brad, you're going to mess it up, don't go down there," Carlos begs.

"I'll pick you up in twenty minutes or I will go it alone."

"Ugh. Fine. I'll be downtown, on West 1st and Olive, text me when you're close," Carlos says with defeat.

I hang up and arrange for a car. This morning I'm making history. I dress in black and wear my darkest shades.

Carlos and I walk into Ramsey Records, straight-faced and with purpose. The elevator ride to the top floor is silent, save Carlos's remark.

"This is crazy," he whispers.

I smile to myself as the elevator door slides open to the familiar top floor of Ramsey Records. I walk straight for Ronald's office with Carlos in tow.

"Oh Brad, we were not expecting you! You know you need to make an appointment," Ronald's secretary stands and speaks with urgency.

I ignore her and open the office door. Ronald is at his

desk and looks up from some papers at me with surprise obvious on his face. His secretary rushes past me.

"I am so sorry Mr. Ramsey, I tried to…"

She's cut short by Ronald.

"It's fine, fine, leave us," he says. "What do you want?" Ronald asks me with a blank expression, not even interested in Carlos beside me.

"What do I want? I want out and I want what's owed to me, and I want it to happen today," I say in an even calm tone.

"Shut the door. Have a seat," Ronald says. I doubt he even realizes what he just said is the name of one of our songs. That's how out of tune with *And Then* he is.

Carlos shuts the office door and we both sit in the chairs in front of his desk. I take off my shades and fold them down one arm at a time.

"Who are you?" Ronald finally asks Carlos.

"Carlos Cortez, I'm Brad's lawyer," Carlos replies.

"Good for you. So, Brad—you want a check, and you want out. First you knock up my young impressionable daughter and now you come here and demand money from me. I took you from nothing and made you into a star. Where's the respect, where's the appreciation?"

"Where is the money?" I ask.

"What money?" He answers.

"I'm a multiplatinum-selling artist that has written every note of every song. CD sales, merchandise, sold-out world tours," I tell him.

"Amazing, truly amazing. Do you realize this entire building works to make all that happen? Do you realize how much that costs? I have given you *everything*."

Ronald's face is red with anger now and he stands up

and puts his fists on the desk. He yells, veins protruding from his forehead and spit flies from his mouth. "You were nothing before I *made* you into something!"

I stand and match his aggressive posture.

"Two percent, you don't think I deserve two fucking percent?" My fist hits his desk on the last few syllables.

We stand off. Ronald has lost something and he knows it. He's lost control over me and it's driving him mad.

"I'm starting a new life and I'm done with this. I'm going to be a father. I just want what is owed to me. Nothing more," I say.

Ronald turns his back to me and looks out the window.

"So, you want to be a family man?" he asks.

"Yes, I do," I say with confidence.

"What kind of family man starts a war?" Ronald asks as he turns from the window to face me.

"It doesn't have to be a war. Two percent over the last ten years, whatever that number is." I take a step closer. "Cut it in half, write a check this afternoon, and we can part ways. We both know our lawyers will make more out of a court battle than anyone. We have one thing in common—we both love Lael, neither of us wants to hurt her. God knows she doesn't need any stress right now. Ronald, you can think of it like you're writing a check for your daughter and your future grandchild, because you are."

"Half?" Carlos asks from his sunken position in his chair.

"Half should be plenty to start over," I explain. "I don't need to be a rich man. I just want to start over—with Lael. I realize you and the company have done a lot to get me where I am, but you have been well compensated for that."

I walk to the door. "Carlos, it's time to go," I call back to him.

Carlos gets up to follow me.

"Wait," Ronald calls to me from behind his desk. I have my hand on the door handle and my back to him. I don't turn around, I am still and he can tell I'm listening.

"What are you going to do?" he asks.

"What do you mean?" I turn to face him with my reply.

"If I let you go, are you going to go to the competition?" he asks.

"No," I answer.

"Then what's the plan?"

"That's not your concern."

"Lael is my concern."

"I'm buying the old theater," I answer. I step closer and closer to him. I want him to know that I'm stating a fact and not asking for permission. "Lael and I will continue to make music, independently."

Ronald eases back into his chair. Looks at the ceiling and smiles to himself. His thoughts are unreadable.

"The old theater," he muses.

"I know I haven't been the best father. Look, Brad, if this is what Lael truly wants..." Ronald drops his hand submissively. "I will give you the full two percent, if Lael owns half the theater."

I'm not sure how to respond. I could not ask for a better outcome, but I'm put off by this human side of Ronald for some reason. I can't find the words so I say nothing.

I stand up and shake his hand. We hold eye contact, his grip is firm and he doesn't let go. I can't read him, I just hold my ground and wait for him to let my hand go. Finally, he does. I head to the door.

"One more condition," he says.

I turn around and raise an eye brow.

"Name the theater after her mother," he says, while writing something. He seems to have moved on to other business already.

"Consider it done."

And with that, I leave Ramsey Records.

When I step outside the air feels different. I feel light on my feet.

"I'll get a car," I say to Carlos. "Wait, something's up here, what does this mean?" I show Carlos the screen on my phone.

"Your credit card declined, pal," Carlos says.

"That's never happened. Damn, my phone isn't working right now!" I add.

"That was fast. He canceled your credit cards and phone." Carlos can't help but laugh. "This is what it's like to be mortal, friend."

"Can you take care of the car?" I ask.

"I'll put it on your bill. You should get what you can from your condo while you can," Carlos says.

I think about my guitar sitting on its stand in the corner, the one Mr. Robson had given me.

Carlos insists on waiting in the car while I go up to the condo. He makes a valid point that I'll need a ride somewhere after I grab my things. As Carlos thought would be the case, I'm already locked out. Thankfully, I've become close with the doorman and he agrees to let me in to grab some stuff. I grab my guitar, and throw a few things in a suitcase. I am in and out in five minutes.

"So, where ya headed?" Carlos asks.

"Sherman Oaks," I answer.

We sit in silence for the entire ride. When we stop in front of Lael's little house, I hand him the realtor's card Sugar had given me.

"How are you at negotiating?" I ask.

"I'll see what I can do. I guess you want me to handle getting that check too? If you do get the theater I assume you will have an incorporation."

"Umm ..."

"I can help you with your plans, don't worry. I'll be in touch very soon," Carlos says, shaking my hand.

"Thank you," I say sincerely.

"Wait until you see my bill," he says out of the open window while the car drives away.

Lael's door is locked and no one is home, so I sit on the front porch next to all my worldly possessions and wait.

I wait for the love of my life.

TWENTY-TWO

LAEL

"**A**re you sure this is a good idea?" Brad asks me as he pushes the cart.

I roll my eyes. "For the last time, yes."

I don't even look at him, just keep my gaze on all the houseware items as we stroll through the market place. Even though I know we've gotten a ton of stuff from the various baby showers, I've become obsessive about getting all the right things. I want the perfect nest to bring the baby home into.

I also don't want to look at him because he's unable to look at me lately without me feeling like I'm under a microscope. He's been non-stop worrying about me for weeks, which in turn makes me feel worried and that's the last thing I need right now.

Zen, I tell myself. *Think Zen thoughts.*

But Brad goes on. "It's just that the doctor said that during the last week before you're due, you should be at home resting."

"Well that's fine for Dr. Anderson to say, but Lael Ramsey likes to go to IKEA."

"I'm also concerned about you talking in the third person."

Now I glare at him. "Lael Ramsey would like you to shut up."

"Maybe we should go back upstairs and get more Swedish meatballs in you."

"I'm fine," I tell him. "Plus there's hot dog and ice cream after we go through the cashiers."

The truth is, I'm hungry as hell all the time, I'm cranky and I'm huge. I've been waddling around in muumuus for what seems like forever and the only thing that's been helping is keeping myself busy and taking my mind off of it.

I'm beyond ready for our baby girl to come out into the world and the more that I think about it, the more anxious and impatient I get.

Hence why strolling around IKEA seems to help my nerves and I'll do anything to get through this last week.

"Are you sure?" Brad asks after a few moments, when I've grabbed a cheap spaghetti strainer and plunked it in the cart. I already have a few but who cares.

"Brad," I warn him. "Leave me be."

"Okay, okay. I just want everything to be perfect, you know."

I nod. "I know. And I don't know how perfect things will be but you know it's going to be fine."

"I know."

The only problem, of course, with waddling with my big fat belly around IKEA (other than knocking items off the shelves) is that I get tired easily. My feet are so swollen and sore they resemble appendages belonging to Jabba the Hut.

I decide to call it a day, happy with my impulse purchases, plus the hot dog and ice cream, and Brad drives us back to our place in Sherman Oaks that we now share.

Christy moved out shortly after Brad lost his condo and had to move in. She got a full-time graphic design job in Orange County so she needed to move closer but we still see each other every weekend. And of course, I wanted the father of my child to live with me and Baby Groot.

Needless to say, the last nine months or so have been interesting.

Sometimes it's been extremely happy, knowing that our baby is on the way. I've never felt so lovingly supported before and Brad has been amazing dealing with the pregnancy.

Sometimes, though, it's frustrating. I never assumed that pregnancy was a walk in the park but the truth is, it's not as fun as some women make it out to be. I'm not glowing and I never was. I've been heavier than I should be and a big sweaty mess, and my morning/afternoon sickness kind of morphed into just an overall feeling of unease that doesn't go away.

I've been bitchy, cranky, and at times it's hard to find the bright side in all of it. It doesn't help that I'm tired all the time. Like, pretty much from the first moment I found out I was pregnant, I've been exhausted. Then there's the brain fog that doesn't go away and the fact that I'm always hungry and yet my taste for food changes frequently. Today the vanilla ice cream at IKEA was delicious, last week the idea would have been revolting. It's hard to keep up.

I've talked it over with my doctor, concerned that

something was wrong or maybe I'm just not a good fit for pregnancy. I mean, I'm young, I thought this was the optimal time to carry a child.

But he assured me I'm healthy and the baby is healthy and it's just not all that it's cracked up to be. Not every mother glows and feels rested and peaceful, full of rainbows and butterflies. Some moms are sweaty and fat and gross and full of farts that can clear a room.

Poor, poor Brad.

This is what he's had to put up with.

Needless to say, we're both happy for when this whole ordeal is over and we can hold our little girl.

Her name is Emma, which was my mother's middle name.

I'm also excited to start being a mom and get back into the music business. In the early stages of pregnancy, I still had the emotional drive and brain power to write songs. But that all faded pretty quickly.

Once Emma is born, I can get back into it and focus on my music career, whether it's just writing songs and helping Brad with his solo career, or gearing up for a side project of my own.

Brad's been doing well. He has plans, especially now with the theater and studio we bought. Things are slowly getting into place. At first he was really adrift, which is only natural after being severed from the only thing he really knew. Like it or not, my father was everything to him and taught him a lot, showed him the ropes, took him under his wing.

It's just that it was a vulture's wing, scavenging on the helpless, always looking out for his own best interests in mind, never Brad's.

It was brave what Brad did. Brave and totally romantic. Picking me, picking Emma, over his band, over his musical career.

But Brad has never been an idiot. And ever since he and my father parted ways, he's been working non-stop. The band has dissolved for now, though he has talked with Switch about getting together to do something of the same. Calvi, of course, has been hung out to dry, that jackass. My only consolation in all of this is that being a tattle tale didn't pay off for Calvi at all. He thought he was going to win big favors with my father by snitching on us but the truth is he hasn't worked since and I doubt he'll have an easy time going forward. It's a small town and no one wants to work with a guy like that. Musicians crave their privacy.

Brad's also been recording some songs somewhere while we wait for our own studio to be completed, and working with various artists. This is the first time he's ever had total artistic freedom as an artist and I think he's just taking his time and enjoying all of it.

Besides, it's nice to have him by my side. He really feels like a partner in all of this and though we have never discussed the possibility of marriage, I know he loves me and is in this for the long haul. He's proved that to me time and time again.

"Do you mind stopping at 7/11?" I ask him as we turn off Ventura Blvd. "I'm craving some nachos."

"Lael, that's not even real food. That cheese is basically plastic. Orange-colored melted plastic on top of GMO chips."

"I know, but I want them."

I give him a look that says not to mess with me.

The pregnant lady always wins.

He sighs and pulls into the parking lot and I ease myself out of the car. He's adamant I stay put but I know it's not just the nachos that I want, it's whatever else catches my fancy as I walk the aisles.

I catch a glimpse of the wine and whimper internally. *Soon, soon, my precious,* I think to the wine bottles. I can't wait to start having wine again.

I go down the aisles, grabbing whatever bags of chips and junk that catches my eye (there's no wonder I'm as big as a house), passing them all off to Brad who cradles them in his arms, then head to the snack bar in the middle of the store.

Fake food or not, I want those gross nachos. I grab them, making sure they are drowning in the cheese, then contemplate hitting it up with jalapenos. I haven't had the stomach for spicy food lately but I know that they can help induce labor (so they say) and at this moment, I want nothing more.

I'm just about to spoon them on top of the nachos when I hear a faint popping sound, like someone has cracked their knuckles.

Only the sound is coming from *me.*

Then a huge gush of fluid comes streaming down my legs like a waterfall and onto the floor, splashing everywhere.

I drop the nachos on top of it in surprise.

The ultimate mess.

"Are you okay?" Brad asks, then he looks down. "Oh my god! Your water just broke! Oh my god! You're going into labor! Oh my god! You can't have a baby in 7/11!"

Meanwhile I'm stunned. A bit mortified that I created the grossest scene to ever grace this 7/11 (and that's saying a lot) but I'm more shocked than anything.

"Let's go!" Brad says, putting his arms around me and trying to lead me out of the store. The water doesn't seem to stop though, it keeps flowing like someone put a hose between my legs. This is nothing like peeing yourself, this is something else entirely and I'm helpless to stop it.

Brad is freaking out, apologizing to the 7/11 employee who doesn't look as concerned as he should be, and then ushers me out to the car, getting me in my seat.

"Are you okay? Are you in pain? Are you okay?" Brad is panicking.

I nod as he clips in my seatbelt. "I'm okay. I just…I guess this is it."

"Okay. Okay, okay, okay. We're one minute from the house, we'll just go there and get the overnight bag and stuff and oh my god I can't believe this is happening. Wait, am I being dumb? Should I get you to the hospital first?"

I give him look, trying to get him to calm down. "Let's go home. You go grab the bag. Call Sally to come pick up Baby Groot. I'm not having contractions yet and you know this can take a long time. In fact, he said if my water breaks, we don't have to rush to the hospital. We can go later."

"No, we're going now. I'm not waiting twenty-four hours to see how this progresses. It's progressing. It progressed all over 7/11. We're going."

"All right."

I'm amazed at how cool I'm being.

Of course, all of that stops the minute he runs into the house to get the supplies.

Then I'm hit with the mother of all cramps.

It's like a charley horse on my uterus.

Holy shit.

I grip the edge of the seat and let out a yelp.

Fucking contractions.

I feared them for months and now they're finally here.

And holy fucking fuck, they aren't any fun.

Luckily, this one ends by the time Brad comes back in the car so I'm able to be calm and collected again.

Unfortunately, we get stuck in traffic on the way to the hospital and I'm hit by two more of them.

"Ow!" Brad cries out as I dig my nails into his arm, the car nearly going off the road. We're moving at a snail's pace but still.

"Ow!?" I roar at him. "You call that painful? Let me show you what pain is really like." I swear I'm seconds from putting my teeth into his arm.

"No, I believe you," he says, shrinking away from me. "But that's three in the last hour, what does that mean? Is this happening quickly? Do we need an ambulance?"

"It's normal," I tell him, trying to breathe like they teach you. It's not really working. What a crock of shit that Lamaze stuff is. "If it's double this, then we're getting close."

"Okay. Okay. You're sure?"

"Just drive, Brad. Shut up and drive."

"Okay."

We get to the hospital just in time. While my contractions didn't worsen in the car, the moment I'm sitting down in the waiting room they come at me with a vengeance. Powerful ones that make me see stars, nearly have me clawing the walls, and they're coming five minutes apart.

Brad wrangles a nurse and I'm put into a wheelchair and wheeled off toward a room.

Everything seems to be happening fast and in a blur.

I'm put on the bed, the nurses do tests and run things to me, my doctor comes by and says I'm dilated by five centimeters and things are progressing fast but smoothly.

It's then that I realize that it's just Brad and I against the world. He has no family. I just have my father. And ever since Brad and him split, ever since he found out I was pregnant, we haven't been close. Just a text sent on birthdays, that's it.

For once, I miss him. I miss having a father around, even though my father wasn't very good at it, he was all I had.

"Are you okay?" Brad asks me as a tear spills down my cheek. "Do you want the epidural after all?"

I shake my head. "No. It's not that. It's just…it's just you and me now."

He squeezes my hand. "You have a world of supporters behind you, Lael."

I nod. "I know, I just…"

And then I'm nearly blindsided by another contraction, the worst one yet.

Oh my god.

I thought I could be brave, I thought I could handle the pain. I thought there's no way in hell I would ever pick getting a needle in the spine over the pain of giving birth and yet here I am yelling, "Give me the needle! Put it in my spine!"

The nurse hovers by me, peering down with a gentle look on her face.

I'd like to spit in that face.

"The anesthesiologist is busy," the nurse says to me. "We can give you a tranquilizer that will make you sleepy and relax you. Either way, you don't have long to go. You're having this baby now."

"But I want the needle in the spine!" I cry out as she brings an IV over to me. "Not in the vein, put it in my spine!"

"I think I'm going to be sick," Brad says, looking like he's going to faint.

And then everything gets a bit hazy. I'm still aware of where I am and the pain has subsided a bit but it's not enough to keep me from screaming with every contraction. And when the doctor starts telling me to push, I'm able to.

Everything really does happen fast or at least the drugs trick me into thinking that.

Before I know it, through the final burst of pain comes euphoria and the sound of a screaming baby.

Emma has been brought into the world.

I'm laughing, crying, overwhelmed by too many things at once. Emma is placed into my arms, her skin pressed against mine, a tiny wrinkled, red-faced little thing.

Brad is beside me, looking down at Emma and I like he's died and gone to heaven.

I've never felt so much love in my life, never felt so complete.

Suddenly the world is whittled down to just the three of us.

Suddenly my heart only beats for my family.

About an hour or so later, after Emma has fallen asleep after her first (successful!) attempt at nursing, Brad leaves the room with an impish smile on his face.

When he comes back, he's not alone.

There's Arnie. Christy. And my father. All crowding the doorway.

I'm so shocked, so happy and touched, I burst into tears again.

My father hovers in the background while Arnie and Christy come by and congratulate me and coo over beautiful Emma.

When they're done, only then does my father come forward.

To my surprise, the moment he looks down at his grandchild, a tear falls from his eye.

"Beautiful, just beautiful," he says. "She has your mother's eyes." He leans over and kisses the top of my head. "I'm very proud of you Lael. I hope you know that now, in case you didn't before. And I'm sorry about what happened with Brad. I do think our parting ways was for the best. But I won't stand in the way of you being a family."

I wouldn't have let him stand in the way but I'm too exhausted and emotional to say anything except, "Thank you."

Then I look down at Emma and say the same thing.

"Thank you, little one, for coming into this world. Thank you for everything."

TWENTY-THREE

BRAD

"**D**on't wake up," I whisper to Emma. "It's okay. I promise you, life isn't so hard." I whisper so quietly, I'm barely making a sound. My beautiful daughter is curled up on my chest, we are in bed and it is the middle of the day. Her name is Emma, she's four months old, and I'm in love.

Her tiny little hand squeezes my finger as she dreams. Other than her diaper she's naked, and I can feel her go through a spectrum of emotions as she sleeps. Slowly, I push back her thin hair. Each time she smiles, I smile back. Her eyes open, and she leaves her little dream for a moment. Her blue eyes are bright and they shine with love. She looks deep into my eyes then closes hers and returns to her little baby dream.

My phone vibrates on the table and I silence it as quick as I can. It's a text from Lael.

Look what came in today!!!

A picture of a large vintage mixing console in our new recording studio is below her message. It is a classic, a Neve, and it cost me almost as much as the theater. I share her excitement. It's the final piece we've been waiting for, almost all the construction is nearly complete.

The theater came with the next building as a package deal and it didn't take long for Lael to come up with the idea to build a recording studio. The theater is our base camp, our creative headquarters. It has always been a sacred place for me and I can't think of a better venue for my family to grow. Most of the old crew still work the live shows and a few of them are helping out on the recording studio side.

I reply to her text:

Yuss! We are on our way!!

Although I want to get to the theater to share the excitement and check out the new mixing desk, I stay here a little longer. My young Emma is peacefully sleeping on my chest and I don't want to wake her yet. Or maybe I delay getting up because I want to make this moment stretch because I am enjoying my time with her. Today is a special day and not only because of the mixing desk.

I've never felt more at home than I do here. Lael often talks about moving to a bigger place but I want to keep things the way they are for as long as I can. Deep down I know it feels so good here because of Lael and Emma and has little to do with the actual house. I'm sure it will feel more or less the same wherever we are. I just don't feel the need to move to a big fancy place. It probably helps that we renovated the space above the recording studio into a condo. Lael loves having a place in the city and I do as well. I have a feeling the next few chapters of our lives will be set in the theater, the recording studio, and the condo. I'm excited about the future, I'm excited about today.

I start getting things together; it's a slow process but I've learned not to rush. One thing at a time and it all gets done. It's taken me some time to learn this patience

Once I locked Emma in the car with the keys in the ignition. I had to call for help, Lael doesn't know that happened. Maybe one day when we are old and grey I'll tell her.

I keep on checking my pocket to make sure of something; for a moment I don't feel it and my heart skips a beat. But then I find it.

I slowly exhale.

It's still there. I repeat this many times.

Emma somehow stays asleep while I strap her into her seat. I check my pocket one more time before sliding in behind the wheel. I finally have a driver's license, Carlos guided me through the process of what he calls being a mortal. Getting my license was at the top of the list. I mean, the guy actually made a list. I think it's safe to say I'm his favorite client.

I glance at sleeping Emma in my review mirror and pull away. Yes, today is a special day.

I make my way through the winding road, over the hills to the city where she waits. It's rare that there's parking available on the street in front of the theater but it's a quiet evening and there is the perfect spot waiting for me. I repeat the process of getting Emma into the car but in reverse. I have her in my arms, her bag over my shoulder and of course I have to check my pocket a couple more times.

The theater looks basically the same, save the new name: The Francesca Theater. I must admit I like the name and what it represents.

Ronald and I have a long way to go, but we have a working relationship now. He actually helped find the infamous mixing desk that is waiting for me. Ronald doesn't get involved for the most part, but he softened up quite a bit when Emma was born.

And Then is a brand that Ronald and his creative team came up with in a board room. I'm proud of the music I've made, I'm proud of every note. But there is no way I can go forward with that name. I release music under my own name now.

Switch wasn't crazy about the idea of releasing under my name at first, but he seems to have gotten used to it. I don't play with Calvi anymore, obviously, it seems to be better that way. We don't have bad blood, per se, we have a lot of history together. But I can't trust a guy like that.

I'm happy Switch is staying with me though, people don't realize how much a drummer changes the sound of a band. I like the way he plays, he makes me sound better.

You can get to the studio from the side entrance, but I choose to go through the theater. As I swing open the door I think about how rare it is that the door is locked. This place always seems to be open, like a library, or a hospital, or a 24-hour diner that never sleeps.

"Hey boss." An old friend that has worked for this theater longer then I've been alive holds the door for me while I enter the foyer.

I laugh dismissively at being addressed as boss. I can't say I'm not moved by the support the staff are giving me, though. They know where I'm from, where I've been, and who I'm trying to be. I could leave for a tour or a family vacation and not have to worry for a moment about the theater. I need them more than they need me.

I do sometimes worry about them pushing themselves too much so I hired one of their nephews who is more brawn than brain to help out with that.

"Look, boss, my daughter is visiting with her family from Vermont tomorrow, do you think I can have the day off?" he asks then shares a smile with Emma.

"You know what, I haven't worked the board in ages, I'll come in tomorrow," I tell him.

"Great, thanks boss," he says as he very slowly waddles away. I feel like all the old staff had a private conversation and agreed they wouldn't call me Kid anymore.

Emma and I take a moment to check on the main hall. I walk through the doors and make my way to the sound desk, I take a seat in the same old chair Mr. Robson would sit at.

"What do you think?" I ask her. "Kind of romantic in a way, owning a theater like this. Your daddy used to live here most of the time and the first time I played was up there. There was a man that worked right where we are that was very special to me and I wish you could have met him, I really do." I speak to her in a calm baby voice and she laughs back. I feel a pang of emotion in my heart thinking about how proud Mr. Robson would have been.

My excitement is pulling me to the construction site that is the new studio. I enjoy the moment I'm having with Emma so I don't rush out. She really is teaching me about patience.

I slowly make my way to the new studio where Lael is waiting.

To get to the studio from inside the theater I have to go into the ticket office, and through the newly-created door that joins the two structures. They did their best to make the door look like it was always there, but the door handle and lock look cheap and modern.

I will have that changed, I think to myself. I check my pocket once again, *it* is still there, right where I put it.

Once in the studio side the feeling is different. It smells of construction; it's the familiar smell when a very old room or building is being renovated. A mix of new wood being cut and old material being torn down. The studio is very close to being completed but there are signs of destruction everywhere. Tools, buckets, rolls of plastic. Another few days and Lael will be hanging pictures and making other final touches. She's really good at creating a home. She calls it "nesting."

I make my way through a common area and down a little hallway. There's a red light in front of the door that has the words *Recording in process* on it. It's flashing on and off.

The door swings open and there she is. Lael looks at us, her eyes are bright and they shine with love just like her daughter's. Lael is contorting herself so she can flick the switch from the control room and see if it's working from the hall where Emma and I are standing.

"Success!" she says in reference to the newly installed light.

"Success," I respond.

"Oh, look at you two. I love you so much," she says as she rushes over and hugs us. She kisses me and Emma smiles at the sight of her mom. She takes Emma from my arms and holds her tight.

"Are you ready?" Lael asks with her fist clenched in excitement.

"Yes I am," I answer.

In more ways than she can possibly know.

I check my pocket once again.

We walk into the control room and there it is. It's slightly smaller than I thought it would be but I still can't imagine how it got in here. The sides and top are beautiful old wood, there are more faders and knobs then I can compute at first glance. There are meters with needles and nothing about this is digital, it's as analog and true as it gets. It's the cinematic setting for a mad scientist and his time machine, or a maybe a wizard's machine built to access another world.

The perfect mix of science and magic.

"We had a little technical difficulty but this is the moment of truth," Lael says. I can tell she's been working hard and it's the excitement that's keeping her going.

The room is full, most of the staff are here, in fact they're all here. The excitement about the studio and especially the Neve Mixing Desk has attracted a crowd.

I didn't plan for a crowd this evening.

Not for what I have planned.

"Come on, take a seat captain," Lael says pulling out the chair.

I sit down at the desk. I don't pull in too close because someone is underneath fumbling with some cables. I push up the master fader for fun. To think of all the creative energy that will be going through this machine, all the memories will be channeled through these tubes and cables. Maybe Emma will one day sing a song through this mixer.

Zap!

"Ahh!" The fella under the desk hits his head when he recoils from the shock. It smells like electrical burning.

"I'm okay, I'm okay, nothing is broken, sorry about that. I am going to need some time here."

I don't recognize him and assume he's the specialist that traveled with this particular unit. These old machines take considerable amount of care and there are very few people in the world that can handle them.

"Oh no! Okay, come check out the live room with me then," Lael says to me, trying not let her enthusiasm waver, even though I can see the live room well from where I sit. Directly above the mixing desk is a soundproof window. You can sit at the mixing desk and look right into the eyes of whomever is performing in the live room.

"Sure, let's check it out," I get up and follow her through the large door. It feels like entering a bomb shelter because the door and walls are so thick. I clap my hands to hear the echo of the room.

"Perfect. This is perfect," I say to her, walking around the room, exploring what's lying around. There's a leather sofa chair in the corner that sticks out. Lael notices me looking at it.

"It's just there for now. It will be moved to the other room," she says.

I chuckle over the fact that she's so concerned about it and look through the glass to see all the grey-haired staff fussing over the mixing desk.

There's something about being in a soundproof room, you can hear your own breath, your own heart beating in your ears. Mine is beating fast. I wasn't planning on doing it like this. But I feel like if I wait for the perfect moment I'll be waiting for the rest of my life.

"Are you okay?" Lael asks.

"Yes, I am. I'm more than okay." I take Emma from her

arms and place her carefully on the sofa.

"What are you doing? She can fall, I can hold her," Lael says with some confusion in her voice.

"It's okay, I'll stay down here next to her," I say as I get down on one knee.

I look up at Lael and watch as her confusion melts away.

She knows what's happening.

And so I take a moment, I don't rush. We look at each other with love. I have one hand on baby Emma keeping her steady and Emma has a silly smile on her face.

I think I might too.

"When you picked me up from the airport my life changed forever," I tell her, clearing my throat. "We have had a wild ride, you and I, and looking around this place I feel like we are just getting started. We're going to travel the world playing wild rock shows, we're going to make music out of this studio, we're going to do it together, the three of us. We're going to live our lives exactly how we want to. I am in love with you. And I want to break all the rules with you. Lael Ramsey I want you to be my wife. Will you marry me?"

I steady giggling Emma again, then reach into my pocket, fumbling for a moment to find the ring.

Lael breaks down into tears,

"Yes," she says, her voice choking.

I put the ring on her finger. All the hair on my body is on end, I don't cry but but emotion is coursing through me in way I can't describe. Lael looks at the ring then pulls me up.

"I love you so much," she says to me.

I pick up Emma. I kiss Lael and hold her with Emma

between us. We are one, we are family.

"Looks like you got it on the first take."

We hear the words coming from the speakers in the corners of the room. Our attention goes to the control room behind the soundproof glass. All the staff are watching us. I notice a few of them have taken off their hats and are holding them next to their hearts. The fella at the seat is holding down the talkback mic, the crew begins to applaud. Then the fella at the desk releases the talkback button to clap his hands.

We watch the entire crew applaud in complete silence. It's a strange sight, all of them clapping and shouting, and not hearing a sound.

Another fella reaches over and presses the talkback mic again, the sound of the shouts and applause make us jump.

"Congratulations!' he says with a large smile.

Lael steps closer to the old-timey looking microphone in the middle of the room that has obviously captured my proposal.

"Thank you, I guess this means the desk works then," Lael says into the mic.

"Everything looks perfect," he says to us over the volume of the applause.

I'm in the theater tonight, doing the sound for the live performance and getting a young band set up for their show. They're a simple trio, bass, drums and guitar. It's an easy one but it's been a long time for me and it's not as second nature as it once was.

As the night progresses though, I'm becoming more and more comfortable with working at the live mixing desk. It's a lot different from the mixing desk in the other studio. First of all, this isn't an analog machine like the one we just got, second of all, it's live music. You're on the spot and there's no room for error, not during a concert.

Even so, I have everything set-up early so I ease back in my chair and watch the theater slowly fill up with concert-goers.

For a new band they have a decent turnout. This is a great place for people watching. There's a young fella at the front of the stage all alone, looking at the equipment. I know what he's feeling, I remember being that kid.

Then I see a crowd of girls come in together, dressed to impress. They are too young to realize that all of this is for them. They are so powerful and I don't think they have any idea, everything here is because of them.

There's a famous guitar player that said there are two kinds of musicians, the kind that do it for the girls and the kind that lie about it. This theater was probably built to impress a girl. The studio next door certainly was. Everything I do now is to impress two girls that are in that studio right now.

"Hey Kid." Sugar comes into my little area with her son, Kevin.

"Hey Sugar, Hey Kevin," I greet them. Kevin is wearing the same clothes and same hat as when I first met him. And he's still too shy to answer me.

"Look, Kid, I have to fly, can you watch my Kid, Kid?" Sugar smiles at the joke. She says it every time and every time I still smile. Even though the years haven't been too kind to her, I still feel I owe her a lot.

I look down at Kevin who's looking down at his shoes.

"I have a show," she goes on. "I am the first one on, I promise I'll be back before this all wraps up." Sugar turns her attentions to her son. "Be good for Mr....*Kid*." She doesn't wait for me to answer and leaves.

Kevin looks up, past me, and scans the whole space with curious bright eyes. I look down at Kevin. He's younger than I was when I first came here and I don't think I was quite so shy, but he does remind me of myself in this very spot all those years ago.

I can't resist from saying it.

"So, your mom let you out of your cage."

The kid smiles at me for the first time and says, "Do you like Dillalo Burgers?"

EPILOGUE
LAEL

Two years later

"Are you ready?" Arnie asks me as he hands me my bass.

"As I'll ever be," I tell him, slipping it over my shoulders.

Okay, that's kind of a lie. I'm ready and I'm not ready all at once.

This isn't just a normal show for me.

This is the first show ever for The New Mistakes.

My band.

I mean, my own damn band.

We've been rehearsing for months, me, my guitarist Bryan, the drummer April. During those months we've recorded an album at Francesca Studios, which Brad and I run together, and we've released that album to critical acclaim. In the day and age where it's hard to make a dime on music, somehow our self-titled album climbed onto the back end of the Billboard charts.

Now it's our first show and it's at none other than the Francesca Theater (which of course is part and parcel of the recording studio).

The show is sold-out. Friends and family and fans are packed to the rafters. Christy and my father are somewhere in the crowd, opting for the real experience this time instead of side stage.

I'm nervous.

Not the kind of nervous like I'm going to puke everywhere, not like I did for my first show with *And Then*. But I'm still feeling lit from within, my stomach doing turns and jumps, my limbs feeling both solid and loose all at once.

The thing is, this is the first show and the first time really playing my own songs in front of fans. I know that Brad says to show them no respect, but I can't help it. They mean everything to me and I want to put on the best show possible.

No pressure, of course.

Then there's my voice. I can sing just fine and have been working on how to really wail on a few songs. I've just got that weird fear, like it's about to turn into a bad dream, the one where you open your mouth to speak or sing and you can't.

What if nothing comes out?

What if I mess up the notes?

What if fear gets the best of me?

And now, now there's hardly any time to worry about it. The lights are going to go on me soon and I'll have to start playing and singing whether I'm ready or not.

Oh god, I don't think I'm ready.

I glance over at the side stage and my eyes meet with Brad's.

He gives me a nod and a calming smile, his way of telling me that everything is going to be okay. In his arms, held up against his shoulder, is Emma.

She's waving at me and grinning, looking ridiculously cute in the oversized headphones she has over her head. She looks like she's about to pilot a plane somewhere far away.

And she's wearing a shirt that says The New Mistakes on her. My heart couldn't melt anymore.

Oh, yes it could, because Brad is wearing that exact same shirt.

My two biggest supporters, my two biggest fans.

After the demise of *And Then*, Brad never really stopped. He went on to do a myriad of different projects, some with artists you'd never think of, like Jay-Z and Elton John. When he's not working with them, he's working with other artists, especially up-and-comers, turning out beautiful albums. Francesca studios has become one of the best studios in the country and we're busy all the damn time.

We've even paired up on our own projects some time. I'm not sure how long The New Mistakes will go on for but I always have room for Brad and he has room for me. One day, when the timing is right, maybe when Emma is older, we'll create our own band together and tour the country, just like we did all those years ago.

Until then though, we have our hands full.

My husband gives me the thumbs up, bringing me back to the present and then mouths something to me.

"Just breathe."

I nod and smile and take in a deep breath.
I throw my shoulders back.
I face the crowd, pick at the ready.
The lights come on.
And I play.

ACKNOWLEDGEMENTS

We're keeping this short and sweet.

Thanks to our families, our friends, and everyone who had a hand in helping with this book. Thanks to our dog Bruce for being our fur baby.

And thanks to YOU for reading Rocked Up. We greatly appreciate it! Writing together was new and challenging at times but in the end it was an amazing experience that brought us closer together and we're thrilled at this labor of love. We hope you enjoyed the show.

Rock on!

ABOUT THE AUTHORS

Karina Halle is a former travel writer and music journalist and *The New York Times*, *Wall Street Journal* and *USA Today* Bestselling author of The Pact, Love, in English, The Artists Trilogy, Dirty Angels and over 20 other wild and romantic reads. She lives on an island off the coast of British Columbia with her husband, Scott, and their rescue pit bull Bruce, where they drinks a lot of wine, hikes a lot of trails and devours a lot of books.

Born in Montreal and raised in rural Ontario, Scott Mackenzie has worn many different hats in his life, from bartending to working as a heavy duty mechanic for the railway, to owning and operating a take-out restaurant. He finally settled down out West, where he lives on an island with his author wife and their dog. Scott can be found exploring the gulf islands on his sailboat, playing and recording music in his studio, or on a hike, thinking about his next book.

This is their first book together.

OTHER TITLES

by Scott Mackenzie
Sex, Love, and Rock n' Roll

by Karina Halle
THE EXPERIMENT IN TERROR SERIES
Books #1 – 9

EDGY SUSPENSEFUL ROMANCE READS BY KARINA HALLE
The Devil's Metal (The Devil's Duology #1)
The Devil's Reprise (The Devil's Duology #2)
Sins and Needles (The Artists Trilogy #1)
On Every Street (An Artists Trilogy Novella #0.5)
Shooting Scars (The Artists Trilogy #2)
Bold Tricks (The Artists Trilogy #3)
Donners of the Dead
Dirty Angels (Dirty Angels Trilogy #1)
Dirty Deeds (Dirty Angels Trilogy #2)
Dirty Promises (Dirty Angels Trilogy #3)
Veiled
Black Hearts (Sins Duet #1)
Dirty Souls (Sins Duet #2)

CPSIA information can be obtained
at www.ICGtesting.com
Printed in the USA
BVOW03s0253091017
497131BV00001B/32/P

9 781546 747505